[Re]Awakenings

An Anthology of New Speculative Fiction

[Re]Awakenings

An Anthology of New Speculative Fiction

by

Alison Buck

Neil Faarid

Gingerlily

Robin Moran

PR Pope

Alexander Skye

Peter Wolfe

Compiled by PR Pope

Elsewhen Press

Contents

Foreword

PR Pope

The invited contributors to this anthology were presented with the theme of awakening. Whether this was to be an awakening into a new experience, environment, or plane of existence, or merely a character waking in their normal life, remained unspecified. As long as the story could be considered Speculative Fiction there was no further constraint placed on genre or style. In response, we have in this compilation stories addressing physical awakenings, natural and supernatural; mental awakenings, self-directed and assisted; magical awakenings, individual and collective; even spiritual awakenings, personal and global. The range of interpretations that the authors have delivered, is testament not only to their imagination, but also to the exciting breadth and diversity of Speculative Fiction.

Here in one volume is a treasure-trove of brand new stories that explore the diverse flavours that make up a good speculative menu. A spectrum of tales from hard science fiction to edgy fantasy to chilling paranormal; styles from clinically serious to joyfully silly. As you read through them all, and you **must** read all of them, you will be taken on an emotional journey through a galaxy of sparkling fiction; you will laugh, you will cry; you will consider timeless truths and contemplate eternal questions. All of life is within these pages, from birth to death (and in some cases beyond). Hopefully, you will also discover that the distinctions between the genres encompassed within Speculative Fiction are often arbitrary and indistinct. Much more significant is what draws them together so successfully into an *über-genre*, that, while appearing to be so utterly modern has its roots in the earliest extant literature. Speculative Fiction is a natural home for writers with imaginations that are crying out to remain unfettered. That is at once both its strength and weakness. Speculation inherently requires imaginative scenarios, pushing the boundaries of the everyday world – the implications of a novel technology or scientific breakthrough, the opportunities afforded by new worlds and races as yet unseen, the dangers of planes of existence previously denied or avoided, the side-effects of tampering with natural laws. Does it also lead to a disconnect with reality? Not if the stories recounted here are any indication. Such a simple theme, one that might at first appear to be no more than a daily, even mundane, experience for each one of us, is nevertheless a rich vein of inspiration for these writers to bring us such a variety of accounts of life within or without, beyond our ken or beyond the stars. Yet the potential for deep and insightful explorations of what it means to be human, to wake into, or from, a life-changing experience, has also provided fertile ground for humour among these stories. The subtle wit of nudging readers' expectations only to wrong-foot them in the final line; the dark irony of rôle-reversal in apparently traditional tales; the dead-pan delivery of a satirical take on modern society; the dry, and very British, humour of a space pilot having a bad day; the whimsy of a narrator who won't play by the rules. Humour in speculative fiction? Whatever next! But it is surely continuing a great tradition that reaches right back to what is widely regarded as the first science fiction story, Lucian's *True History*, a satire on the incredible 'truths' that his 2nd century contemporaries were peddling, which starts with an exhortation to the reader not to believe a word he says as he's made it all up. Thus was science fiction born out of a joke.

I was invited to contribute to this collection of stories, and then asked to act as compiling editor. As well as being quite flattering, such an invitation quickly becomes a daunting prospect with responsibility for the compilation as well as some of the content. At first my concentration was directed to my own contributions. Once they were written I was keen to see what my fellow contributors would deliver. As each one arrived I was lucky enough to get to read it first. I was especially pleased that many of these authors are previously unpublished, having been invited after impressing the editorial staff of Elsewhen Press with their work. Crafting a good short story can be much more difficult than writing long form narrative; there are fewer words and less time to develop a character or set the scene, the reader's attention must be grabbed almost immediately as there is no time for waffle or flabby preamble. In all of the contributions to this book, the short story format has been used to great effect, in some cases to lead the reader to an apparently logical conclusion, only to present a twist in the end that completely subverts the reader's assumptions and requires a re-appraisal of the whole tale. I love to get to the end of a story and be so surprised that I immediately want to read it again to look for the clues I must have missed. We have stories like that here, I hope you enjoy reading them as much as I did.

Part of my rôle as compiling editor is to introduce the collection as a whole and explain or justify the choice of work included. However, I think the best justification for each of the stories included in this collection is the writing itself. I find anthology compilers who feel compelled to provide a summary of each included story (albeit only a sentence or so in some cases) are often guilty of ruining the surprise that is one of the delights of a diverse collection such as this. To paraphrase a well-known film character, an anthology is like a box of chocolates – too much detail in the contents list can stop you tasting at random and enjoying a pleasurable new experience. So instead I shall try to explain the compiling rationale, such as it was. The quality of all the stories made my job as compiler easy and yet at the same time quite onerous. Choosing the tales to include was straightforward; the opportunity to incorporate stories representing a wide range of the genres that together make up Speculative Fiction was very welcome and will hopefully entice readers who are fans of each of those genres, tempting them to stray into other areas of writing that they may not have previously considered. However, that has, in turn, made it more of a challenge to put these tales together in an order that makes some sort of sense. Apart from the underlying theme there is a plethora of other ways in which these different stories share interesting topics and premises and it is those that I have tried to use to plot a path through this veritable universe of stories. I resisted using genre to corral them, indeed I held out against any identification of genre for each story – some will no doubt criticise this approach for removing their ability to choose just the stories they expect to like (using that overly detailed chocolate box contents list); but I encourage you yet again, dear reader, to read all of the stories (which is where my chocolate box analogy falls apart, because even I wouldn't keep all the chocolates to myself). Taste away, praline and gianduja, fantasy and science fiction, you might find that they aren't so very different after all!

PR Pope, London
October 2011

Podcast

Alison Buck

Like all of us, Alison Buck has led many lives.

One as a sensible, hard-working type, employed in financial systems, graphic design and web site development. Another as a writer, scribbling away, committing her stories to disc and eventually publishing several to reasonable acclaim. Throughout all of them, the mother of two and wife of one.

Skilled at exploring the psychology and interior lives of her characters, Alison delivers stories that range from chilling tales of horror through insightful contemporary drama to thought-provoking science fiction. Her empathy with her protagonists, her rich descriptive prose and her use of gentle humour serve to ensure that, whatever the setting, her stories are always a rewarding read.

Light.

I open my eyes.

Must try to stay awake.

I think I'm managing to remain conscious a little longer every day; the sedative they're giving me must be wearing off... It's a struggle to stay alert, but I have to make the effort; I have to be ready to grab any chance of escape.

Escape? Who am I kidding? I can't move. I can barely breathe. I don't know if I'll ever be able to get out of this pod, let alone get off the ship and back home.

Home.

Home seems so far away and it probably is by now; light years maybe. I mustn't let the memory fade. I will get out of here. I have to keep believing that. But how? How am I going to get out? They keep me in here, in the pod, at least while I'm conscious, so I've never seen any other parts of the ship. I've never seen any of the crew either or, if I have, I don't remember. Sometimes I feel like they've forgotten about me. And maybe that's a good thing; I don't want probes in my brain and shit like that but, hell, other times I wish they'd just kill me and get it over with.

Stop that!

Get a grip!

Can't let myself think like that.

"Reckon it's the fear that'd kill you," Martin always used to say. Yeah, like he knew! "I reckon, if the Greys take you, the important thing is to remain calm, stay cool and not give in to the fear. That's the only way to master the situation. Greys experiment on humans on board their ships, but they don't kill you. When they're done they put you back, so you just have to stay strong till then. Problem is, of course, they keep coming back for you. Wherever you go, they'll find you. You never really escape."

Greys? Spaceships! Martin really believed all that UFO shit: thought he knew it all. Mind you, he had read every book and seen every documentary so I guess he knew more than most. He used to spend hours online, having insane conversations with his crazy, conspiracy theorist friends around the globe. They'd read and seen everything too, but none of them said it would be like this. For all their talk, they didn't really know. How could they?

Weird thing is: Martin would probably kill to be here now; on an alien ship! But, after all these years, having to listen to him going on and on and on about visitors from other worlds and government secrecy and bloody alien abductions, the aliens bloody take me! Some sort of sick cosmic joke that is: why didn't they take Martin? He'd have been in his element. Spaced out nutter; he'd have loved all this.

Hell, now I know I'm in a bad way: I miss him. I actually miss Martin; the single most dull man alive: the guy could bore for England! Actually, it's not just Martin: I miss everyone. If only there were someone to talk to. Anyone. Please don't let me be the only one here. Please.

OK. Calm down.

Stay in control.

Think.

Martin might be several spanners short of a toolkit, but he had a point about the fear: it may not kill me but, if I don't stay in control, I will go mad in here.

Concentrate.

On what? There's nothing to do, nothing to see.

The pod. Describe the pod. Take a deep breath and describe the pod.

OK. OK, the pod... Let's see... It's made of... Actually, I don't know what it's made of. It could be something completely new: some weird alien material. Whatever it is, it's not hard or rigid, not like metal or glass, and it's thin enough to let some weak light through. The walls feel firm and smooth. I guess it could be organic; like the ship is an organism, like I've been eaten! Shit! Come on, concentrate! You're a scientist, well, near enough, so act like a scientist. Keep calm, be logical... Describe the pod... OK, the pod is a flexible, translucent container. I'm suspended inside it somehow, in a liquid, like some sort of specimen in a lab. I'm not wearing a mask but I'm breathing without any problem, so I guess the liquid must be saturated with oxygen, like in that film where they put the rat in the tank of water, or something. I forget the details...

Thinking about it, I never get injected or anything like that, so the sedative must be introduced into the liquid. But I've never noticed a change in the taste. I never know when they're doing it; I just start to feel sleepy. I've tried to fight it, tried to stay awake, but it's no use. And the poor lighting doesn't help. It's like a photographic dark room in here; a dull glow over everything. Maybe their eyes see in a different range of the spectrum. Maybe they can't see blue and green. OK, plenty of time to speculate. For now, just stick to the facts...

The liquid is warm. It's always warm. And it tastes salty, so it's not just water. Sea water maybe... What was that film called? I forget... I just remember the rat in the tank.

That's me now: the lab rat in a tank...

The pod's too small for me to stand up and it's so cramped that I can barely move. I don't think I'm in restraints; I can't feel any ties on my arms or legs. My muscles ache; it may be difficult to move but it's even harder to stay completely still. I'm trying not to react to anything, in case they realise that the sedative dose is too low. I need to be awake when they come next time. I need to know who, or what, I'm dealing with and it could be my only chance.

The strain on my muscles is terrible and sometimes I just have to stretch. Some time ago, or maybe it was only yesterday (it's so hard to keep track of time in here), I lost it. I just couldn't take it. Suddenly everything got too much for me and I lashed out. I was desperate to be free but it was a stupid thing to do. Alarms went off; great, booming noises, almost drowning out the thumping background sounds of the ship. It took quite a while for things to calm down again and then I guess they put an extra dose of the drug into the liquid, because I fell asleep again. Going crazy like that was a stupid self-indulgence. I mustn't let it happen again.

I wish there was some way of recording all of this; I could die out here and no one would ever know what had happened to me. Hell, I don't even know what's happened to me. I keep trying to remember the actual abduction, but there's just a gap in my memory. I remember, just before it, I was driving. It was night and it was raining. I clearly remember the sounds: the engine, the hammering rain, the water splashing under the tyres and the wipers thumping on the screen. There were lights. I remember the wipers sweeping the rain across the screen and making everything pulse; cars, lorries, streetlights. Then, suddenly, there was silence; absolutely no sound, but lots of really bright light. And I was here.

No sensation of movement. No flying through the air, no 'beam-me-up', no nothing. Just here; in this bloody pod.

It feels like I've been here a really long time, but I've no idea how long it's actually been since I was taken. Could be weeks. Could be years. There's no way of knowing but, in all this time, I haven't seen anyone - or any 'thing'. No little green men. No Greys. No nothing. Lately, perhaps because the sedatives are failing, I've begun to hear sounds above the ship's engines. The sounds aren't there all the time. They could be some sort of communication but, if they're voices, they certainly don't sound human and, whoever is doing the talking, I don't think they're trying to communicate with me.

I suppose it's possible that the whole ship is automated, even down to selecting and abducting mugs like me. Don't know whether that's reassuring or not. If the ship's flying on autopilot I guess it could be programmed to travel the galaxy for centuries. I could spend the rest of my life in here, slowly going insane. Hell, I could get old and die and rot in this bloody pod. Oh please don't let me be the only one here... Oh please...

Oh shit...I feel so sleepy... I must try to stay awake... I must...

I open my eyes.

Light.

Another day in the tank! Nothing to do and no one to talk to. It's a scary thought, but I have to face the possibility that I am alone. It is possible that I was the only one taken. But, if aliens had the entire human race to choose from, why the hell would they choose me? What would anyone want with me? I doubt if anything has come to a shuddering halt because I'm not there. Hopefully someone's looking after the dog, but I doubt if anyone at the office has even noticed I've gone or, if they have, it won't have been anything more than Alec grumbling, as usual, about unreliable bloody contract programmers. He'll have hired someone from the agency to replace me same day and then forgotten all about me.

I wonder if anyone back home actually misses me. Mum and Dad are gone, so I guess my only family is the dog. Friends? Now that is sad; the only person who might actually care that I'm not there is Martin. He'll be down at The Feathers, pint in hand and no one to talk to. He'll have missed me, if only because he'll have had to find someone else to listen to his UFO conspiracy crap. Except, of course, I know it's not crap now. I wish I could be there, at The Feathers. I'd have something to tell him. He was right, all along. Sorry Martin. Sorry I didn't believe you, mate.

I open my eyes.

Light. Very bright light.

Something is wrong. The pod's surface is pulsating, not with the usual rhythm of the ship, but as if the pod itself is alive. What the hell's going on? A malfunction? Shit! I wanted to get out, but not like this.

The pod is shrinking and the pressure is becoming unbearable. What's happening? I'll be crushed if it shrinks much more. I have to get out. Shit! What if the air out there is poisonous? What if I've been kept in here for my own safety. I don't want to die just because some technical fault spits me out into a poisonous alien smog.

Alarms are going off everywhere. It's getting really cramped in here. And it's painful. Really painful. I have to move. More alarms! I don't care, alarms or no, I have to move. I have to get out of here!

Suddenly there's a rush of liquid leaving the pod. Metal arms are gripping my head, dragging me, crushing me.

Shit!
  My head! Head... being crushed! Close my eyes.
  Can't breathe.
  Falling...
  Dying.

Eyes open.
  Light! Lots... light!
  Mind going...
  Can't remember.
  I don't... I...
  Can't think.
  Just screaming.
  Mind going.
  Gasping.
  Cold.
  Fear.
  Mind
  ...gone.
  Scream!

"Well, there's clearly nothing wrong with his lungs!"

The doctor releases the forceps and quickly performs a practiced assessment of vital signs.

"Congratulations! You have a healthy and very noisy baby boy!

Worth it

ALEXANDER SKYE

Alexander Skye has been obsessed with sci-fi since before he was born. Since those early experiments with time travel, he has read and enjoyed every branch of science fiction; from the most realistic of hard SF, through the most cynical of cyberpunk and the most Victorian of steampunk, to the most exuberant of space opera. He's enjoyed other genres besides, most especially fantasy, with which he has had a long-running affair. It began as a child, reading *The Chronicles of Narnia*, and *The Lord of the Rings*, and has never really abated. His first and greatest love, however, will always be science fiction.

Having spent so long merely reading and admiring, he decided that it was finally time to try and tell his own stories and hopefully you'll enjoy them as much as he enjoyed writing them; if not, he'll be forced to find a different job, which would be tragic since they're all so boring - after all, how many other professions let you stare wistfully at the stars on a cloudless night and call it research?

William looked down at the road below and watched as the city shook off its slumber and began its Monday. He watched his wife pack the twins off to school, straightening tie and skirt. Their uniforms were spotless, the deep green of Cooper's Court Primary School, the best school in the city. The most expensive too. In fact, he thought, looking about at the world around him, this was the most expensive area in the city. Clear skies above, a rarity in Godsbridge, gleaming buildings of metal and glasswork, so different from the brick and mortar of the poorer districts. Not to mention the well cared for roads, and the fancy fronted shops. They really had come a long way from their home in the docks.

The sun began its leisurely way across the sky and the road below, covered in moisture from a cold night, gleamed under its gaze. William looked away, his state of mind so at odds with the city's awakening. He was so very tired.

But it had been worth it. The children went to the very best school, they had the very best friends. His wife, Catherine, had everything she had ever wanted and more – she had never expected, or even dared to dream of a life in the upper city. She'd hoped to leave the docks at least, with their dirty air and dirtier ground, but to come so far in such a short time.

Such a horribly short time.

But it had been worth it. It would've been nice to have

all the details, but it had been worth it, just to see the look on his family's face.

William looked down at the page in front of him for what must've been the fiftieth time.

"Mr Keyes, if you're having second thoughts, there's no need to worry yourself. You're under no obligation to sign."

William looked up again.

"I know that Mr Harcourt. I just," he paused, "It's a lot to come to terms with. Can you go over the details of that last part again?"

"But of course. And please, call me John."

The large man seated on the far side of the ancient oaken desk ruffled through the pages he held, his brows knit closely together as he skimmed each page.

"Where were we? Oh, yes, of course. The 'suspicious death' clauses."

William nodded.

"Well, they're actually very simple Mr Keyes." He paused a moment to readjust the small glasses perched daintily and precariously atop his nose.

"In what I must admit is rather obtuse language, they state that if the contract holder - in this case your fine self Mr Keyes — if the contract holder dies under any circumstances deemed suspicious by the appropriate authorities, the contract holder and his or her family lose all rights to the money promised them in this contract. However, on the other side, we as a company also lose all rights promised us in the contract. Simply, if your death, far off may it be of course Mr Keyes, is in any way strange or suspicious, the contract is void. This protects you against attempts on your existence by us, and protects us from your family attempting to cash in early, as it were."

William nodded again, slower this time, considering Mr Harcourt's words.

Mr Harcourt, for his part, set down the papers and leant forward in his chair, lacing his hands together in front of him as he leant upon the table.

"Why is it you care if my family cash in early? Surely you don't have to wait as long that way?"

"Well, that's true," agreed Mr Harcourt, "but a death in suspicious circumstances is always fraught for everyone involved. That kind of atmosphere does no good at all for our business. It's much the same as if the contract holder is, say, killed by warfare in His Majesty's service. Hence the earlier clause prohibiting members of His Majesty's armed forces."

"Ah, I see. I'm sorry Mr Harcourt, it really is a rather daunting prospect. I'm really not taking it all in as well as I'd like, but it all does make sense once you've gone over it with me."

Mr Harcourt positively beamed.

"I'm happy to help Mr Keyes! My job here is specifically to make sure that all our contract signees understand entirely what they are signing and what it entitles both their family, and the company, to in the long term. Perhaps you would like to look at the sort of numbers your family can be expecting from the company, in the event of your demise?"

William nodded dumbly.

"Don't worry Mr Keyes, I'm sure it'll be a long time off yet. Besides, it's quite the legacy to leave to your family, as you'll see."

William forced a smile, and reached for the next page of the hefty booklet.

"It's on page fifty-three."

Once they had both reached the correct page, Mr Harcourt took a moment to stroke his chin, perhaps imagining a Machiavellian beard in place.

"As you can see, our rates are incredibly generous."

William could indeed see. It would be more than enough to set his family up, quite happily, for life. If he lived to a decent age, it would be even more. In fact, if he died in his nineties, his grandchildren could retire then and there.

"Everyone always asks why we pay out so much. You're wondering the same, I presume Mr Keyes?"

Once more, William nodded.

"It's very simple really. We tend to find that, just like wine, things are better when they've been aged well. With a contract holder living into their nineties, even with our generous payouts, the company can more than offset the cost with the possible income from it. That profit then goes back into supplying more areas with cheap and reliable power, and paying more people like yourself Mr Keyes, should they become contract holders. The system works spectacularly well." Mr Harcourt paused in his, quite evidently rehearsed, speech and glanced down at William's details.

"Ah, from the King's Wharf I see? We recently expanded our energy supply into that area of the city, I assume you've seen the benefits?"

"I have. The street lamps alone have made a huge difference. It's nice to have the heating for our house as well." William paused. "It's actually what made me consider coming down to look at your contracts. See if I could make a difference to some families in cheaper areas myself sometime, you know?"

Mr Harcourt took his turn to nod, leaning back in his chair and smiling knowingly at William.

"You're a good man Mr Keyes, that much I can see. I can tell you that our next plan of expansion is to power the outlier areas to the south of the city — the farms and industrial areas. After that, we plan to do the same for the lower levels of Godsbridge, and then we plan to move northwards to bring power to the shanties to the north. That won't be for a while of course, so you could well go on to help the very poorest of the city. I myself have a contract signed in one of these drawers," he gestured to the immense wall of filing cabinets that towered behind him, "so I can someday help those same people. We can do it together, Mr Keyes."

16

William had walked out of that building a short time later feeling like a new man. He had a generous signing bonus in hand – one which would go on to buy the family's way out of the crumbling house they lived in.

It'd set them up in a nice new area, he could carry on his job in the docks – he'd get a bicycle or something to get to work quickly. Catherine could take up a little job in one of the customs houses or banks nearby – she was cleverer than him by far, and knew her reading and writing perfectly. In no time they'd be better off than anyone in either of their families had ever been, and wouldn't that be something?

He bitterly remembered all these thoughts he'd had. The world had been so full of hope, so wonderful that afternoon. And for three years, it really had gone that way. The extra money coming in meant they could afford to save here and there; they could afford to send the children to a better school once the current year ended. They would even have enough to send them to secondary school – almost unheard of in the Keyes family.

And then, he'd died.

Obviously he knew it would happen one day – you don't get far beyond childhood before you realise that. He'd just hoped it wouldn't happen so soon. Especially not before he saw the children grow up. But, as his grandfather had always said, Fate is a cruel mistress.

But it shouldn't have been like this. He should've died, and that should have been the end of it. But it wasn't. Harcourt had never told him what would happen when he died. Maybe the man hadn't even known himself. But all William knew was that between moments, he had died. On the one second, tick, he was alive. He heard someone above him call out a warning and looked up. The other second, tock, he was dead. And yet, not dead. He was no longer alive, his body buried in a graveyard to the north of the city – a step up from the rest of the family who were buried in the river far below, like most lower-dwellers. And yet, here he was, watching the world go by. He had no idea how it worked, and yet, here he 'sat', a crystalline lattice in a lamppost, watching Godsbridge go by. It was a lucky co-incidence that his family had moved to this same street with the money they were paid for his soul. At first it had been horrible seeing them go about their lives and unable to say anything.

But then he had realised the truth.

Mr Harcourt had been right. He was helping people. And on top of that, he could watch his family grow up, see his children prosper – whether Thomas would become an officer in the navy like he always wanted, whether any of Marianne's prospective men were up to scratch. And he would always be able to watch them. In a way, it was better like this.

Yes, he reflected, watching Catherine and the twins as they turned the corner of the road, it was better like this. It was worth it.

If only he could close his eyes and rest.

THE MERRY MAIDEN WAILS

ROBIN MORAN

The Merry Maiden Wails is Robin Moran's first published work. Born in Yorkshire she happily resides in Leeds after finally escaping the insanity and chaos of London although Cyberdog and South Bank are greatly missed. Horror is her comfort zone, having read twisted tales and bone chilling stories since she was young so it's no surprise it has warped her writing mind. By day she's a teaching assistant, watching over children who enjoy screaming 'TEACHER' in her face. By night she writes and occasionally gets distracted by her Draenei Shaman, Medua, who is not impressed by Robin's writing and desperately wants to reach level 85.

On October 20th Kerrywood was bleak, silent and abandoned. If passers-by drove through the village they would notice that the temperature dropped; teeth would begin to chatter while their breath became visible. October was usually cold and windy; the atmosphere mild and damp. But Kerrywood was icy, nipping and biting at the faces and fingertips of strangers who entered the village on their way to their actual destination.

The place was a ghost town. A mystery that was still haunting the news.

Around the Village Green all the buildings still stood. Dark with no signs of life. The Merry Maiden pub and the church had gaping holes in their roofs.

The theory was abandonment. People simply disappeared from the village. Why? How? Nobody knew. Nobody knew where the residents had gone. Police and news footage had shown houses with personal belongings left inside. There was no good reason for any of this to have happened. But for any villagers that were out there – *if* they were out there – there was a good reason that even the most sceptical of residents would have eventually come around to believing.

Before Kerrywood had become the nation's shocking ghost town, the village was alive with busy local businesses and plenty of community events. There was also an ugly statue that stood in the fields leading off Cannon Lane. Her arms were outstretched, fingers spread as if desperately reaching out for help. Her mouth was opened in eternal anguish. A silent scream that had never ended as her pain continued. Her eyes had been carved wide, full of sorrow and heartache. If she could, the tears would have flowed and the wails would have been constantly heard across the village. The Merry Maiden used to stand in that field, surrounded by dead grass.

And she stood alone.

*

"She's an ugly, mossy eyesore," Kerrywood's newest resident stated, "I want that gawping statue off my land."

In the front row of the audience Jimmy Casey sat silent, listening to the verbal agreement from some of the villagers and watching others nod their head.

"It *is* an eyesore."

"That statue gives my child nightmares."

"Ugly. Absolutely ugly."

Jimmy began to open his mouth but stopped. Beside him Eric elbowed him and dipped his chin, opening his eyes wide and then gesturing with his head to where Daniel George stood. Jimmy shook his head and closed his mouth.

"Got something to say? Hmm?"

Bugger, Jimmy thought and glanced up to see the smarmy git staring right at him.

"Yes he does," Eric snapped.

"Care to share with the audience then?" Mr George asked, pointing to the spot next to him. Jimmy's eyes darted to the side and he swore under his breath.

"That statue you want tearing down is part of my friend's family history," Eric continued.

"Thank you, Eric," Jimmy said, "I'll take it from here."

He smiled weakly at his friend, but there was a hint of a

grimace and he found himself hesitating to stand up and say his piece. After all, he was only going to talk about that statue's goddamn history again; this time to a person who would only find the tale amusing and come up with his best snarky comments. Mr George was a tall, stocky man who looked like he could easily defend himself physically despite the wrinkles that were setting in and greying hair. But from Mr George's speech tonight, Jimmy saw a man whose razor sharp tongue was probably worse to deal with than his physical strength.

Towards the back of the audience Harry Goodman raised a hand. "Aye. I got some stories about that statue." He paused to grind his teeth. Mr George glanced over at the old man as he tried to keep his teeth in, rolling his eyes.

"That Merry Maiden is a strange thing," Harry continued. He stopped again, raising a finger and frowning as he tried to remember what he was going to say next.

"Merry Maiden," Mr George scoffed, "She doesn't look so merry."

"It's actually a reference to her last act, given by sympathetic villagers and her family," Jimmy said, "It was apparently…" He paused when Mr George looked his way.

"Merry," he finished.

"Someone once vandalised the statue with graffiti," Harry began again, mostly to himself, "Poor bugger was dead the next day. Just like that. Strange."

"I don't care if she's merry, angry, or menopausal. She's on my land and I want her off it. And I think many people will agree with me that she needs to go. Right?" He turned to the audience with arms spread wide.

"Hear, hear," a woman said from the back. Again there was a ripple of verbal agreement throughout the audience.

"Well…" Jimmy started. He sat up straighter in his seat

and raised a hand, "If you don't mind, I'd like to – excuse me, I'd like to explain if I could…"

"I think somebody also tried to tear it down," Harry murmured. "Many years back. When they went to get rid of it their dog became anxious and vicious if anyone tried to calm it down. Then it just collapsed dead. Yes, very strange…"

"Can you all shut up for a minute and let the poor man speak?" Eric asked loudly. He scoffed when everyone continued to talk and shout out words of encouragement for Mr George.

"No bloody manners these days," Eric muttered to Jimmy.

As he stood up, Vicar Samson's voice echoed across the room, booming confidently. "Can you all *please* be quiet?"

Gradually the room fell silent as the murmurs died down in mid-conversation. All that was left was Harry's soft mumbling voice.

"But somebody actually tried to do something good for that statue. They wanted to plant flowers around it to brighten it up – it really did need some cheeriness to it when that girl's face is not a pretty sight –."

"Harry," Vicar Samson said gently.

"Dad," Harry's daughter whispered and shook his arm.

"But the flowers didn't grow. A few did but they were dead in a day…"

"Dad, please. It's Jimmy's turn to talk." Jacqueline said.

Jimmy nodded once at her. "Thanks Jackie." He took a deep breath and stood up. Mr George was waiting, with a smirk on his face.

Vicar Samson waved a hand towards the farmer as he looked at Jimmy.

"I understand the Merry Maiden has a very important connection with your family, Jimmy. Perhaps you can enlighten Mr George on the myth?"

"Okay. Well, the rest of you already know the myth," Jimmy began, "So you know that the statue of Brigit O'Cathasaigh has been an important part of my family's history since the seventeenth century when my ancestors came from Ireland to England." Now he faced Mr George squarely. "You'll find this completely absurd. I do too sometimes. I look at that statue and think it's stupid how it has kept my family stuck here, too afraid to move on and start a new life somewhere else. My family have been stuck in Kerrywood all these centuries with every single new generation forced into staying here to make sure nothing happens to that statue."

"Then I'm doing you a favour. I want that thing down and you're free to move if you wish to," Mr George told him.

"Let me finish? I still feel like I can't leave that statue. Like Harry said, strange things have happened to people who have messed around with her. I've seen it. I was a kid when the previous owner of your farm tried to take it down. That dog went nuts. I can be a sceptic Mr George, but something is weird about that statue and I wouldn't feel comfortable abandoning it. I worry that the myth is true and something will happen. May I explain how that statue came about?"

Mr George sighed and nodded.

"Could do without a family history lesson but fine. Go on."

He sat back down in the front row.

"My dad told me that the Merry Maiden was an ancestor of ours. The eldest daughter of Cormac O'Cathasaigh, when they migrated to Kerrywood; Brigit was immediately considered odd by the villagers here. I've heard different reasons why. She may have had a disability, physically or mentally, that people would have been ignorant about. I think this was around the time when people were being accused of witchcraft if they didn't appear to fit in with or conform to social norms. The story says she didn't want to go to Mass on a Sunday. It was a hot, summer's day and she wanted to spend it in the sun. She went to the fields that are now part of your land Mr George and when people left the service she was caught dancing and singing in the field. The priest confronted her, accusing her of sin and not respecting their God on the Sabbath so he damned her. As soon as he did there was a sudden storm and thunder roared above them. Lightning flashed, apparently so bright everyone seemed blinded by it and all they could hear was a scream. When the storm disappeared Brigit was gone and in her place, where she had been standing, was a statue. The one everyone can see on your land."

At that point a mild wind fluttered through the gaps of the town hall's doors. It gently breezed past the audience, stirring their hair and clothes. A low wail echoed too and even Mr George frantically darted his eyes around the room, turning to stare at the door where the moaning seemed to be coming from outside. Jimmy watched people in the audience shiver and murmur between themselves.

Eric rubbed the goose bumps that had risen on his arm. "I hate it when that happens. Gives me the creeps when I hear her."

The farmer shuddered and turned back to face Jimmy. For a moment he frowned but suddenly laughed nervously and stood up.

"Her? Look at all of you! You're haunted by someone who probably didn't exist. That was the wind. It had to be."

"It's my family's duty to watch over her and make sure she stays put; they've kept this promise for centuries. I've been told what happened to my ancestors when they tried to take her away after her transformation. The village suffered. People started dying –."

"It was the seventeenth century. England was constantly being attacked by plague epidemics," Mr George argued. "Look, I noticed everyone's reactions back then when the wind howled – and *yes,* that was the wind."

"And notice that he's failed to point out how he went a shade of white when he heard the noise?" Eric asked his wife.

Daniel George continued. "That statue has you all scared for no good reason. It controls you all and you can't keep living like that. I think it's time for that statue to come down then nothing will haunt you anymore. Vicar, can we call for a decision? Everyone raise your hand if you think she should go."

Jimmy went over to the councillors' table.

"Please. The Merry Maiden is supposed to be protected by my family. It's my duty and I *really* do not want to find out what could happen if I broke that vow. I can't stress that enough."

"I'm sorry, Jimmy, but look at the show of hands," Ms King said.

The majority of the audience had raised their hands. Harry was one of the few along with Eric and his wife, Diana, who kept their hands down; the old man shook his head.

"This isn't going to end well," he said to his daughter.

"The land does belong to Mr George now. It's on his property," pointed out Vicar Samson, "I know other farmers in the past have been okay with the statue staying there but Mr George has voiced his dislike for it and he has a right to be heard and ask for it to be removed. And I think most people in the village will agree with him." Vicar Samson looked at Jimmy, "Have you considered moving the statue onto your land?"

"Doesn't matter if we move it to another location. The tale says she has to stay there in the spot she was petrified into."

"Jimmy you talk about how insane you think these stories and vows are yet you suddenly become reluctant to let go. Maybe this is the perfect time to forget any fears you've had and I *do* think you keep this vow out of fear. You're frightened of 'what if' scenarios."

"Do you believe in her?" Jimmy asked.

Vicar Samson shrugged lightly.

"Honestly, no. I don't."

"So is this settled?" Mr George asked, "Can I get rid of that statue? Mr Casey, if you want it moved to your property I'll help do so. But I don't want that thing on my land for much longer."

"Fine," Jimmy said, "If people agree then there is nothing I can do about it."

Outside the wind howled louder and smacked violently against the doors.

*

"And it's gone," Jimmy sighed. He looked out of the living room window, staring at the spot where Brigit used to stand. Now it was just a dead patch of grass, brown and thin. Maybe with the statue gone the grass would actually grow there now.

His son and wife were asleep on the sofa, too tired to continue watching David's favourite film. David's stuffed nose made him snore lightly while activity sheets from Sarah's class slowly slid off her knee. Jimmy had to smile, thinking of all the doors that would now be open for his son. When he got older he would have complete freedom in whatever he wanted to do with life. No statue to watch over.

I think this will be better for us, he thought. *But mum won't be pleased to hear the news.*

In her sleep his wife mumbled and her hand began twitching. David stirred beside her when she jumped, and yawned as he opened his huge green eyes. Jimmy picked the boy up in his arms and reached out to touch his wife gently on her arm while his son rested his head onto his father's shoulder.

"Sarah," he whispered.

She shook her head and one of her hands flew up as if trying to shield herself. She cried out again and one of her legs kicked out.

"*Sarah.*"

"Get away – what?" she sat up, rubbing her eyes and then scanned the room with a frown.

"Nightmare?" he asked.

She sighed and held her forehead, slumping back into the sofa. "Oh, that was horrible!"

"What was it about?" he asked and sat next to her, still cradling David in his arms.

"The statue," she said and stood up to move to the window. She stared out, observing the dead patch, "I have that bloody statue on my mind."

"She was in your nightmare?"

"I dreamt I was out in the field and I was just standing near the place where she used to be. And the statue wasn't there but this girl was and she had her back to me." She shuddered. "I heard this terrible wailing around me and she suddenly turned around. Her face was awful. You know how her mouth was carved like she was screaming? It was still like that and her eyes were red and puffy from crying. Then she started moving towards me and the screaming got louder and angrier." She stopped and shuddered again, "Didn't your dad mention something about those kinds of dreams?"

"When he first started telling me about Brigit he

mentioned something about warning dreams or visions. If you do wrong by her she'll punish you and you'll know about it beforehand. You'll hear her wailing and even see a vision of her."

Sarah licked her dry lips.

"Do you really think the stories are true?"

"I was always afraid they were. All those stories I heard about really got to me over the years. I remember when I was a kid and first heard them I couldn't sleep for days and was scared to go anywhere near her. She was my personal bogeyman."

Sarah chuckled, "I guess they've got to me too."

"Apologies on behalf of my superstitious family."

"Still… do you think it could be true? Think I'm in danger?"

"I think we need to stop letting childhood fears haunt us. I won't admit this to that smarmy jerk over there but I think he actually did this family a favour. You probably dreamt about her because she's been the topic of everyone's conversation the last few days and she's been a burden to this family. The more I think about it, the more I'm glad she's gone."

David stirred in his arms and Sarah reached out for him.

"Let's get him to bed. He needs as much sleep as possible if he's going to get over this cold."

She stretched out her arms as she walked over and Jimmy slowly passed the boy to her, moving him gently so he didn't wake up. His eyes opened slightly as Sarah held him but closed again and he wriggled in her grip to put his arms around her neck. She picked up his stuffed monkey and Jimmy kissed him on the head.

"Night, little guy. Feel better," he whispered.

"And don't you worry," he told Sarah.

"I'll try not to," she said, walking out of the living room. "You know, I actually felt sick when they tore it – ow!

Oh, these *toys*!"

Jimmy laughed, flicking through the television channels. "Stood on one again?"

"I almost impaled my foot on it! Honestly!" she sighed, nudging the plastic fire truck out of the way with her foot, "As soon as I put them to the side they're scattered all over the floor again."

Jimmy smiled but that was quick to disappear when he saw a flash of lightning outside. Rain began to smack against the window. Slowly at first and gently, but it soon turned fast and frantic. A low rumble could be heard and, soon after that, another flash of lightning brightened up the sky for one second. The rumble responded again almost immediately. A slow grumbling at first that seemed to go on for ages until finally Jimmy heard the sharp, loud cracks above his house. He hoped Sarah wasn't already freaking out but when he continued to hear her walk up the staircase, listening to the stairs creak as she did, he figured everything was fine. Otherwise she would have been running down the stairs by now, babbling about the Merry Maiden.

Jimmy had to enjoy this newfound peace he felt, even with the wild storm outside.

Maybe we could move away. Somewhere closer to the city, he thought.

In his head Jimmy saw a modern semi-detached house with a spacious parking area where they could hear the sound of a main road nearby. Not right next to it, but near enough for the sound of traffic to not be a pain and let Jimmy enjoy hearing civilisation around him rather than irritating horses and cows.

Rain continued to slap rapidly against the window and another roll of thunder roared above the house. The back door in the kitchen rattled against the force.

And the howling wind grew louder and high-pitched.

*

The storm had died by the morning and the sky had been left cloudy and grey with damp in the air. It was cold for a late September morning; where a light jacket over a long sleeved top wasn't enough to stop the shivering. The scarves and gloves were whipped out of hibernation, finally leaving the drawer under the bed; Jimmy stood at his front door, glancing around at his muddy garden and all the new leaves that had fallen off the tree covering the garden. Wonderful. Just when he'd finished raking up all the others. The gazebo he had left up was now on the ground in a crumpled heap, defeated after facing a strong wind and storm all night. The bins had been knocked over and the bags inside were spilling out.

"How's the garden?" Sarah called from inside.

"A mess," Jimmy answered and went back inside where the smell of bacon, sausage and egg guided his nose to the kitchen. He grabbed a spatula to get his breakfast onto the plate. David sat at the table, munching loudly on cereal and playing with the dinosaur pencil topper he'd just found in the box.

"I'll get the bins sorted before I go and sort the gazebo out when I get back from work."

"The gazebo was knocked over?" Sarah sighed and served her own breakfast. "And how's the weather."

"Freezing. It feels like winter's here already."

"Right…" She sighed again as she sat down and Jimmy stared at the dark shadows under her eyes. She yawned before taking a bite of toast.

"Didn't you sleep?"

Sarah shook her head. "I kept having that nightmare. Same one, over and over again. And each time it seemed to get worse. Like her screams would be louder and more high-pitched or she'd get closer to me. And her face was terrible! She had this twisted mouth, frozen in a scream and she was a really unhealthy white colour. It looked like something out of a Japanese horror film.”

“You did watch one last night before bed,” Jimmy smiled. “Mind doing a favour? Don’t mention any of this to my mum? I worry what it’ll do to her health. She hasn’t been completely well herself since dad died so I’d rather keep this whole matter quiet.”

“That’s fine. I remember your mum was quite afraid of her too. I can’t see her being thrilled about the whole situation.” She brushed the crumbs off her top. “David, sweetie, we’ll leave in a few minutes and drop you off at Aunty Olive’s.” She placed her hand against his forehead. “No temperature and you’re eating. That’s a good sign.”

*

The cold weather outside slapped Jimmy in the face; a horrible contrast to the cosy warmth of his house. His breath was visible and his teeth smacked against each other uncontrollably. He was standing in the doorway again, glancing around his chaotic garden when, in the corner of his eye, he noticed something fall. He looked down to see an icicle was melting on the welcome mat.

His eyes darted up; on the frame of his front door, icicles had formed, small and pointed. The wind smacked him in the face, stinging him with its frosty touch but he forced himself over to the bins rather than retreating back into the warmth. He heaved the wheelie bins up, almost tripping over the bags that had spilled out. The wind nipped at his ears and he constantly needed to stop to pull his hat down over them as he muttered to himself about the weather. Above, he was sure he heard a rumbling and looked up at a sky with clouds that seemed darker than earlier. They threatened to chuck rain down on the land, making the whole morning seem absolutely miserable, when the air should be fresh with the smell of burning leaves from around the village and the weather comfortably cool and breezy.

Mr George was strolling over to his gate, waving merrily.

"Good morning!"

Jimmy responded with a quiet groan.

"It blew away my garden table and chairs all the way to the gate," the farmer said and stuffed his gloved hands into his coat pockets, "Well, no animals went berserk and died on me."

"Good to hear," Jimmy muttered and threw one of the bags back in.

"Everything seems to be fine. I didn't wake up covered in boils or anything of the like."

"Wonderful news."

"How are things for you?"

Jimmy managed a weak smile.

"Fine." He dumped two more bags back in and started sorting out the cardboard and the plastic bottles that had fallen out of the recycling bin.

"The witch hasn't been banging on your doors or shaking furniture about all night?" Daniel flashed a toothy grin at him and chuckled.

"No." Jimmy continued with his chores in silence.

"Well, I'll be at home all the time. Stop over when you're ready to thank –."

Both of them froze when they heard Sarah's cry from the house. There was loud thumping and David screaming.

Jimmy raced to the house with Mr George sprinting up behind him. Sarah was lying at the foot of the stairs.

"She's not moving!" Jimmy yelled, falling to his knees at her side. His hands stretched out but paused and he stared down at her body. Her eyes were open, staring up at him blankly; her head tilted at an odd angle.

"Oh *god*," he whispered.

"David, come here," Mr George said and took the hand of the little boy who stared up at him. His mouth was opened and his eyes had begun to water.

"Mummy…"

"Your mum's had an accident. Come to the kitchen, lad," he said gently and guided him there. The little boy wouldn't move at first, pointing at his mother on the floor. Mr George took his hand, "Just come into the kitchen. Just for now. Jimmy…"

Jimmy turned his head, opening and closing his mouth. Tears ran down his cheek.

"I'll call 999," Mr George said.

"She's – she's not moving. She's not even breathing."

Mr George nodded. "I'll get an ambulance here."

"Thank you…" Jimmy sat back, slumped on the floor unable to take his eyes away from Sarah. One of David's toys lay next to her feet; a slinky dog with its face crushed in. He touched it lightly with his fingertips.

In the kitchen Mr George was already on the phone.

"Ambulance, please. It's an emergency."

Jimmy was trudging into the living room. David was running out of the kitchen, stopping to stare at Sarah before going to his dad who brought him into his arms.

"Dad?"

"It'll be okay. Mummy's had an accident."

"Daddy, she's not moving."

"I'm sorry, David."

He held his son tight and found his eyes wandering outside to Brigit's former spot. The screaming wind he heard last night echoed in his head and his stomach churned. He bit his lip to avoid crying out in front of Mr George and his son.

*

People murmured silently between themselves. Jimmy sat next to David never leaving his side as the small boy nibbled on the plate of chips in front of him. He kept his arm around his son's shoulder, gently squeezing now and again to ensure the boy felt safe.

"Have you tried eating something?" Vicar Samson asked, sitting at their table.

"I don't have much of an appetite at the moment."

"How're you doing kid?" he asked David who smiled timidly at the vicar. "You'll be fine," he told him and looked at Jimmy.

"It was a beautiful service. I'm sorry I couldn't lead it at our church."

"Not your fault. How's the repair going?"

"Very slowly. The builders can't do much in this weather and there was quite a lot of damage from the storm."

"My wife had a nightmare that night about Brigit. It was like the nightmares my family told me about if any of us ever abandoned our responsibility."

Vicar Samson nodded but his mouth was pursed.

"I know you think this whole business was absurd –."

"Your wife fell down the stairs because she tripped. Accidents like that are *not* paranormal. It was a tragic thing to happen to your family but this isn't because of an angry spirit." He patted Jimmy on the shoulder and stood up. "You can always come to me if you want to talk."

"Thank you, Vicar," Jimmy whispered.

"And son…" Vicar Samson reached behind David's ear and produced a pound coin. The boy gasped, lifting a hand to his ear and then laughed. He reached out for the pound and mumbled a shy 'thank you' to him. "Look after your father. He'll need you more than ever right now."

David nodded, leaning to the side and hugging his father.

Jimmy stroked his son's hair.

"How're you doing, kid?"

"I miss mummy."

"Me too," he said gently, "We'll be fine. Guys sticking together?"

David nodded. He yawned and started rubbing his eyes, snuggling up more into his father who held him close and kept thinking to himself: *We'll be fine. We can do this.* In doing so he also tried his hardest to keep away the tears that were blurring his vision and he turned his head to wipe them away, eyeing the crowd in the room to make sure no-one saw him cry. And he almost believed he had got away with it until he saw his mother-in-law looking his way and then politely excusing herself to come over.

"Didn't hide that as well as you thought you did," she said and sat down.

Jimmy wiped away more tears.

"I'm so sorry."

"I keep telling you to stop apologising. You're not to blame." She reached out for his hand. "Is there anything me and Keith can do?"

"I think we'll manage. I promised David we'll have her favourite meal tonight."

"That sounds nice. And I hope you'll still come to ours for Sunday dinner?"

"Sure."

David stirred in his arms and his voice was almost a whisper. "Daddy, can we go now?"

"It'll be over shortly. I know you're tired."

"I don't feel well." He sat up and let his head hang down. Jimmy touched his son's forehead with the back of his hand.

"He feels a little warm," he told Mrs Gordon. "David,

do you feel sick again?"

The boy nodded, pouting. When Mrs Gordon reached for him he went over and hopped onto her lap.

"Keith and I will take him back home if you have to stay and wrap the reception up."

"I shouldn't be too long. Just put him straight to bed with some water. There's chicken soup in the kitchen cupboard if he feels hungry. That usually makes him feel better."

David stayed in his grandmother's arms as she stood up, gripping him and balancing him on her hip. "You know, your mother used to be exactly the same. Chicken soup and pineapple juice always perked her up if she was feeling under the weather. Her favourite film always helped as well." She waved goodbye to Jimmy, moving towards her husband who welcomed the young boy with open arms. "Let's tell each other stories about Mummy."

Once David had left with his grandparents, Jimmy stood up and walked towards the crowd. Some people turned to him, forcing eye contact and smiling before patting his shoulder and quietly apologising for his loss. Eric dutifully came to his side.

"I can wrap everything up for you if you need to escape," he offered.

"No, I can do this. I can do this," he said, repeating it in his head like a battle cry. He forced the corners of his lips to tug up, quietly thanking anyone who came to offer their condolences.

"Oh love, I'm so sorry. She was a lovely woman," Mrs Candershaw said. Jimmy glanced down at the small, plump woman.

"Thank you. You're not with your husband?"

"No, Malcolm's ill. Food poisoning." She paused for a second to glance over at Mrs Berkham who ran the local café. She was busy talking with Vicar Samson, not noticing the scowl on Mrs Candershaw's face.

"I hope he feels better," Jimmy said.

"If there's anything you need, you let me know," she told him, shrugging her duffel coat on. "I'm always here to help," she added and left, only to be replaced by more villagers and friends who came with the same questions and sentences.

"I'm so sorry for your loss."

"Sarah was a lovely woman."

"My kids loved having her as their teacher."

"If there's anything you need…"

Jimmy nodded and smiled his way through the rest of the afternoon, keeping his answers brief and letting his voice become a deadpan whisper. Whatever he tried to do to distract himself – whether it was ordering another half a pint or repeating conversations with guests – his mind still flashed to the image of his wife on the floor and then to the statue, thinking about what his wife had seen in her nightmare. Brigit O'Cathasaigh was still haunting his mind, desperately reminding him that she would not be gone for good.

There was a sceptic somewhere inside of him and he was determined to reach for it and pluck it out to the surface to wipe away any lingering paranormal paranoia.

He trudged his way through the rest of the reception with Eric at his side and breathed a sigh of relief when, finally, he hopped into his friend's car and slumped back in the passenger seat.

"Survived?" Eric asked.

"Barely. I just need to get home now."

*

It was another night alone in a cold bed, listening to the screaming wind around the house and the rain splattering against his window. His alarm glowed red in the dark and he watched the minutes go by painfully slowly. Four past two. Five past two. Six past two…

He rubbed his eyes and sighed, sitting up to turn over his pillow and then turning onto his left to settle down. He closed his eyes and lay there, feeling his head sink into the pillow. But then his shoulder ached and the pillow felt hard and lumpy again. He turned onto his back again and opened his eyes, glancing to his bedside table.

Seven past two…

He sighed and muttered to himself, swearing as he sat up and moved to the window to look out at the dark land around him. The wind had yet again blown things about in his garden with the bins back on the ground and the bags spilling out. He groaned and rested his head against the glass, flinching at the coldness of it.

"Daddy?"

David stood in the doorway, clutching a blanket to himself and pouting when Jimmy turned to him.

"You're not feeling well?" Jimmy asked.

"I still feel sick."

"Come here." David trudged over to him and his father knelt down, stretching out his hand to feel his forehead. "You're still very warm. Have you been sick?"

David shook his head.

"But I feel cold."

"That's a temperature. Can't you sleep?"

"I did. But then the scary woman woke me up."

Now it was Jimmy's turn to feel nauseous and he could feel the hair at the back of his neck stand on end. No amount of heating in the house could stop the shivering and goose bumps rising on his arms.

"The woman?"

"In my dream. There was a woman and she was crying but then she stopped and started screaming. She was in my room and I woke up." David threw himself into his father's arms and hugged him tight. "I think she's hiding.

I don't want to go back in there."

"I'll check your room. Make sure she's gone. Okay? If she's there you can count on me to get rid of her."

The wind wailed louder and Jimmy couldn't help but glance outside. He clenched his teeth, desperately fighting the need to throw up. David was still in his arms and he clutched onto his son tighter, holding him close with the fear that any minute he would be taken away if he loosened his grip just a tiny bit. His mind struggled to think logically but fear was too powerful for any remaining rationality. The hairs continued to stand on end and the temperature seemed to drop as he began shaking. The sound of the wind outside felt like it surrounded the house, trapping everyone inside as it waited for the perfect moment to strike. The shrill howling began to feel like it was just a disguise to hide what was really making that sound.

*

The morning came but sleep had failed to do the same. Jimmy stood outside his doorway, hoping that the fresh yet freezing air might brighten him up somehow as he held a steaming cup of coffee in his hands. Daniel George was already up and about at the farm up ahead, wrapped up from head to toe in thermal clothing while he angrily shouted at a smartly dressed stranger. The man, younger than the farmer, presented him with papers as he nodded calmly and attempted to speak every time Mr George took a break to huff and wave his arms about. After a while Jimmy's neighbour gradually stopped shouting and shrugged feebly, hanging his head. Brusquely he took the papers and shook the stranger's hand with a frown on his face which changed to sheer disgust as the visitor left. The snarl stayed on his face when he came towards Jimmy, realising he had been watched all this time.

"Enjoyed the show?"

"Something wrong?" Jimmy asked, deadpan.

"My animals have to be slaughtered. Goddamn Foot and Mouth Disease."

"Oh. Sorry to hear."

"Yeah, you sound so sympathetic," Mr George snapped.

Jimmy sipped his coffee.

"When did it happen?"

"A couple of days ago. Like I hadn't had enough trouble already. My dog died the day after the statue was torn down."

Now Jimmy lifted his head up with an eyebrow raised and he edged closer to the gate.

"Oh?"

"Don't start. I know what you're about to say."

"Wasn't going to say anything. Just curious."

"Well I found him dead at that spot. You know, where she stood?"

Jimmy pursed his lips together and looked away.

Mr George scowled.

"I know you're thinking it."

"Haven't you noticed what's been going on lately? It's chaos here. The church and pub have been damaged. The weather and the strong winds. My wife. Food poisoning at the Berkhams' cafe and your animals. Ever since –."

"And I can provide an explanation for all them. The buildings were hit by tree branches because of a storm. That's not uncommon. Again, neither is this weather. We all know this is what England can be famous for. Foot and Mouth Disease is a plague lurking around the corner for all farmers. There are thousands of reported cases all over the world. I faced this back in two thousand and one. You're quick to blame the supernatural when there is a logical explanation for everything that has been happening and frankly I'd prefer it if you kept that bullshit to yourself. I don't want to hear about that fucking statue anymore."

"Sorry about your animals," Jimmy said quietly and wandered back inside, leaving Mr George at the gate. He went straight upstairs to David who was tucked up in his bed, nibbling at a slice of toast very slowly with a warm blanket wrapped around him.

"We're going to the doctors at eleven," Jimmy told him and felt his head, "You still have a temperature."

"I kept dreaming about that lady."

"It was just a nightmare, son."

*

Jimmy still couldn't stop thinking of that waiting room. They had been completely surrounded by people coughing and sneezing. Most of them had been shivering just like David, who had seemed paler by the time they arrived at the surgery; some were sweating like it was a hundred degrees outside but all of them sat slumped and dazed.

Susan, the receptionist, was frantically rushing about, calling patients and directing them to their doctors and answering the phone to arrange more appointments.

"Is a bug going around?" Jimmy had asked.

"Looks like it. We've been fully booked for days and more and more people keep coming in with flu-like symptoms."

"When did everyone start getting sick?"

"I think our first patients came in after the storm."

Jimmy had clutched David's hand tighter but Susan had been quick to reassure him.

"Oh don't worry. It's just a bug. That time of the year. People are getting better; it's just they're getting sick easily. Don't worry about it. Your son is going to be fine."

Now, lying in bed, Jimmy could hear his son's bed creaking as he coughed loudly and sneezed; he lay awake yet again feeling like this house, this village even, was a living force working against him now, under the complete control and manipulation of Brigit's spirit.

His eyelids were getting heavier, drooping every now and again as his head felt lighter and settled into his pillow, relaxing better than he had done the previous night. The bedroom around him changed, taking him outside into the village that was dark and dimly lit, with complete silence. No-one seemed to be present. It was just him, standing in the middle of the Village Green dressed in nothing but his pyjamas, with a frown on his face. A frost covered the grass and houses while his breathing was a clear white from the cold, but the temperature didn't bother him. When he moved, his body seemed to take ages to respond, moving in slow motion and he simply walked around the Green like he was having a casual stroll, taking in his surroundings. No lights were on around the village, not even the lampposts yet somehow he could still see clearly.

One lamppost came on. Underneath there was a figure. Somebody dressed in white shabby clothes who was a blur; Jimmy reached up, checking if his glasses were missing. He felt his knuckles knock against the frame. Yet the figure was still blurry.

It was also moving.

Slowly.

With the empty village around him and this one unfamiliar figure walking in his direction Jimmy began to back up, turning his head to find the path to his house and run there to lock himself away. As the figure moved closer his hairs stood on end. His heart raced. He was panting, finding it difficult to catch his breath, and winced when he felt like there was a pressure on his chest, right in the middle.

The silence in the village came to an end when a howling began. Shrill and far away at first, the noise grew louder, giving the impression that it was creeping towards him. And so was that person.

His movements remained slow. He attempted to run but his muscles did not want to move at a faster pace. He cried out desperately, forcing his legs forward. The footsteps of the stranger could be clearly heard now as they walked across the muddy grass. The squelching continued, quickening and soon he felt ice cold breathing down the back of his neck. He stopped, clutching his left arm. The pain shot up it, reaching his jaw and snaking its way across his back. He groaned, gasping for breath, and stumbled as his vision darkened. Turning around to his follower he yelled out, falling back onto the grass, still clutching his arm.

Brigit looked down at him, clenching her rotten teeth together and baring them at him. Tears ran down her unhealthily white cheeks.

And she started screaming. High pitched, piercing into his ears. Jimmy moved his hand away from his arm and up to one ear. Then back again when the pain in his arm made it feel like it was being ripped away from him. His vision blurred, continuing to darken while the screaming continued.

He was dragged back into reality as he fell off his bed.

But the pain was still there. He tried to get onto his knees but he was on the floor unable to move and now clutching his heart as he opened and closed his mouth frantically trying to breathe. The thud of him hitting the floor had luckily woken up Sarah's parents and he groaned out when he heard rushing footsteps.

Mrs Gordon shrieked at the doorway. "Jimmy!"

A figure loomed over him and he recognised the blotchy, chubby face of Mr Gordon.

Jimmy gritted his teeth and his hand went to his chest. Every time he opened his mouth to speak all that came out were short, panicked breaths.

"Heart attack. Penny, call an ambulance now. Take David downstairs and stay with him."

Jimmy opened his mouth again.

"Don't try and talk."

"Da…"

"David's going to be with Penny. You'll be fine. The ambulance will be here soon."

Outside thunder roared and forks of lightning could be seen in the distance. The wind increased, wailing around the house and Jimmy squeezed his eyes shut to hold back the tears as sweat from his forehead drenched his face. His vision remained blurred.

Then darkened again.

And slowly the pain seemed to fade. Mr Gordon's voice sounded far away and distorted. But a loud scream could be heard, piercing into his ears.

More blackness.

And more screaming.

*

In the Village Hall hardly anyone breathed a word. They sat in groups at the tables, staying mainly with their friends or family. Mr and Mrs Gordon sat with Georgina Casey whose handkerchief was damp from constant tears. Vicar Samson sat with them, tensed up and looking down the whole time. His mouth tightened now and again as his eyes wandered back and forth from Jimmy's mother to the glass of water he was clutching onto.

"How's the boy?" he finally asked.

"Still very sick," Mrs Casey whispered. She looked pale and drawn; hand shaking as she dabbed at her eyes with a tissue, "Sarah's sister has been looking after him today while we attended the funeral."

"His condition is worsening?"

She nodded.

"The doctor confirmed it's pneumonia. He's very weak right now."

"I'll keep David in my prayers. And if you ever need to talk –."

"He isn't going to get any better," Mrs Casey interrupted, "We all know what has been happening and I'm going to lose my grandson now. He's next."

"Mrs Casey –."

"I know what you're going to say Vicar. But this village let that statue get torn down. Open your eyes and look at what's happening here. Something is going wrong everywhere and my son and daughter-in-law are dead. My grandson is also dying."

The rain hit the windows frantically. Mrs Casey nodded to the window.

"Storms like that are not normal, Vicar," she continued and guests turned to stare at her as her voice grew louder, "And from what I know you've been plagued with them since you tore her down. After David she's finished with my family but she hasn't finished with your village." She glared in everyone's direction. Most people flinched when she did, casting a gaze outside. Some shuddered. Some immediately looked away, remaining silent and letting their head hang down.

"It'll continue," she warned them, "Food poisoning and damaged buildings won't be the worst of your problems."

Outside the village hall everyone heard the wind wail.

And some were convinced they also heard sobbing echoing around outside.

If you go into the woods today...

Peter Wolfe

Peter Wolfe lives the life of a hermit, desperately trying to avoid the mysterious and terrifying 'Real World', preferring instead the varying realities that inhabit his bookshelf and his mind.

Peter lives in Leeds with his girlfriend and their cat, who has the joint function of being Emperor of the Known Universe and Chief Editor. His Lordship seems to disapprove of Peter's writing, forever stealing his pens and or leaving indecipherable comments by walking across the keyboard.

'If you go into the woods today...' is Peter's first published work, though with luck many more Science Fiction and Fantasy stories will soon follow.

On a more personal note Peter finds writing about himself in the third person quite peculiar and fears that if he doesn't stop soon he might do a Jack Torrance. After all, All Work and No Play...

The Woodcutter slipped the knife into his belt and took his axe from its spot behind the door, pausing to kiss his wife goodbye, as she handed him the satchel that contained his lunch, and smile at the baby playing in her cot. The Woodcutter joined his fellows near the trees where they always waited and together they headed deep into the virgin forest which bordered their little village. They travelled down winding woodland paths and after an hour's walk they arrived at the copse of trees that was to be their work that day.

The Woodcutter worked hard all morning and, after several hours, a large pile of wood was stacked near the horses so the men decided to stop for lunch, spreading out to sit among the trees. The Woodcutter collected the satchel his wife had packed him, from the tree branch where it had been hanging and settled down with his back against a stump. Inside he found the usual hunk of bread, cheese wrapped in a cloth and a small skin filled with cheap wine. Before he had even lifted the skin to his lips the Woodcutter heard a scream from nearby. Scrambling to his feet he ran towards the sound, dropping his food and snatching up the axe. Behind a large bush, the Woodcutter stumbled upon one of his fellows sprawled on the ground with a huge white wolf muzzle deep in his chest.

"Help...me..." gasped the fallen woodsman as the wolf snacked on his innards. The creature raised its head, muzzle stained red as it noticed more woodsmen arriving and, giving a fierce growl, loped off into the forest.

"Go, I'll look after him," one of the woodsmen told them as he dropped down beside the injured man. At his words the Woodcutter and his colleagues chased after the wolf, weaving between the trees. The wolf, being faster than them stayed ahead easily, teasing the woodsmen by allowing them glimpses of him through the trees. One by one the woodsmen fell behind as they ran out of breath or gave up, until eventually it was only the Woodcutter who still followed. The Woodcutter finally began to gain ground as the wolf climbed a small hill and soon he was only a few feet behind, almost close enough to reach out and grab it. Suddenly the wolf gave a great leap and glided through the air. Too late, the Woodcutter saw the sharp drop ahead of him and, unable to stop, fell. Rolling down the steep slope the Woodcutter's axe was knocked from his hand and his head smashed against a rock as he splashed down into a shallow stream. The world began to spin and, as the Woodcutter felt consciousness slip away, his last sight was of the great white wolf staring down at him from atop the slope with blood drying on its jaws.

When the Woodcutter finally awoke, darkness had enveloped the forest. Groaning, he picked himself up and gingerly felt the back of his head. It was sore but the bleeding had stopped. What surprised him more was his luck. He could just as easily have landed face down in the stream or the wolf could have finished him off while he lay helpless. Overall, he had got off lightly. Quickly searching around he found his axe and knife but his clothes were ruined. The fall had ripped holes in both shirt and trousers and they were soaked; heavy from the stream's cold water. Carefully he climbed back up the steep slope and once at the top tried scanning the area for anything that might tell him where he was or which way home might be. Instead all the Woodcutter could see was darkness. He couldn't find his footprints and there was no sign of any other living thing, man or wolf. The Woodcutter weighed his options. He could wait until morning and use the light to find his tracks and follow them back to the village. But dawn was many hours off and it was only going to get colder. Besides, the wolf could also still be nearby. His only other choice was to pick a direction and hope it led him to safety. There were many other villages along the edge of the forest and even a few cabins hidden within the forest itself. Any of these would give him somewhere to rest safely and dry off. Shivering, the Woodcutter decided that it was his only hope; looking around he saw a tree which he felt was familiar and set off in that direction.

Knowing how easy it was to get lost in the woods the Woodcutter marked each tree he passed by scraping off some of the bark with his knife so that he could find his way back to the stream if it became obvious that this was the wrong direction. There was no moon and the only sounds were the wind in the leaves and the occasional owl far off and out of sight. Without light to guide his way the Woodcutter found it slow going, stumbling on hidden roots, his clothes catching on bushes and branches which clawed at him from the darkness. Just as the Woodcutter began to think that he had gone the wrong way, he stumbled on something and while picking himself up from the ground noticed that the forest floor around him was paved. The brickwork was old with weeds poking from the cracks but it was a sign of civilization and the Woodcutter seized on this hope, following the old path through the trees.

The path went on for miles, winding through the trees before emerging into a clearing with a small hill. An old chapel was built upon it. The years had not been kind to the place. The windows were smashed and an apple tree was growing through one of the window openings. Peeking through the doorway the Woodcutter found that the roof had partially collapsed, forcing him to duck under the rubble to get inside. The Woodcutter's boots crunched on broken glass as he searched the ruin. Most of the roof was still intact but the Woodcutter could see that it would take little more than a strong wind to bring the whole thing crashing down. He also found scores of broken shields leaning against the walls, each displaying a different heraldic device. Lions lay beside griffins and wolves while dragons slumbered between great castles. The wood of the shields was rotten and many of the images on the shields had faded with time. Deciding not to stay under the crumbling roof the Woodcutter made his way outside and searched around the hill. The darkness made it difficult but his effort paid off when he found a number of blackberry bushes and the Woodcutter's hunger made itself known. He quickly stripped one of the bushes bare and had started on a second before his hunger was sated, both his hands and lips stained with the dark juice. His hunger dealt with, the Woodcutter decided his next priority should be to light a fire. Carefully he made his way around the forest's edge collecting dry wood and soon had a blaze going. There the Woodcutter sat as the fire warmed him and his clothes dried. Warm and full it was not long before he began to doze.

When the Woodcutter awoke the fire was out. The ashes were cold and the sun was already high in the sky. Standing, he stretched; the aches of the hard ground adding to the pains from his fall. He made his way around the hill until he found the blackberry bushes again and enjoyed a breakfast of the remaining fruit, trying his best to wipe the dark juice from his hands on what remained of his trousers. Deciding to make a search of the clearing by the light of day, the Woodcutter carefully explored the hill but found little that he hadn't seen the night before. His only new discoveries were the occasional pile of small animal bones or abandoned rabbit holes. As his search brought him back to the fire the Woodcutter noticed movement at the forest's edge and glimpsed a figure entering the trees. Shouting he made a dash down the hill and into the forest. The Woodcutter gave chase but the figure was always just out of sight; all his cries going ignored. The Woodcutter was just about to give up hope when he emerged into another small clearing. Stood in a circle on the far side were four beautiful women and, in the middle of the clearing, the figure he had been chasing, a young woman more beautiful than any he had ever seen.

At the Woodcutter's appearance the women all quickly turned to face him, clasping their hands behind their backs. All five women were of stunning beauty and were dressed in long elegant dresses, the colours of autumn leaves and all matching their long flowing hair. They seemed shocked at the Woodcutter's arrival despite his shouting; the woman he had been chasing quickly backed up towards the group, making sure to keep her hands out of sight.

"I'm sorry. I...didn't mean...to frighten you," the Woodcutter gasped as he tried to catch his breath, "I...don't want...to hurt you." He took a few deep breaths and steadied himself before straightening up, "I'm a bit lost. I was wondering if you could help me."

The women remained silent, staring at him. He noticed one glance at the axe in his hand.

"Don't worry I won't hurt you," the Woodcutter lifted the axe slightly. "This is just for cutting down trees."

The women continued to stare while a couple of the group began to whisper in the ear of the woman he had chased.

"You are lost?" she eventually asked.

"Yes." The Woodcutter looked at the group of women. "Would you know the way back to the edge of the forest? I know I could make my way from there."

The women glanced at one another again and began to smile.

"You are deep in the forest my friend. Few people come this way anymore," the woman he had followed told him, "You must be tired. Sit with us a while. We will take you home when we are all rested."

The smile on her face was beginning to unnerve the Woodcutter. This wasn't like the smiles his wife gave him; this was the smile a wolf might give a deer. The smile of a predator. It was hungry and dangerous. He tightened his grip on the axe.

"Thank you for your hospitality but that isn't necessary, I'm quite rested. All you need do is point me in the right direction..."

"Nonsense, you must join us." The woman took a step closer still keeping her hands behind her back and making the Woodcutter wonder what she might be hiding; what was it they were all holding in their hands?

Nervously the Woodcutter asked the other question which had been bothering him since his arrival in the clearing, "Begging your pardon but if we are as deep in the woods as you say, what are five ladies such as yourself doing here alone?"

The women exchanged another look before responding.

"It is our home," one of them told him.

"We are the wives of the wood," answered another.

The woman who had led the Woodcutter to the glade gave the others a look to silence them before turning back to her pursuer, "Are you sure you won't put that heavy axe down and join us?"

"No. Thank you though."

The woman took another step towards him, "That is a shame. In that case..." With a blaze of speed he would not have thought she possessed, the woman leapt at the Woodcutter.

In the blink of an eye she was in front of him with her arms outstretched. Now the Woodcutter could see what she had been hiding, he had been expecting a knife or some other weapon but what he saw was far worse. In place of hands the woman had three long claws which she now slashed towards him. The Woodcutter felt a sharp pain in his chest before the woman barrelled into him, knocking him to the ground. Glancing down he saw blood bubbling from deep cuts on his chest and, before he could move, the woman was on top of him and lapping at his wounds with a long, inhuman tongue. Disgusted, he pushed her off and rolled back to his feet hefting the axe and swinging it at her. As it flew towards her she leapt aside easily with a laugh.

"Come sisters, he's delicious," she called to the others and they began to advance across the glade. Looking again the Woodcutter saw that the woman's once beautiful face was marred by her hunger, she seemed far more feral now, his blood staining her lips just as the blackberries had earlier stained his.

The Woodcutter hefted his axe again, keeping it between him and the woman who was now trying to circle behind him, cutting off any chance of his escape. He swung at her again causing her to back up towards her approaching sisters.

"Look sisters, he wants to play with us," she smiled at the Woodcutter sending a chill down his neck. "Mother always told us to play with our food."

Suddenly the woman gave another lunge. Her claws were aimed at the Woodcutter's throat but by sheer chance the Woodcutter had chosen that moment to take another swing at the she-devil and the axe caught her in mid leap; its head embedding itself deep in her throat. The other women all stopped their advances; the shock on their faces mirrored by their stricken sister. Blood oozed from her wound accompanied by a gurgling as she tried to speak. Ignoring her, the Woodcutter placed a foot in the centre of the creature's chest and wrenched his weapon free causing her to drop to the ground while a puddle of blood spread out from the twitching corpse.

The other wood-wives quickly recovered and began to hiss and spit at the Woodcutter like feral cats. Slowly he backed away into the forest but step by step they followed, keeping their distance until level with their fallen sister. They paused; one of them sniffing the air before she bent down licking at her sister's wound. She straightened up, her sister's blood still on her lips, and growled to the others. Suddenly the Woodcutter was forgotten and the group pounced on their fallen sibling, lapping at her blood and tearing into her flesh with their monstrous claws. Using this distraction the Woodcutter turned and fled the horrific scene.

The Woodcutter didn't stop until he reached a small stream, where he collapsed against a tree and retched. When he was done he washed the foul taste from his mouth with water from the stream and set to cleaning the wound on his chest. With the blood washed away the cuts didn't look as bad as they had back in the glade, though just to be sure the Woodcutter took what remained of his shirt and ripped it into bandages. Sitting back against the tree he took stock of his situation. He was lost deep in a forest where there were murderous monsters and he was bleeding, aching and exhausted from the ordeal. He knelt down beside the stream to pray. After some time he stood again and set off, picking a direction away from the glade.

The Woodcutter's travel through the forest now seemed much more unsettling. He no longer felt as safe, now that he knew there were more dangerous things than wolves amongst the trees. Every movement around him had suddenly become the leap of some monster out to get his blood; every tree had enemies lurking on the other side and every sound now seemed to be some beast tracking him. The Woodcutter wandered for what seemed like hours, following animal trails while clutching his axe tightly. Eventually he noticed the trees starting to thin and he began to hope that the forest's edge might be close at hand. Instead the Woodcutter found a small ramshackle cottage; a chair beside the door and smoke drifting from the chimney.

Having learned his lesson the Woodcutter approached the building cautiously and was just reaching out to open the door when it swung outwards making him jump backwards and raise the axe. There in the doorway looking even more surprised was a little old lady.

"Show me your hands!" he demanded of her. Carefully she stepped out of the cottage and raised two frail but perfectly normal hands. Slowly the Woodcutter lowered the axe, keeping a tight grip on it. "I'm sorry. There were some women back there. They weren't human. Their hands. They...." His voice trailed off.

"So you ran into those clawed bitches, did you? Don't worry about it dearie, they would set anyone on edge." The little old woman shuffled forward and in the soft light that filtered through the trees the Woodcutter could see her properly. She seemed human but then again so had the wood-wives. She was tiny, about half his height, and her arms and legs were thin and frail. The old woman was wrapped head to toe in filthy animal skins and her long white hair was thinly spaced on her head yet her smile was kindly.

"Tell me young man, do you often wander through the woods half naked? Hmm?" She picked up a dusty blanket from the chair beside the door and threw it to the Woodcutter. "Wrap yourself in that before you catch your death or the neighbours see you and set to gossiping."

Looking around, the Woodcutter wrapped the blanket around himself. The cottage was the only building he could see.

"You have neighbours?"

"Well no, but you never know who might wander past. Besides my daughter should be back soon and she don't need no encouraging." The crone pushed her way back inside the cottage and soon emerged struggling to drag a wooden chair. "Here, sit yourself on this and I'll make some tea." she told him. Again she disappeared into the house and this time was gone some time before appearing with two mugs of steaming tea.

"Now dearie, what are you doing all the way out here?" The old woman asked before settling back in her chair, slurping as she sipped the tea.

Still a little suspicious, the Woodcutter sniffed the tea before taking the tiniest sip. All seemed fine so he took a deep draught, feeling its warmth spread through his body.

"I'm afraid I got lost."

"Ahh, and that's how you ran into those bitches back there right?"

"Yes Ma'am," the Woodcutter nodded.

"Don't call me Ma'am. You'll make me feel old." Suddenly the woman began to cackle to herself. "Hah suppose I am old aren't I? Want a biscuit?"

"Erm, no thank you."

"Well I do." With that the crone hopped down from her

chair and vanished back into the house, and while the Woodcutter could hear the sounds of her crashing around in the cottage he took a closer look at his surroundings. Trees grew all around the house but a small garden had been made to one side where herbs had been planted and a small stack of logs leaned against a stump. The old woman soon came scuttling out trying to chew on a biscuit.

"Do you live out here alone?"

"A poor old lady like me? No, no, no. I live with my daughter and her daughter. They're off gettin' some firewood. Should be back soon." She started to dunk the biscuit in the tea to soften it up.

"No men? Don't the wolves bother you? Or those creatures?"

"Oh no, no, no. They don't bother us. What trouble could we possibly be?" She flashed him a toothless grin, "Besides, old women are very tough. You'd need better teeth than mine. Oh look here they are." She stopped dunking her biscuit and called out to someone behind him. "Girls look we've got someone for dinner!"

Turning around the Woodcutter could see two figures making their way through the trees, one tall and elegant; the other about the same size as the old woman. As they drew closer the Woodcutter could make the pair out more clearly. The tall woman was of the same age as his wife and was pale as snow with lips as red as rubies. She was almost as tall as the Woodcutter but moved with much more grace, seeming to glide rather than walk across the forest floor. The smaller of the pair was a young girl of about nine with a mess of golden curls atop her head. Both were clad in furs, though much cleaner than those of the old woman; and the young girl wore a floor length red cape, its hood draped down her back. At their approach the Woodcutter stood respectfully, being careful to keep himself covered, and greeted them with a courteous nod. Mother and Daughter moved over beside the Grandmother.

"Who is this charming gentleman you have found us?" The Mother asked.

The Woodcutter gave her a nervous smile, "I was just a little lost and your mother was kind enough to make me some tea. I don't mean to impose."

The Grandmother handed her tea to her daughter and hopped to the ground, "Oh it's no imposition. We like having strangers for dinner. We'd have them all the time if we could catch them." The old woman gave another little cackle at her joke but the Woodcutter began to feel a little unsettled again; his eyes flicking to the axe which now lay on the ground by his feet. He suddenly realised he had somehow found himself in the same situation as before: alone with strange women he didn't know. These women hardly seemed any threat, but then again neither had the wood-wives at first.

The pale woman watched her mother make her way into the house still cackling away.

"You poor dear. My mother hasn't been talking your ear off I hope."

"Not at all. She has been very kind," the Woodcutter told her.

"He met those bitches by the church before he found his way here," shouted the Grandmother from within the house.

The Mother flashed him a look of sympathy, "I hope they didn't hurt you. This forest can be quite grim if you don't know your way around."

"Just a scratch," answered the Woodcutter. The young girl who had been staring at him intently leaned forward and poked him hard in the chest where the wood-wife had scratched him.

"Darling, what have we told you about poking people?" The mother scolded her daughter, "I hope she didn't hurt you?"

"Not at all," the Woodcutter told her, trying to hide his grimace.

"You've got big muscles," the little girl told him, "and a big axe."

"All the better for cutting down trees," he said trying to smile.

Behind him the Grandmother re-emerged from the house carrying more cups which she passed to the new arrivals.

"Grandma, can we keep him?" Mother and Grandmother shared a quick look after which the Grandmother gave a shrug.

"You know you can't dear, you always forget to feed them." The Mother turned to the Woodcutter, "You know how young children can be. Sorry, but we will give you a head-start."

Beside her the little old lady nodded smiling.

Fear was once again beginning to fill the Woodcutter, "What's going on?"

"Well dearie it's like I said, we'll be having you for dinner. But first we have to work up an appetite. The hunt is the best part after all."

Sitting there the Woodcutter didn't understand the fear spreading through him. As strange as they were the little old lady wouldn't be able to hurt him in a fight, neither would the little girl. The mother might be dangerous if she had a weapon but still not a serious threat, even if they all attacked together. Feeling a little braver the Woodcutter made up his mind. "I've had enough of running through this forest thank you. What if I don't want to run?"

In her chair the Grandmother smiled. "It's your choice

dearie," she turned to her daughter and granddaughter. "Come on dearies, let's change for dinner."

The Mother helped the old lady to the ground where she started stroking the fur belt at her waist. When the Grandmother smiled at the Woodcutter again, teeth he hadn't seen before appeared from her gums and she straightened up, stretching so she was no longer half his height but instead towered over him, seven or eight feet tall. The hair on her head started to fill out and began to sprout on her hands and face while the furs she was wearing fused with her skin to become part of her. Claws emerged from once tiny hands and her feeble arms and legs now bulged with powerful muscles.

Transformation complete, the Grandmother stood before him. A monster. Behind her both Mother and Daughter were stroking their own belts and undergoing their own transformations. The thick fur that covered the Grandmother was white as snow, the Mother's was a coarse black and the Daughter's was auburn. Bravery forgotten, the Woodcutter dropped the blanket, snatched up his axe and sprinted away from the family. Stumbling as he ran, he heard the sound of a howl behind him and then two more voices joining it. Primal fear began to set in and while the Woodcutter put on another burst of speed it turned out to be in vain. From the corner of his eye he could see something moving beside him through the trees and, glancing left, saw the Mother loping along, effortlessly keeping pace. Panicking, the Woodcutter glanced right and saw the Daughter also running beside him, while a sense of dread told him that the Grandmother was somewhere close behind. Realising this, the Woodcutter knew what was going on. They were playing with him. Suddenly he burst into a clearing and the sunlight momentarily blinded him, causing him to trip on the uneven ground. He was sent sprawling onto the grass, the axe flying from his hands and landing in a nearby bush.

As he picked himself up and blinked away the spots of light in front of his eyes the Woodcutter searched around desperately. The wolves hadn't emerged from the forest yet but he knew they were there. He could hear laughter from among the trees. The clearing, it turned out, was a familiar one and the chapel looked down on him from atop its hill. Somehow he had come full circle. Glancing once more at the forest the Woodcutter ran towards the open doorway. Already exhausted from running, the Woodcutter's legs cried out in pain as he climbed the steep slope towards the ruin; but he put it aside and pushed himself harder when he saw three hulking shapes shoot from the forest's edge, closing the distance between them and him with awesome speed.

Stumbling the last few steps, the Woodcutter fell through the doorway as a powerful set of jaws snapped shut, narrowly missing his leg. The Woodcutter pulled his way under the collapsed section of roof and leaned, energy spent, against the stone wall waiting for the creature to kill him. But the death he was expecting didn't come. Peeking under the gap the Woodcutter couldn't see any sign of the family, in either form. Thinking this might be another part of their game, he took a chance and crept deeper into the chapel searching for anything that he might be able to use as a weapon, something which could replace his axe. But there was nothing of use, only rotted shields and broken glass. Suddenly the Woodcutter heard a sound outside and pulled himself up to one of the high, open windows. There he could see the Daughter grinning at him with teeth the length of his finger.

"Woodcutter! Woodcutter! Come out and play!" The beast spoke to him in the little girl's voice.

"Don't make us come in there Woodcutter. We won't

be pleased, and if we aren't pleased we might not kill you right away." This time it was the Mother's voice calling from the other side of the chapel. "Have you ever had someone chew off a leg while you still live? The screams are almost as delicious as the leg itself."

"Come out dearie," the Grandmother called to him through the doorway, "We'll let you run some more, if you like? Fear adds to the flavour. Just like dunking a biscuit." Her grin showed the Woodcutter a mouth which could swallow his head in one quick bite.

"I'm not coming out!"

"Oh go on dearie, it's more fun if you do."

"No. Come in and get me!"

Suddenly realisation struck the Woodcutter, "You can't can you? You can't come in!" Outside the wolves growled confirming his suspicions. "What's the matter? Not church people?"

The Grandmother's jaws snapped shut and she disappeared from view. The Woodcutter could hear the three of them circling the chapel.

"Think you're clever do you?" The Mother snarled from near the back wall, "If you don't play nice then maybe we won't."

The Daughter's giggles echoed off the stone at her Mother's words. "Maybe we creep through the woods and visit Mrs Woodcutter and little baby Woodcutter? Maybe we bring them back here and eat them in front of you. Let you hear their screams as they die slowly and all because you won't play with us."

Inside the chapel the Woodcutter stayed silent, trying to control an anger which was brewing inside him.

"Didn't know we knew about them did you dearie? We could smell them on you before you even arrived at the house."

"I want one!" The Daughter demanded causing the

Grandmother to cackle with laughter again.

"Good idea dearie. We'll munch on old Mrs Woodcutter and make the little baby one of us. What say you Woodcutter?"

The Woodcutter snapped, "I will kill you all! I won't let you hurt them!"

"Sounds like someone wants to play after all. Oh and just so you know dearie, we can come in whenever we like. True, these bodies don't like that nasty old church but we have more than one don't we?" The Grandmother gave a little cackle, "And don't worry, we don't need teeth and claws dearie. I think we'll come in and get you then go get your darling daughter."

The Woodcutter could hear huffing and puffing outside and, lifting himself back up to the window, watched the three stroking their belts and changing back into their human forms. All the noise gave the Woodcutter an idea of how he might kill the family and escape. While they were busy the Woodcutter raced to the tree that grew from the floor, climbed until he reached the roof nearest the window and waited. Only moments after he was in position the three witches came crawling through the doorway and spotted him, seemingly about to escape.

"Stop him!" The Grandmother shouted and the three of them ran towards him. Jumping up the Woodcutter grabbed one of the rafters that struggled to hold up the roof and pulled with all his might. After a tense moment the rafter came away from the crumbling stone and all around him the roof started to collapse, crashing to the ground. The witches, seeing this, all made desperate dashes to escape; the Daughter trying to scramble back out of the doorway was crushed as the roof there gave way. The Mother tried to jump and climb out from one of the windows but was hit in the head by falling masonry before having more of the roof collapse on her, crushing her like her daughter.

Angered, the Grandmother threw herself at the tree causing the Woodcutter to lose his balance and fall backwards out of the open window. With a crash that knocked the wind from him the Woodcutter hit the ground and was sent tumbling down the hill. When he finally came to rest, the Woodcutter gingerly climbed to his feet and watched the last of the roof collapse into the chapel, silencing the scream of the Grandmother trapped within. The Woodcutter stood and watched until the final stone had fallen and the clearing was silent and peaceful once more. Walking carefully around the outside of the clearing the Woodcutter collected his axe from under its bush and cautiously approached the pile of stones which had been the chapel. After some searching he found a frail dead hand poking from the rubble and he began to dig. When the last stones had been moved aside and he could see her clearly the Woodcutter paused. The old woman's dead form looked little different from when he first saw her in the doorway of her home, she once again looked ancient, frail and even friendly, the falling roof having done little damage to her body. Looking down at the little old lady who had made him tea and offered him a biscuit the Woodcutter swung his axe and chopped her head clean off.

It was many hours before the Woodcutter had finished his work but when he was done three heads were piled a short distance from the chapel's ruins. Like the old woman, the Daughter's face was barely changed in death, still young and innocent, and the Woodcutter, feeling pity for the girl, covered her face with the red cloak she had worn. The Mother's extraordinary beauty was gone though, falling debris had pulverised her face and the mess that remained could barely be recognised as human;

but the Woodcutter could feel no sympathy for the creatures that had threatened his family. Gathering more firewood the Woodcutter made a pyre around the pile of heads determined to make sure that the witches would never have any chance to harm his wife or child. When the blaze was lit and the flames reached their highest, the Woodcutter took the three belts he had gathered from the bodies to toss them into the fire's heart. One at a time they were thrown into the pyre and each time the flames licked at one of the belts a deafening wolf howl echoed through the clearing.

By now evening was setting in and, after the last belt had been destroyed and its howl had faded, the Woodcutter took a torch he had prepared and lit it from the pyre, setting off into the forest once more, determined to return home. An hour or more he walked before stumbling onto a tree that bore one of his markings and soon he had found his way back to the stream where he had banged his head. Here, the Woodcutter paused and, before he could set off anew, noticed a distant light through the trees. Carefully he extinguished his torch in the shallow water and crept silently through the trees towards the light. As he grew close he began to make out voices and, peeking around a tree, saw a group of men gathered around a fire. It took a moment for his eyes to adjust to the bright light again and when they did the Woodcutter realised he knew the men, they were the woodsmen he had set off with more than a day before.

Excited, the Woodcutter leapt out from behind his tree, surprising the woodsmen and making them drop the bowls of food they had been eating. Warmly they greeted the Woodcutter, telling him of their search for him and of his wife worrying back home. The woodsmen asked him to tell of his adventures but none believed his tale and before long they were setting off back to the village, the hour's long journey seeming no time at all to the young Woodcutter. Upon seeing his front door and the lit window the Woodcutter burst into a run, throwing the door open and grabbing his surprised wife in an enormous hug.

"You're back!" His wife exclaimed as she hugged him tightly. When she finally let him go, tears of joy in her eyes, the Woodcutter carefully sat on the edge of the bed while his wife went to check on the baby who was gurgling in her cot and straining to get towards her father.

"Are you alright?" The Woodcutter asked his wife as she carried their daughter over to him, nested safely in her arms.

Handing him the baby his wife sat down beside him, "I am now. I thought I'd lost you." She kissed him tenderly on the cheek. " I'm so happy you're back. I thought I'd never see you again." She kissed his hand gently. "What happened to you?"

"Nothing much," he told her. "Nothing to worry about anyway." He kissed her gently on the lips and they lay down together with their daughter giggling between them.

Afterlife

PR Pope

Accidentally pushed through a time-space warp as a child, PR Pope found himself in our dimension. Lucky enough to find a surrogate family in his exile, he had a fairly normal upbringing: school, university, research institute, international prizes. Drawing on his innate technological superiority over earthlings, he proceeded to 'discover' many of the advances that we take for granted in a modern networked society - frequently passing the credit to others to avoid arousing suspicion. In the process he made and lost a fortune, but is nevertheless still happy. He has decided now is the time to commit to print some of the tales with which he was weaned on his home planet.

Caroline blinked in surprise and squinted slightly as her vision started to adjust. She was sure that she must have died, in which case this was paradise. The light was clear, bright, almost clinical. Distinctly different from what she had envisaged. It was also rather noisy, if strangely subdued. Not quite the angelic choirs her upbringing might have led her to expect, more like the waiting area of a hospital accident and emergency department. That thought jarringly reminded her of how she came to be here. She shuddered as the memory came flooding back, feeling that metal pole piercing her chest, the acute pain and then the abrupt cessation of everything. Until now. She couldn't see anything sticking out of her chest. In fact, there was no evidence that there ever had been anything untoward in her torso. She was still wearing the same clothes but they were apparently undamaged and there were no bloodstains to be seen. Gingerly she tried to sit up and was amazed to find herself entirely unimpeded. Paradise? It didn't seem to be much like any vision of the 'realm beyond' that she had ever seen.

Perhaps she wasn't dead after all. She could look around now and was surprised to find herself in a large area that did indeed appear plain and unadorned like a hospital. But there were no obvious patients as such. The few people she could see were not exhibiting any signs of injury or disease.

'Psychological ward maybe,' she thought, 'perhaps I

imagined the accident.'

Swinging her legs around and over the side of the trolley on which she had been lying, Caroline carefully slid off and took her weight on her feet while steadying herself on the trolley's metal frame. Having failed to collapse or otherwise sink to the ground she pushed herself away and took a step. She was fine. There was obviously nothing wrong with her. She breathed a deep sigh of relief.

'In which case, where are the nurses?' she wondered.

She started to walk towards the nearest person, a middle-aged woman sitting in a chair with her hands clasped together in her lap. Just at that moment she felt a gentle tap on her shoulder.

"Caroline. There's no need to disturb Agnes, she's having a little trouble acclimatising. Would you walk with me and I can answer any questions you may have."

Caroline turned to look at her manifest minder. A tall, beautiful, androgynous person was standing beside her. Dressed in a long white outfit he, or she, was looking relaxed and serene yet confident that Caroline would comply. Having decided that this person would not be a threat, Caroline nodded and the two of them headed away from the oblivious Agnes towards the centre of the room.

"Do you understand where you are?" asked the lofty beauty.

"I've come to the conclusion that I'm either dead or in a funny farm."

"Well done. But which?"

"Funny farm?"

"Try again."

"Dead?" Caroline sounded less flippant this time.

"Right. Welcome to Afterlife."

"How did I get here?"

"You died, obviously."

"That big pole was real then?"

"Very real, very big, and very messy."

"But…" Caroline looked pointedly down at her intact chest and pristine clothes.

"How you remember yourself from before the accident. That's quite normal. Occasionally someone remembers themself as they were after whatever eventually caused their death, especially with long drawn out diseases. That can be quite distressing for them when they get here, but we can usually deal with it and re-engineer their self-image a bit. Accidents invariably happen so fast that the victim has no time to imagine themself in any other way than undamaged. Anyway, that's all irrelevant for you so let's not dwell on it. We have other things to discuss."

"Okay. Where are we going now?"

"You have to choose your Final Destination."

"I'm sorry?"

"This is just a way-station, a waiting room or transit area if you like."

"On the way to…?"

"The Final Destination. Generally it's dependent on cultural upbringing, religion, personal beliefs and that sort of thing. So a Catholic might be expecting to go to Purgatory on the way to Dante's Heaven, a fundamentalist Christian may be hoping for Paradise but expecting to be consigned to pits of fire and brimstone, or any of the other religious visions of what we call H3."

"H3?"

"Heaven, Hell or Hades. Fashions change too, of course, so for example Valhalla isn't terribly common any more and we rarely get to cross the Styx these days. Oh, but the Void is extremely popular with fundamentalist scientists. Actually they don't even come through here on their way as it would completely upset their belief system." She grinned.

"Right." Caroline looked thoughtful for a few seconds.

"Do you have a name?" She asked.

"Of course."

Caroline waited a few more seconds and tried again.

"What is it?"

"Raphael."

"Like the archangel?"

"Not like."

"You mean you are the archangel Raphael?"

"For you."

"What does that mean?"

"Those with an Abrahamic upbringing expect Angels. Anyone heading for Valhalla wants a Valkyrie. For Buddhists it's Devas and Hindus have Apsaras. Classical traditionalists expect nymphs; and, of course, Charon. Pagans have spirits. All the same really."

"So you appear differently to each person?"

"No, but how they interpret me is different."

"No wings though!" Caroline grinned.

"Well, it's considered rude indoors." Raphael smiled back, a serene calming smile.

"So, the Final Destination?"

"Your choice."

"Any?"

"Yes. But it's a once-only decision. There's no trial offer or fourteen day cooling-off period."

"What's the catch? Apart from living with your decision."

"Not exactly 'living' with your decision!" Raphael corrected Caroline.

"You know what I mean. But don't avoid the question. Is there a catch?"

"Not really. However if you choose somewhere that you don't actually believe in, it can be a great disappointment. An ever-lasting disappointment, of course."

"But I'm not limited to choosing Purgatory or Hell? I could head for Valhalla if I thought it would be more fun?"

"Not that good a choice for a young woman actually, but there's nothing to stop you. Except your family."

"Family?" Caroline looked confused. "What have they got to say about it?"

"Nothing directly. But you may want to consider where your relatives and friends might already be, or where those coming along later will expect to find you."

"Hmm."

"Tarquin for example."

"Tarquin?"

"Didn't you both make a vow to be re-united on 'the other side' and whoever was left behind would remain faithful?"

"How did you know about that?"

In reply Raphael just raised an eyebrow.

Caroline thought for a moment.

"So, you're telling me that I need to choose my Final Destination to be wherever Tarquin is going to expect to find me in fifty years time?"

"Fifty years, or tomorrow."

"Tomorrow? Why, what happens tomorrow?"

"I don't know. That's the point. I don't know. You don't know. If he does come here tomorrow then he'll probably be looking for you in Heaven. In fifty years time, who can say? By then his beliefs and expectations may have radically changed and he may be looking for you somewhere different."

"So even if I choose based on where I think he's likely to look for me it may eventually be the wrong choice." Caroline was thoughtful for a few seconds and then continued. "I should leave a message, to tell him where to find me."

Raphael winced slightly, but nonetheless perceptibly.

"Bit of a logistical nightmare managing an infinite bulletin board across the whole of history."

Caroline looked at Raphael's pursed lips and slightly cocked head, but couldn't decide whether it was a joke.

"Is that a no?"

"Yes."

"Yes it's a yes, or yes it's a no?"

"Yes, it's a no."

"Sometimes you don't make it easy to understand…"

"Mysterious ways and all that." Raphael smiled that serene smile again.

"Of course," Raphael began again, "you don't have to take any notice of what others have done or may do."

"So, if I chose, say, Valhalla…" Caroline started to ask but was dismayed by Raphael's re-raised eyebrow,

"…or wherever, and then Tarquin comes along at some time in the future expecting to find me in Purgatory. What would happen?"

"He wouldn't find you there."

"Well obviously. But could he then come looking for me elsewhere?"

"Caroline. It's called the Final Destination. Think about it. Not very final if you can change your mind and try again. If nothing else, imagine the logistics of managing all those indecisive people who would change their mind every other day and want to try something different. No, far too disruptive. The dolphins would be furious."

"What?"

"Never mind. Look, the point is that you need to make the right choice for you but in the context of whoever you are expecting to meet 'on the other side' and whoever might eventually be expecting to meet you there. If that is a significant concern for you then you need to be predictable! If not, then live a little. Or in fact, not, of course."

"Very droll!"

Raphael looked at Caroline with that serene smile once more.

"What should I do?"

"It's not for me to say. You must decide."

"Why?"

"Rules is rules."

"Rules are for breaking," ventured Caroline.

"Not this time."

"How quickly do I have to decide?"

"Take your time." Raphael laughed. "Sorry, IN joke. We're effectively outside time here."

"What does that even mean? Time obviously passes here, we've been talking for about five minutes. Things happen in sequence. You tapped me on the shoulder, then I turned round. Cause and effect. So how are we outside time?"

"Very good. We're outside time in the sense that your perception of time here is unrelated to the passage of time in your old life, as it is being experienced by those you left behind. When you opened your eyes here five minutes ago it was 10 o'clock on the 10th of October for Tarquin. The time we've been talking here doesn't even register as a significant fraction of a second there. For him it's still 10 o'clock."

"Like Narnia."

"If you want."

"So… inside time rather than outside time?"

"That's a good description, but keep it to yourself. Most who come through here don't think about such things as deeply as you obviously do. The distinction may be lost on them, or it may confuse or even frighten them. Generally they're happy with 'outside time'. It's what they expect."

"Okay." But Caroline wasn't entirely convinced.

"To be frank, you're probably focussing on the least significant details of your situation. Although that's not uncommon among the smarter souls we help to pass on."

"Souls?"

"What did you think you and these others here," Raphael swept a hand over the room, "were?"

"I don't know. I hadn't thought about it."

"Well you're all souls that have been liberated from the physical realm and now you're here you need to move on."

"Why?"

"What do you mean why?"

"Why do I need to move on. Why can't I just stay here."

"Because this is just a way-station."

"So?"

"Logistics, yet again. It would fill up very quickly if everyone hung around for too long. This isn't an infinite resource you know."

"You seem very concerned about logistics for a spiritual being."

"Just trying to relate to your human experience. You were a project manager weren't you?"

"Yes I am. ... Er, was."

"There you are then."

"But I still don't understand..." Raphael touched a finger to Caroline's lips.

"Precisely. You don't understand. You won't understand. You can't understand. You have to accept some truths for what they are and move on. Literally." That smile again. Caroline was now beginning to find it smug and irritating rather than serene.

"You died," Raphael continued, "less than a second ago in Tarquin's world. He is only just realising it as the alarms from the monitoring equipment around your bed go off. He's very tired as he's been at your side since you went into the coma…"

"Coma?" Caroline interrupted. "Hang on, what did you say the date was?"

"Tenth of October."

"So the accident was over a month ago?"

"That's right. You've been in a coma ever since and the doctors decided this morning to switch off life support. Tarquin disagreed but his opinion doesn't count and you have no family, so it was up to the hospital. Now both of you have to move on. In many ways you have the advantage over him. You know what's coming next whereas he doesn't."

"Can't I tell him? As a ghost or something?"

"He wouldn't be able to see or hear you."

"I could find a medium to interpret."

"You've seen too many films! It's not really like that. It's a one-way process. If it wasn't, after thousands of years there wouldn't still be any doubt about the afterlife would there?"

"It seems so unfair."

"I think that's exactly what Tarquin is saying right now."

"Oh." Caroline thought for a few more moments. "Can I at least see him?"

"Not advisable."

"But possible?"

"Difficult. As I said we're outside time."

"Inside."

"Whichever. The point is that seeing Tarquin would be like looking at a still frame from a film. Whenever anyone has tried, it has been very disconcerting, even frustrating for them. Almost all have regretted it."

"Almost all. But not all?"

"I know of one person who was reassured, but he had

gone to watch his wife die seconds after him, so he knew they were about to be re-united - as they were. Everyone else has been haunted by the experience. Sorry, no pun intended."

Caroline frowned.

"I really would advise against it," Raphael continued firmly.

Caroline was standing next to a simple armchair. She sank onto one of the arms, put her left hand to her forehead and looked down at her feet.

"I don't know what to do. You said I could take my time deciding?"

"Within reason."

Caroline looked up at Raphael as a thought struck her.

"Do you meet and guide everyone who arrives here?"

"No, there are a few of us."

"Do you choose who to guide?"

"In a way."

"So you could choose to guide Tarquin when he comes here?"

"Indeed."

"How good is your memory?"

Raphael was apparently surprised by the non-sequitur but replied calmly.

"Perfect." From Raphael this didn't sound like a boast but a statement of fact.

"So you would remember what I choose to do and could tell Tarquin when he gets here?"

"I could."

"Would you?"

"If he asked me. I'm not supposed to encourage a soul to make a specific choice. But if I'm asked a direct question I will tell the truth."

"Okay. I've decided. I'm going to Dante's Heaven, I guess that's via Purgatory."

"Right. Let's go."

Caroline stood up again and started to follow Raphael who had turned to walk towards a large doorway at the end of the room. Caroline hadn't noticed the door before.

"One last question." Caroline had caught up with Raphael.

"Of course."

"Did my Mum and Dad choose Purgatory?"

"I don't know."

"Why not?"

"I haven't met them. When did they die?"

"About fifteen years ago."

They had now reached the doorway. Raphael stopped and turned to face Caroline.

"Here we are. Go through this door and you're there. If Tarquin comes through I will choose to be his guide. If he asks me where you chose to go I will tell him. Goodbye."

Caroline was lost for words. It now seemed so sudden and abrupt. She pushed the door open and started to step through, then turned to ask one last question.

"Are you sure you don't know where Mum and Dad went?"

"Yes. Fifteen years ago this system wasn't in place. Sorry."

"System?"

"Afterlife 2.0. Tarquin's insurance covered you."

As Raphael was speaking Caroline felt herself being pulled through the doorway as if by suction.

The door shut behind her.

Raphael smiled a serene smile.

Through tear-filled eyes Tarquin watched the monitor next to Caroline's bed. The small flashing red light changed to steady green and a message flashed up on the display:

Brainwaves secured
- Upload complete -
Thank you for choosing Afterlife 2.0

Dreamers

Alison Buck

Like all of us, Alison Buck has led many lives.

One as a sensible, hard-working type, employed in financial systems, graphic design and web site development. Another as a writer, scribbling away, committing her stories to disc and eventually publishing several to reasonable acclaim. Throughout all of them, the mother of two and wife of one.

Skilled at exploring the psychology and interior lives of her characters, Alison delivers stories that range from chilling tales of horror through insightful contemporary drama to thought-provoking science fiction. Her empathy with her protagonists, her rich descriptive prose and her use of gentle humour serve to ensure that, whatever the setting, her stories are always a rewarding read.

The old man's grey-green eyes faded as he began to drift away. With a parting smile, he gently opened his fine, long fingers to reveal a tiny golden bird resting in the palm of his hand. He eased it onto the sill of the open window, where it remained completely motionless and silent. Lucia thought the animal must be frozen or perhaps a statue; an incredible work of craftsmanship, until, with the faintest ruffling of its golden feathers, the tiny creature suddenly dropped its head to one side and fixed her with its black diamond eye. Lucia felt herself smiling in return. She looked up to share the moment but, even as she watched, her old friend paled to invisibility and was gone.

Alone with the strange golden bird Lucia felt no alarm and indeed was oddly comforted. Its intense dark stare looked deep into her. Deep, deep into her soul.

Lucia closed her eyes.

It was cold now; the air chilling through her thin gown. It was time to reopen her eyes.

The window was wide. Far below, on the spiky, winter-grey lawns, the gravel paths seemed to writhe and twist like pale, sliding snakes. Then, as Lucia stared down, a light snow began to fall. From all around the rim of her vision, slow, ragged flakes tumbled silently past, seeming to converge to a single point; deep in the glossy evergreen of a holly tree far below. It was mesmerising: breathtaking.

"Lucia?"

The woman's voice was hushed. Lucia continued to stare down into the dizzying tunnel of falling snowflakes. She didn't move, but was listening intently and aware, directing her attention to the voice, waiting for it to continue.

"Lucia?" it came again, still soft, but uneasy, "Lucia, can you hear me?"

The urgent gentleness in the voice was clearly an attempt to mask some underlying distress and Lucia was anxious for her, sensing her hidden pain. The voice seemed uncertain, suffering, reaching out for comfort, and Lucia could never ignore a cry for help. This time the appeal was unusual; the voice was somehow aware of her and, most bizarrely, it knew her name. How could that be? Lucia puzzled over this as she waited for the voice to speak to her again. Trying to sense its location, she leant forward, her toes now at the very edge of the window sill.

"No! Lucia, stay still!" a terrified shout, "Don't move!"
Lucia froze.

As she waited she was aware of the softest tingling against her skin, as snowflakes lightly brushed and melted on her bare feet; a delightfully ticklish sensation. Lucia smiled, in spite of herself, but she obeyed the frightened voice and didn't move.

After a moment's tense silence, when the voice began again, it was clearly struggling to regain its previous evenness.

"Lucia, can you hear me? Don't move." and then, shivering, whispered, "Oh god, where are they?"
"Who?"
The voice made no reply.
"Let me help you," Lucia coaxed, taking care to remain still.
"What?"

"Let me help you." Lucia repeated gently, "Where are you?"

"What?"

The woman now sounded utterly confused so Lucia spoke more slowly. Steadying her breathing though she was shivering with the cold, she made her tone as calm and encouraging as possible.

"Can you tell me where you are. I want to help you."

"Lucia, I'm here. I'm right here; by the door."

"The door?"

"Lucia, I'm here, in the room."

Involuntarily, Lucia began to turn. Again the terrified shout.

"Please, I'm begging you, stay still. Don't move."

"I'm sorry. I didn't mean to frighten you. I won't turn round or come any closer if that's what you want, but please let me help you."

The voice said nothing and, for a moment or two, there was absolute silence in the icy room.

"Are you still there?" Lucia asked.

"Yes," said the voice, "I'm right here. Please, Lucia, just try to stay still."

This was very strange, Lucia thought; it almost felt as if the voice was really with her, in the room. She wondered where the woman actually was and why she was so desperate to remain hidden. Why was she afraid to let herself be found? Not a fugitive, surely? That was too far-fetched. Was she worried that Lucia might be shocked by her appearance? Deformed perhaps, or badly scarred? Here in the hospital Lucia had met many lonely, lost and often beautiful souls housed within malformed or damaged bodies. It was of no consequence to her; the outer person meant nothing to Lucia, who saw the soul beneath. Unfortunately, the world outside did not have Lucia's sight and was frequently cruel. Was this the pain that Lucia could sense in the voice?

"Please let me help you." she said, making only the slightest of movements to turn.

"For god's sake, Lucia, stay still!" The voice was agitated; shrill with alarm.

"OK," Lucia soothed, "I'm sorry. Try to stay calm and breath deeply, in and out, slowly, like this. And don't worry, I won't move again, I promise."

"Thank you." the voice sighed.

"That's OK. I'm sorry but, for some reason, I can't feel what the problem is; maybe because I'm not with you. You're going to have to tell me."

"Tell you what?"

"What's happened to you. If you don't want me to come to you, that's fine; we can just talk. Just tell me what's happened and don't worry; I promise it will go no further. First, would you like to tell me your name?"

"My name?"

"Yes. But only if you want to; only if you're happy to tell me."

"You know m-," the voice broke off suddenly, then leapt with relief, "At last! Where the hell have you been? I rang for help ages ago. Quick, get her in."

Lucia felt someone strong grab her left arm, gripping her wrist, pulling her. She swung off balance, pirouetting about her left foot, her right leg and right arm swinging out into cold, thin air. Spinning back again, her right hand was suddenly grabbed and she was hauled forwards and down, into a confusion of light.

The woman, not frightened now, tried to prevent her being given drugs. But she was over-ruled. Lucia felt the sting as an injection pressed into her arm. She felt her eyelids closing and she slipped into unconsciousness.

"Lucia?"

This voice was very different. This voice was used to being in charge. A man.

"Lucia?" he repeated, "Can you hear me?"

Why, Lucia wondered, did they always ask her that? If she couldn't hear their question, she wouldn't give them an answer, would she? Also, a person might be able to hear perfectly well, but simply choose not to answer, or even answer 'No'; his question was a silly one.

"Lucia I need you to open your eyes because we need to talk. I want you to tell me what the matter is."

Lucia hadn't yet decided if this person was someone with whom she wanted to exchange the merest everyday pleasantries and she was certainly miles away from the sharing of opinions, hopes, secrets or deeply-held dreams with the owner of this officious voice. But she was getting ahead of herself. First things first; should she acknowledge hearing? She was lying in her bed and presumably had been asleep for some time. If she lay still and said nothing, he would most likely conclude that she was still asleep and he would go away. That would buy her some peace, a few hours, a day perhaps; who knew the passing of time in this place?

"Lucia." the tone was no longer questioning but brusque, his patience ebbing fast, "Open your eyes."

His voice was economical, the words clipped to avoid wasted time. Lucia had a mental image of tiny clipped segments of typewritten words falling from the lips of a large and preposterously formal man. The snippets of text were piling up around him, their unintended juxtapositions forming bizarre new words; 'busy-nonsense', 'better-wasting' and 'other-bother' among them. It worked like a translation into a new language she mused; he asks foolish questions and the clipping translates them into nonsense by way of answers. That made a sort of sense. Lucia particularly liked 'busy-nonsense'; it seemed to sum up this tiresome and overbearing doctor's attitude to perfection. She smiled.

Her smile was seized upon immediately.

"You're awake. Good. Open your eyes."

The voice expected her compliance. It was used to being obeyed. But Lucia had decided finally that she didn't like this person and she didn't want to talk with him. She scrunched her eyes tight.

"I'm a very busy man, Lucia. Open your eyes."

Lucia heard his brisk and, no doubt, manicured fingers tapping in irritation.

"I don't have time for this." he was talking to someone else now, "Let me know when she starts co-operating."

Lucia heard the door swing shut and slowly opened her eyes. Angelique was standing over her, a knowing smile on her broad, unlined face.

"You shouldn't do that, Lucia."

Lucia didn't reply, but stared up at the nurse's face.

"You know, Angelique," she said at last, "Your face is like the African sun."

The nurse threw back her head and laughed a high, infectious laugh.

"Goodness, Child, what makes you say that?"

"It's obvious; warmth just pours out of you. You're one of the kindest people I've met in my whole life."

"Hush now," said Angelique, becoming embarrassed, "I'm just doing my job."

"No, you do much more than that, Angelique. And you do much more than that ridiculous man will ever do; you give time and you give love. Your caring makes people feel good and that's when they start to recover; when they begin to regain hope."

"Hush now."

"I don't care what you say." Lucia's voice faded to a

whisper, "You're the only sunshine in this place."

Lucia closed her eyes again, weakened by the exchange.

When Angelique spoke again she was insistent, the concern clear in her tone.

"Lucia, Honey, if you don't co-operate, the doctor is going to start treatment and medication and, Honey, that's a road you don't want to go down, believe me. Please talk to him. Tomorrow, when he comes back." Angelique paused a moment, hoping for some sign of acquiescence in her patient. She started tidying the bed, tucking the sheets around Lucia's wasted body, "I know he's an arrogant so and so, but everyone says he's really good at his job; he's the top man. Please let him help you. You don't want to be in here forever, a pretty girl like you. You want to be out, having fun."

Lucia's eyes fluttered open for a second.

"I want to help people, Angelique."

"I know you do Honey, I know."

The nurse paused, shaking her head. Gently, she touched Lucia's cheek, the gesture conveying all the maternal love she felt for this fragile young woman, really little more than a child.

"But Honey, right now you need the help."

Lucia was dreaming again.

She was drifting high above the snow-covered lawns, oblivious to the cold. Feeling herself drawn to one of the other hospital buildings, she floated towards it and passed with ease through the old red brick walls with their crumbling lime plaster. She stopped, or was stopped, at the bedside of a small sleeping child, a little boy.

With a whisper like that of air slipping smoothly over silk, the golden bird flew to rest on her shoulder. Lucia had not expected the bird to be here, indeed, until it suddenly appeared, she had no recollection of ever having seen it before. And yet she was immediately at her ease and familiar with it, remembering now that it was the gift of the gentle man with the sorrowful grey-green eyes. The tiny bird nestled against her neck and, feeling its comforting warmth, Lucia relaxed, letting her mind wander freely.

Images formed. Daylight. The boy was on his way to school. It was his birthday. Lucia saw him running in the street, kicking a gleaming red football. The ball was new, a present from his grandmother, Doreen. Next, Lucia saw the ready smile creasing the old woman's face as she watched her grandson opening his birthday gift. When he saw the shiny new football, his own face glowed with gratitude, returning Doreen's loving, toothless smile. Suddenly, remembering that she did not have her dentures, Doreen clapped a thin hand to her mouth, but she need not have been concerned; the boy had not noticed and would not have cared if he had. He loved his Nan, she was the best Nan ever and anyway, for the moment, his attention was fixed on the shiny red ball she had just given him.

Lucia smiled.

The images winked back to the street. The ball bounced away from the boy, rolling under the parked cars on the opposite side of the road. At the same time, Lucia saw the delivery van turn the corner, its young driver moaning tunelessly to the music on his radio, his body jerking to the thumping beat and his palms keeping up the rhythm, on the wheel. For an agonising moment, the young man suddenly froze, seeing the boy run out in front of him. Then panic gripped him and he grabbed at the wheel, pulling it hopelessly to the side. He knew he was going to hit the child and, in the slow motion of the last second, Gary, the young driver, shut his eyes. Lucia, though, could see it all. Time slowed; becoming viscous. Lucia watched, appalled, as the unyielding metallic solidity of the van slammed into the soft and vulnerable body of the child, punching the air from his lungs, shattering several ribs and breaking both his legs, before hurling his dislocated body clear across the road. The boy was unconscious even before he hit the pavement and from Lucia's viewpoint, high above his fallen body, everyone and everything seemed frozen, save for the widening shadow of blood pooling around the child's head. Then the silence ended, with a sudden, headlong rush of noise and frenzied action. In an instant everyone came back to life; running over to crowd and jostle around the tiny prone figure.

Without warning, Lucia was tugged away and back to the bedside.

Motionless under crisp, white sheets, the boy looked strangely more broken now than he had done lying on the street. Bandages and plaster seemed to enclose him entirely, grossly distorting the proportions of his limbs; his own small body seeming somehow lost beneath it all. Wires and tubes connected him to machines humming quietly at the head of the bed. Unaware of Lucia's presence, a nurse checked and re-checked the monitors' displays every ten minutes. Lucia knew that Josh had already bettered the expectations of the medical team in having survived the many hours of emergency surgery. She also knew that he would be luckier still to survive the night.

Lucia's own chest was tight with anxiety for the boy, but she knew she must remain detached while she investigated what help was needed. She steadied herself, again letting the warmth of the bird at her shoulder calm her, then closed her eyes. From a tiny glow in the palms of Lucia's outstretched hands, a golden aura pulsed and grew, gradually encompassing both her and the boy lying tiny on the oversized bed. In the clarity of the searching light, Lucia could see that, given much time and care, the boy's shattered bones would eventually mend. However, it was also clear that Josh would not have that time; a large blood vessel had just ruptured and was discharging blood into the fluid below his fractured skull. The pressure on his brain was building very fast. Alarms began to sound and medical staff began to converge on the bed. Unseen by them, Lucia reached deep within herself and focussed all her attention on the damaged blood vessel, sealing it and forcing down the pressure in the fluid around Josh's brain. Baffled, the nurses checked and rechecked the monitors and bleeped the on-call doctor. While they worked, Lucia maintained her link with Josh, rejoining the cracked bones of his skull and willing him the strength he was going to need to get through the next few hours.

Conscious of another presence, Lucia looked up. The man with grey-green eyes was there again, watching her. He was bathed in the same golden light and he was smiling. It was a smile of pride in what she had just done. And though Lucia could not quite remember precisely who this man was, she knew that he knew her and was very important to her; a mentor perhaps, or maybe the ghost of her long dead father. Whoever he was, his smile and his approval meant all the world to her.

Lucia looked back to the boy, but both he and the bed had vanished. She was somewhere outside. The man again smiled at her and she was filled with such happy contentment that she literally danced for joy. Floating lightly on the chill night air, she span around once last time and was back in her own room. The man was gone.

A smile still playing on her lips, Lucia sank back into dreamless sleep.

"Lucia? Wake up, I know you can hear me."

It was a friendly voice: Angelique. Lucia opened her eyes.

"Good girl. My, you're tired this morning." Angelique coaxed Lucia to a sitting position and fitted the cuff around her arm, "Now Honey, listen to your Angelique. Mr Pleasance will be doing rounds again later so please talk to him. I know you don't like him; I've seen the way you act when he's here. But if you keep this up he's going to think you've really lost it and he'll start you on the drugs. And, Honey, you don't want that. Please just talk to the man. For me, Lucia, please."

Lucia sighed.

"I'm not mad, Angelique. There's nothing wrong with my head. I just go away sometimes. People call to me. They need help and I go to them. That's all."

"In your dreams?" the nurse's tone was anxious, "People call you in your dreams? When you're asleep, right?"

"Yes."

The nurse relaxed.

"One time I thought someone was calling to me when I was awake, but it was only Nurse Jacobs."

"You give her a fright, standing in the window like that."

"That's because she doesn't know I can fly."

With renewed concern, Angelique looked deep into Lucia's eyes.

"No one can fly, Child."

Lucia merely smiled, which further worried Angelique. She decided to change the subject.

"I've got some good news. You'll never believe what's happened down in PICU."

"PICU?"

"It's where they look after the really seriously ill children. My friend Evie was on duty yesterday when a boy was brought in. He'd been hit by a truck and he was in a really, really bad way. She said he was rushed into theatre and they worked on him for hours. They did absolutely everything they could, but no one really expected the poor lad to get through the night. And then, guess what? When the doctor examined him this morning, his skull fracture had gone; healed!"

Lucia smiled again, but said nothing.

"Lucia, you don't understand; bones don't heal like that! Evie said she saw the X-rays with her own eyes and she heard the consultant say the pressure on the brain might be out of control." Angelique shook her head, "Evie's never seen anything like it. Never. None of them have. They don't know what to make of it. I tell you it's unbelievable; absolutely unbelievable." Angelique wrote Lucia's blood pressure and temperature in her notes. "OK. I'd better get on but, please, remember what I said about Mr Pleasance."

"I will. I promise. And Angelique?"

"Yes, Honey?"

"Would you ask Evie to give Josh a hug from me?"

"Of course I will. Honey. I think she'll have to wait her turn though; he's a darling little lad by all accounts. See you later."

To please Angelique, Lucia did speak to Mr Pleasance on his morning rounds.

Sweeping into the room, surrounded by a gaggle of anxiously competitive students, the consultant addressed his questions to the room as a whole, rather than to anyone in particular: patient, nurse or students, but Lucia obediently answered every one. As before, his brusque interrogation conjured, for Lucia, the image of the ticker-tape mountain of clipped words. 'Balancing-liquid', 'eat-teaching' and 'hungry-vomit' were her favourite new words today.

Before leaving at the end of her shift, Angelique came to thank Lucia for co-operating.

"I'm proud of you, Honey. Now, hopefully, they can start to sort out the problem."

"I'm OK, Angelique, really. Don't worry."

"But I do worry. You're looking so thin, Honey. Promise me you'll eat something at lunchtime."

"I do eat. I eat at every meal. Honestly, I do."

"Good." Angelique sounded unconvinced, "I'm glad to hear that, Lucia, but Mr Pleasance will know what to do. He'll soon get you well and out of here."

"There's no need. This is exactly where I need to be."

Dreaming again, Lucia found herself floating high above the old surgical wing. The bitterly cold night air was ice clear, the stars, brilliant diamonds in the cloudless sky above her. Every tile on the roof below was edged in frost and sparkled in the sharp, brilliance of the full moon. Enchanted as she was by the transformation around her; of the familiar, utilitarian hospital blocks into glittering, starkly beautiful palaces, Lucia was nevertheless still listening for the call that had summoned her. Quiet and intermittent, the voice was hard to pinpoint. It came again now and drew Lucia down towards it.

Drifting through the walls and into the ward, Lucia felt the call again. She came to a stop at the bed of an elderly lady. As the golden bird landed silently on her shoulder, Lucia again felt its reassuring familiarity. She extended her arms, golden light pulsed around her and images began to form in her mind.

Joan was in the Post Office. Lucia watched as she pushed the money into her purse and snapped her handbag shut. In turning to leave, the old lady accidentally bumped into the impatient young man who had been waiting to get to the counter in her place. The images snapped forward to Joan approaching the door of her house, pausing to catch her breath at the gate. Then, again, to a moment of quiet anticipation, as she waited for the kettle to boil for a reviving cup of tea. At the same time, Lucia saw the young man walking slowly towards the house. He had followed Joan to her home and was now crossing over the road towards the gate. He stopped there, looked up and down the street several times and then darted up to the front door. Joan heard a knock at the door and Lucia watched the old lady walking stiffly along the corridor. She also saw the young man, Kev, who had run around the side of the house and was now crouching at the kitchen door.

Joan called through the locked front door.

"Hello? Who is it? Who's there?"

Suddenly, glass smashed behind her. Kev was breaking in through the kitchen door. Joan shrieked and Lucia watched helplessly as the old lady struggled to reopen the front door to escape. Shouting abuse, Kev ran up and grabbed her. Dragging her to the kitchen, he threw Joan to the floor.

"Is there anyone else in the house?" he snarled.

Joan, whimpering with shock and the pain of a broken ankle, managed to shake her head, so Kev began to ransack the kitchen. He stole all the money from the purse and then raced from room to room pulling open drawers, emptying their contents; smashing and destroying Joan's precious belongings with malicious glee. Meanwhile, in the kitchen, Lucia could see further disastrous events unfolding.

Eventually, Kev smelt it: acrid, choking smoke. In the kitchen, he had carelessly thrown some tea towels onto the hob where the kettle rested over an open flame. By the time he became aware of it, the fire had taken hold, creeping up the wall and across the polystyrene tiles on the kitchen ceiling, generating the noxious black smoke that began to fill the house. Burning drops of molten polystyrene were spreading the fire and falling on Joan as she tried to drag herself towards the door. Ignoring her, Kev tried to save himself but was overcome by the impenetrable fumes. Lucia saw him die. Lying on the floor, below the level of the smoke, Joan was still alive when neighbours, alerted by the black cloud belching from the broken kitchen window, risked their own lives to drag their friend from the inferno.

Now, lying unresponsive in her hospital bed, Joan was sedated, on ventilation and with antibiotic and fluid lines in place, but Lucia knew that she would not survive her injuries without her help. Focusing, Lucia calmed the inflammation along Joan's airways, clearing the fluid that had seeped from the damaged tissue. Then Lucia lifted her gentle probing to the level of Joan's damaged skin and began to heal the terrible burns that peppered the old lady's head, arms and legs. Detaching and removing the hardened plastic, enmeshed deep within the wounds and coaxing the layers of skin to then reform and heal over, took time and immense concentration. Lucia felt herself weakening, but the golden bird nuzzled closer, its warmth reviving her. Despite this extra surge of energy, Lucia was close to exhaustion as she sealed the final area of injured skin. She wondered, briefly, whether she was capable of making one last effort and repairing Joan's broken ankle. As if in reply, a hand gently reached across and rested on hers. Lucia was not startled, but looked up. Of course, he had been there all the time and now, seeing him, she realised that she had felt his presence throughout the healing.

"Enough." he said, his beautiful eyes full of concern, "You've done enough."

Lucia closed her eyes and felt herself sinking down, floating back. In her own bed she quickly slipped into a deep and well-earned sleep.

"Lucia, Honey, wake up. You need to eat something. Come on, wake up for me."

Angelique kept up her gentle pleading until Lucia opened her eyes.

"That's better. Good morning, Sleepyhead. I was beginning to think I'd have to eat your breakfast for you."

"You can have it, if you like. I'm not hungry."

"No, no, you need to build your strength up, but I'll stay for a few minutes while you eat, if you like."

Sitting up, Lucia forced herself to eat a few mouthfuls while Angelique made lively conversation.

"It's happened again. Everybody's talking about it."

Lucia, her mouth full, raised a questioning eyebrow.

"This time it was an old lady. She came in yesterday after a dreadful fire at home. She was barely alive, and her poor grandson died in the flames."

"Her grandson?" Lucia was shocked.

"Yes, I shouldn't really be telling you any of this, but I spoke to one of the nurses, who spoke to one of the policemen, and he told her that it must be her grandson, but the fire was so fierce that he's not not been formally identified yet so they don't have his name. It looks like the old lady left something on the stove and forgot about it. Poor lad never stood a chance. I really feel for her; she's going to feel so bad, I mean, when she realises she caused a fire and her grandson is dead. It's so sad." Angelique paused, "But there is some good news too, even out of such a tragedy."

"Good news?"

"Yes, the lady was in a terrible state when they brought her in; the smoke had damaged her lungs and she had burns all over her poor body. But then, this morning, guess what? All she has is a broken ankle! Can you believe it?"

"That's incredible. Do you know if the policeman said anything about the house being upside down?"

"Upside down? What do you mean, Honey?"

"Do you know if he said anything about the house being in a mess?"

"Lucia, Honey, the house was completely burned out; of course it was a mess."

"No, I mean, did it look maybe like there'd been a break-in or anything?"

"No, not as far as I know. Why do you ask that?"

"It's just, I was thinking that he might not have been her grandson. And, whoever he was, he might have been in the house for the wrong reasons. He could have broken in to steal her stuff. He might have caused the fire, not her."

Angelique was appalled.

"Lucia, I'm surprised at you! That poor boy's lost his life. He's dead and he was only about your age. It's an absolute tragedy and it's really wicked to say things like that about him."

Lucia had never before seen Angelique angry, but she was angry now.

"Now finish your meal and no hiding any of it."

Angelique stood at the end of the bed, for once making no effort to hide the fact that she was monitoring how much food Lucia had eaten. That done, she left, still shaking her head disapprovingly. Lucia watched her go in silence.

Angelique was uncharacteristically quiet for the remainder of the day and Lucia began to realise just how much she relied on the nurse's friendly visits to pass the time. Even on those days when Angelique's shift meant that Lucia saw her only during routine checks of vital signs, the nurse's concern and friendship had become intrinsic to Lucia's life. Today, the hours between meals and sessions with the therapist dragged by and the resulting boredom gave Lucia plenty of cause to regret having spoken so hastily. She still felt the need to defend Joan, but she knew she had handled things badly.

Thankfully, when Angelique came back the following morning, she had clearly decided to forgive Lucia her callous outburst. She breezed into the room with her familiar, beaming smile and Lucia could not conceal her relief.

"Angelique, I'm so sorry; I shouldn't have said those horrible things. I don't know what I was thinking. Are we friends again?"

"Of course we are, Honey. And I'm sorry too; I shouldn't have taken it so badly and, anyway, you were partly right; turns out the old lady has two granddaughters, but no grandson."

"What's she said about how the fire started?"

"The old lady?"

"Yes."

"Oh, nothing yet; she's still under sedation, but she's doing really well. Evie says the police are hoping to talk to her today."

"Good. She can tell them what really happened."

Angelique looked at her with a curious frown.

"Why are you so sure that she didn't start the fire? Old people are often forgetful like that; it happens all the time."

Lucia wondered for a moment if she should tell Angelique everything, but concluded, as she always had before, that this was not the time. It was clear that the general consensus among medical staff was that Lucia was in need of inpatient psychiatric care, indeed her therapist had suggested she might refer Lucia for residential care at a specialist unit. The staff were concerned and their approach was thoroughly professional, but Lucia felt that Angelique was the only one who really saw her as a person rather than a diagnosis. Treasuring that bond, Lucia decided not to jeopardise it by telling Angelique too much.

"No reason. It just don't think she should be blamed until all the facts are known."

A few days later, Angelique returned to the hospital on her day off. Hurrying to Lucia's room, she was surprised to find the nursing assistant, stripping the sheets from the bed.

"Hello Denise. Where's Lucia?"

"Who?"

"The patient. Do you know where she is?"

"She's gone."

For a dreadful moment Angelique feared the worst.

"What do you mean? What happened?"

"I think a place came up at the Gatfield. She was transferred first thing this morning. Why? Is there a problem?"

"No, no, I just wanted to show her this."

Angelique turned the newspaper over and Denise leant forward to read the headline. In bold, black capitals, it read, 'Local woman's miraculous survival as arsonist thug dies in inferno!'

"She knew. I don't know how but, somehow, she knew."

In the Gatfield Clinic, a large Victorian house that served as a residential unit for the treatment of eating disorders, Lucia was feeling very much alone. There were six other patients in residence; girls and young women, but, while they had chosen to be there, Lucia felt she had been forced. Given no alternative, she had been torn away from the hospital; away from Angelique and away from those who might need to call to her for help when all other help had failed.

Months earlier, Lucia had herself been close to death on admission to the hospital. Slowly, she had been nursed and coaxed back from the brink, and it was during this period of recovery that her dreams had become open to the silent, desperate appeals from others hovering at the edge of life. Lucia had not felt any need to understand why this ability had suddenly awakened. As her condition improved, it seemed to her entirely just that this unasked for gift had emerged; it gave her the means with which to repay the debt she felt she owed for regaining her own life. She accepted it. More than that, she welcomed it, as giving a purpose to her existence; something she had never felt before.

Both staff and patients tried to welcome Lucia into the community at Gatfield, but her unhappiness and resentment kept everyone at bay. For an entire week her dreams were undisturbed and she felt bereft that her talent, her calling, was going to be wasted. Her sense of worth, always fragile at best, began to slip away.

The call, when finally it came, was different from the others; less urgent, subtle, almost a polite request. Completely ignorant of the local area, Lucia had to trust herself entirely to instinct. She relinquished control of her dreaming self and, rising up, let herself be pulled gently away towards a complex of low buildings a mile or so from the clinic. The buildings had the look of purpose-built accommodation for the elderly; single storey with picture windows. There were ramps and sturdy grab handles at every door. Lucia let herself be drawn into the brightly decorated entrance hall, passing a sign that read, 'Welcome to St Catherine's Hospice'.

Unseen, Lucia finally came to rest at the bedside of an elderly man. He opened his eyes; beautiful grey-green eyes, and smiled up at her.

"Hello Lucia."

Lucia was completely overwhelmed.

"It's you!" she cried, "What are you doing here?"

"I think you know the answer to that one, don't you?"

"No, you can't be; I've only just found you."

Her dear friend smiled.

"I can heal you." Lucia gasped, only then realising that some element was missing.

"Are you looking for this?"

He lifted his painfully thin arm and held out his palm. As Lucia watched, the tiny, golden bird began to take form there, resting quietly in his hand. Lucia again had the sense of remembering something long forgotten. She smiled.

"What is it?" she asked.

"She is my imagining of the gift that we both share. I like to think that the spirit of all those who have preceded us live on in her too, but that might just be unfounded fancy." he tried to smile through his pain, "I've always seen her as a bird and I've always referred to her as 'her' but she will assume whatever form seems most natural for you."

Lucia shook her head.

"She's beautiful just as she is."

He smiled again.

"She certainly is. Take her. She will stay with you now and she will help you as she always has me."

"I can't take her. She's yours."

"Lucia, I have no more need of her. You know that."

It was true. Lucia knew her friend was dying but still she fought against it; not wanting to believe that she would lose him.

"Can't you heal yourself?"

"No, my dear Lucia. That I cannot do."

"Then, please, let me heal you."

Lucia's eyes began to fill with tears; knowing what his answer would be.

"Shh, don't cry. My time is ending. This part of life is over but you, of all people, know there is more to life than this." he waved his hand to describe the room, "I'm not sad. I have lived a long, long life and I have always known that this little bird would, one day, show me who was to take over but, Lucia, I waited so long that, I must confess, I began to lose heart."

"How long were you looking for me?"

"Goodness, I was old and searching for you a century before your grandparents were born." he sighed, "Lucia, I wish I could spare you this sadness, but I have to tell you that long years are a burden that comes with this gift."

"A burden?"

"Yes, Lucia, I am so sorry, but eventually, you will lose all those you know and care for; they will all die before you. The world will change, but you will live on. One day, many, many years from now, this little bird will show you that the time has come for you to rest. She'll show you who will take on your burden and you'll teach that person, as I taught you."

"How will I know who's the one?"

"You'll know."

"But how?"

"Be calm. Believe me, you will know."

"But how? How did you know I was the one?"

He drew a shallow, ragged breath and managed a faint smile, amused at her persistence.

"Very well. Give me a moment."

He rested for a few minutes.

"Some months ago, I was having trouble with my breathing so they took me to the hospital. I had been there less than a day when a young woman was brought in. A young woman with the gaunt, brittle body of a starving child. She was very near to death, but it was not her time to go. She called to me."

"That was me."

"Yes, Lucia, that was you. When you called, this little bird shone out like she had never done before. The glow around us was alive with reds, golds, purples, blues; swirls of every colour imaginable. It was so very beautiful. Take my word for it, Lucia, you will know it when you see it."

"And did you just know that I'd want to do this?"

He shook his head slightly.

"Remember, Lucia, I had seen you at your lowest ebb. I've watched over you since then and seen this gift fulfil a need in you. We were born to do this, you and I. It completes us." Exhausted, he began to close his beautiful eyes, "Now, I'm sorry, but I need to rest. Will you stay with me?"

Lucia simply nodded; she couldn't trust her voice to speak the words.

As the the minutes went by, nurses, oblivious of Lucia's bedside vigil, realised that their patient was quietly leaving them. One of them drew a chair to the bedside and sat, taking his hand in hers to let him know that she was there. He made no response.

Lucia heard his breaths become increasingly shallow and infrequent. She could not bear to see this; to lose him so soon.

"Please don't go! I've got so many questions."

She thought she saw the tiniest hint of a smile, but nothing more.

"Please!" Lucia was weeping now, "I don't even know your name."

If he heard her he gave no sign.

"I can't do this." Lucia whispered, almost to herself, "I can't do this without you."

His chest rose for the last time and he whispered a reply, no louder than a sigh.

"You will."

COURTESY BODIES

PR POPE

PR Pope has spent many years perfecting the art of avoiding being noticed. Usually to be found just outside the centre of attention, he has been present at most of the recent decades' significant scientific breakthroughs. Now that he has decided to commit some of his tales to paper and ink (or pixels as the case may be) he is being forced to be less reclusive. However, convinced that no-one ever reads author biographies anyway he feels it unlikely that anyone would be able to use this information to track him down. But for the benefit of any such intrepid (or sad) reader he describes himself as four Roman cubits tall, one point six gigaseconds old with a mass of approximately sixty four thousand yottadaltons

Ben opened his eyes to a blurry vision of mangled metal, slick with rain that reflected and refracted flashing red and blue lights. He tried to shake his head to clear the image and immediately regretted it. Was that thumping in his head, in his ears or in his blood? Slowly he remembered what had happened and suddenly he panicked.

"Teresa?" No answer.

"Teresa?" Louder this time, but still no answer.

He tried to move and realised that he couldn't. He was obviously being held in place, not just by his seat belt but by parts of the car that must have become wrapped around him.

"Sir?" A voice, not one he recognised. He couldn't turn his head to see who had spoken.

"Sir, can you hear me?" A young man's voice. Ben's mind finally started to get back into gear. Ah, the flashing lights.

"Yes. Are you a doctor?"

"Paramedic sir. I need you to tell me how you are. Don't try to move yet. Can you see alright?"

"Yes, yes. What about my wife?"

"She's still unconscious. My colleague is with her, I need to check you."

"No. I'm fine, look after her."

"You're sure you're okay?"

"Look young man, I can see, hear and talk just fine."

"Is anything hurting, can you feel anything broken or

damaged?"

"Damaged? What sort of question is that? I'm stuck in this chair and I can't move, something is pinning me down and stopping me from turning my head to look at Teresa. But I'm fine. You should be worrying about her."

"I'm worrying about you for now sir. You say you can't move."

"Obviously not, with all this wreckage trapping me."

"But that's just it sir, there is nothing trapping you in place. Your seat belt is still on but otherwise you're quite clear. If you can't move it's because you've suffered some trauma, maybe your spine. No, don't try and move. We'll have you out of here very soon and then we can assess the damage more thoroughly."

"Okay." Ben's voice trembled as he spoke, he didn't sound quite so confident any more.

"But what about Teresa?"

"I'm just going to check her now sir, don't worry."

~

Teresa sat in the wheelchair and watched Ben intently. She pushed the button on the side of the hospital bed to raise him into a position where she could see his face. She smiled as he woke up and focussed on her.

"Oh my love, are you all right?" he asked.

"Better than you, it seems."

"But you're in a wheelchair?"

"Which at least means I'm mobile. You're stuck in one position."

"What happened? Well I think I can guess what happened, but how … ?"

"A lorry. They think it jumped the lights and hit us. Luckily it just clipped the front wing, span us across the road and into the corner of a building. An eighth of a second later and we would probably have been crushed. Still, the car's a write-off."

"Me too by the look of it!"

Teresa was relieved, if his sense of humour was still intact then he would probably be okay.

"No change there then," she grinned at him.

"And you?"

"Broken bones in my legs, the original impact was on my side of the car and there was some 'intrusion into the passenger compartment' according to the police. Which means that a carbon fibre panel crushed one leg and deformed the other."

"What happened to me?"

"Nothing in the impact from the lorry, but as we were spinning your head got thrown about and you must have twisted your neck. Your spinal cord was damaged. That's why you can't move."

"Paralysed for good?"

"No, of course not. They can fix you, but it will take some time to re-grow the nerve tissue. Now you're awake again they can prepare you for that. I'll tell the doctor you're conscious and she'll explain what's going to happen. It's just as well we've got that medical insurance."

"It's expensive?"

"Not just the cost, but the time. Don't worry she'll explain." Teresa smiled encouragingly as she rolled her wheelchair backwards and turned it round to go out of the door.

~

The doctor explained everything very clearly to Ben. Teresa had heard it before but she sat there anyway just in

Ben's sight so he wouldn't feel so nervous. He would put on a brave face, but he was inherently squeamish and might stop listening. She would keep him calm enough to pay attention.

A short, very pretty Chinese doctor, Ming Hu had a very effective bedside manner, which immediately put Ben at his ease. After describing the damage that had been done to the nerves in his spinal cord, she told him exactly how it could be repaired. Following the initial surgery, it would take about two weeks for new nerve tissue to grow and would require his body to be completely motionless, immersed in a bath of electrolytes and nutrients for the whole time. In the past this had been achieved by a combination of trance induction and drugs causing paralysis of most of the voluntary muscles, but it had always been unbearably frustrating for the patient. Now, with the advent of Courtesy Bodies, it was becoming much easier, almost routine. In fact, Teresa's bones could be knitted together and fully healed much more effectively in a similar way. That too required immersion and immobility, and hence would also be immeasurably eased by the use of Courtesy Bodies. The two of them could take a holiday together in temporary bodies while they waited for their own to be repaired.

~

"How much do you know about Courtesy Bodies?" Joshua Burke asked Ben and Teresa.

"Not a lot more than the adverts on TV," said Ben.

"and what the doctor here has told us," added Teresa.

"Okay, I've got a little vid clip here on my tablet that will give you the basics and then I can answer any questions you have. Shouldn't take very long. Does that sound like a plan?"

"I'm not going anywhere." Ben sighed as he focused on the wall where Joshua's tablet was projecting an image of a young couple running through a field of poppies.

The vid clip was effectively an extended version of the advert that they had seen on television from time to time. A young couple, identified merely as Andy and Sam, doing all the things that couples do in soft-focussed dreamy sequences in romantic films: running through a field, hand in hand on the beach, riding a bicycle together (that always looks quite uncomfortable, thought Ben), having a picnic in a park and so on. Then, when they're flying together in a glider, a sudden downdraft causes them to lose control and spiral down, crashing to the ground. Clean-cut doctors patch them up but they both have broken legs and arms; they'll be okay in a few weeks. 'But we're getting married in two days time' they say. Cut to the Courtesy Bodies corporate headquarters, and then to a room where they're each lying on a couch and have a small cap placed on their head. After a few hi-tech lights flash and graphs wiggle, a display says 'Upload complete'. Another young couple are lying on separate couches wearing similar caps. More lights and graphs and a display of 'Download complete'. The second couple open their eyes, look at each other and smile. 'Now I can still walk down the aisle' says the bride-to-be. Cut to a wedding ceremony with the second couple swapping vows 'I Samantha Myers, take you Andrew Briggs as my lawful wedded husband...''. Another dreamy sequence, of a honeymoon on a tropical island. Cut again to the Courtesy Bodies room where the honeymoon couple are lying on the couch and the display shows 'Upload complete', followed by the real Andy and Sam (no longer with their limbs bandaged) and 'Download complete'. As Andy and Sam walk out of the room chatting excitedly about their great honeymoon, the Courtesy Bodies logo appears and a voice over says 'Ask your medical insurance advisor about Courtesy Bodies today'.

Joshua touched the screen of his tablet and, with a small click, the logo vanished from the wall.

"Your medical insurance included Courtesy Bodies for any treatment that would take longer than a week, so you're both covered while the damage from your accident is repaired."

"So it's only used in medical situations like ours. Accidents?" Teresa looked quizzical.

"There's no technical reason why it couldn't be more widely available to anyone that can afford it. But so far there has been quite a bit of discussion on ethical grounds so there is currently a regulatory oversight body that limits how and when it can be employed. It's quite safe, there's never been any question about that."

"So what is the issue?"

"The length of time it is fair to keep an Angel placid."

"Angel?" Ben snorted.

"Yes, we call anyone who volunteers to be a Courtesy Body an Angel. I think you'll agree that it's really rather appropriate."

"What happens to them?" Teresa asked.

"That's easiest to explain if you understand a bit of the science behind Courtesy Bodies. Every person exists as the combination of two separate things, a soma and a psyche. The soma is essentially the physical body and, although in general it's what we think of as the person, what they look like, it's really just a container for the psyche. Nowadays thanks to medical science, with so little disease and the effects of ageing under control, it's really only accidents that we need to worry about."

"Your generation might not have to worry about ageing young man, but we were already too old when those breakthroughs were made."

"Oh, sorry, that was thoughtless of me. Still, as you're demonstrating right now, a significant problem is damage to the body caused by external events. The body can be repaired, extended and, to a certain extent, replaced. But what continues to make the person unique, irrespective of changes to their body, is their psyche, the mind that is the essence of the individual. It's separate from the body but is normally unable to interact with the rest of the world without one. Some years ago there was a very brilliant Nobel-winning scientist who discovered a way to remove the psyche from the constraints of a soma and store it in a quantum environment, effectively an electronic brain. Obviously an important part of the process is to be able to restore the psyche to the soma. Once that was achieved it was realised that the psyche could be removed from the soma while particularly traumatic procedures were being performed such as surgery. It could be stored and then replaced once the surgery was over. Some early experiments were done for patients undergoing life-threatening operations. They were very successful and gradually the researchers increased the length of time that the psyche was stored, until it was quite possible to store a patient's psyche for the duration of their whole treatment; reducing the need for excessive pain management drugs and all the side effects, as well as significantly increasing the recovery rates because more aggressive treatments could be contemplated. At Courtesy Bodies we have further perfected the techniques. We can upload a psyche from a body, leaving behind an empty soma. We are able to store many psyches simultaneously in a quantum storage device the size of a pinhead, in a state we call placid. We can download a psyche back into its soma to reunite the original person, and they're none the worse for it. Then we realised that as well as storing the psyche while the soma was being repaired, we could store the psyche from a healthy person and temporarily download someone else's psyche into their soma. That way, someone who had been incapacitated could continue with their life while their own body was being repaired. But, of course, we needed volunteers to offer their soma for use by a patient. We obviously want healthy and fit volunteers so we started by talking to students in the research labs where the early work was done - we knew they would understand the concepts and issues. We decided to call our volunteers Angels, but even so we realised there would need to be some sort of benefit for them - students always need help with their finances! Whenever we need a soma for a patient we call a suitable Angel from the volunteer list into our lab. We upload their psyche into placid storage and then download the patient's psyche into their soma. A few days later the process is reversed, the angel goes home with a significant amount of credit and the patient's psyche is reunited with their own soma which is now as right as rain. Everyone's happy."

"What does it feel like when your psyche's in this quantum placid storage?"

"I don't know personally, but we can provide artificial stimulation to the psyche while in storage to simulate experiences if they want. We offer them some options to simulate sleeping, being on holiday (the tropical beach is very popular), reading, even studying, and some choose to be doing something a bit more active like dancing."

"What non-stop for days on end?" asked Teresa, raising her eyebrows.

"At least they wouldn't run out of energy after one twirl on the dance-floor, like we do these days!" Ben laughed.

"Actually," Ben continued, "that prompts a question I have. You said 'suitable angel' just now. Does that mean that you try and match the angel to the patient?"

"To a certain extent, yes. As I said, most of our Angels are students which means they're usually in their early twenties, although not always. We give them all a thorough medical examination and make sure they're fit and healthy, not on drugs or otherwise addicted. We will always use an Angel of the same gender as the patient, ideally one with similar interests and activities if possible."

"Why what difference does that make?"

"Even if an Angel is fit, if the patient wants to participate in activities that require special skills it is often better if the Angel's body has been previously exposed. For example, an Angel who is not particularly active would suffer more muscular pain after a skiing holiday than one who has skied before."

"So the patient can use the angel ..."

"the Angel's soma"

"...can use the angel's soma to do things like go on holiday."

"Sure."

"Any constraints?"

"Obviously the patient has to agree to bring back the soma in the same state of health as when they were downloaded into it. If there is any medical attention required then the patient's health insurance must cover it. They agree not to take unnecessary risks or to commit any illegal acts that could be detrimental to the future life of the Angel, which obviously includes things like drugs. They also sign a sworn affidavit that they are responsible for any actions and liable for any consequences during the period in which they are downloaded into the Angel's soma. That's why we have a notary on hand during the upload and download processes to ensure accurate timekeeping."

"So you've had problems with dodgy patients then?"

"No, not yet. But you never know." He shrugged.

Teresa had been quiet for a while, looking very thoughtful. Ben glanced over at her.

"You okay love?"

"Yes, I'm fine." Teresa answered.

"So, Mr. Burke…" Teresa looked at Joshua.

"Joshua please."

"Well Joshua." She continued. "I think we understand the principle, if not the science. What we need to know is exactly how this would work for us."

"Of course. For a start I'm afraid that we have no Angels on our list who are even close to you in age. In fact you'll be our oldest ever patients."

"Does age make any difference? Might it not work?" Ben interrupted nervously.

"Absolutely not. As I'm sure you're only too aware, the mind stays as young as you want whatever the body does. So the psyche is just as easy to upload however old the soma is."

"Surely the mind and body, my psyche and soma, are the same age? Unless you believe in re-incarnation." Teresa asked.

"Let's not get into a spiritual discussion. If there is such a thing as re-incarnation then it's just nature's way of performing a download into a new soma." Joshua grinned.

"What about the soul? Is that part of the psyche?"

"The honest answer is that I don't know. There has never been any scientific evidence for or against the existence of the soul separate from the mind. So as far as we're concerned, the psyche encompasses whatever isn't the soma - if you believe that includes the soul as well as the mind then that's fine by me. We've never had anyone who's been reunited and felt that they have become soulless."

"I can't tell if you're making fun of me." Teresa scowled at Joshua.

"Absolutely not. I can assure you that we have had patients of various religious beliefs who have not had any cause to complain. That includes a few priests, a couple of bishops, monks and a lama."

"It works on animals too?" Ben asked, straight-faced.

"Ben! This is serious." Teresa scolded him.

"I'm sorry. Please finish what you were saying about how this will work for us." Ben looked contrite.

"Right. We have found a suitable couple on our list, which would be more appropriate than two separate Angels who are strangers, for obvious reasons."

"You mean while we're them we can, err…."

"You're not them, you're you. But you're using their soma, and yes you can. Just remember nothing risky or illegal."

"At our age?" Teresa was trying to look shocked but Ben noticed a twinkle in her eyes.

"We won't be our age, we'll be theirs." Ben's eyes widened.

"What are they like? Can we meet them?" Teresa asked, almost absent-mindedly.

"We generally feel it's better not to meet in advance, but I can show you a photo of them. They're both in their mid twenties, they live together and are both studying for their doctorates. They plan on getting married at some point when they can afford it. They volunteered a while ago, but only want to be angels if they can do it together. Here's their picture." Joshua had been fiddling with his tablet while talking, now there was a click and a photo sprang onto the wall for Teresa and Ben to see.

"This is Joe and Carly. Joe is the one with the beard."

"You don't say."

"Now Ben, don't tease," scolded Teresa again.

"As you can see, they're smart, healthy…"

"Pretty," interrupted Ben

"…and ready to be Angels at a few hours' notice."

"Have you told them about us?"

"No. First I need to know what you want to do."

Ben and Teresa looked at each other. Joshua couldn't tell what unspoken communication was going on.

"Do you want me to leave you to talk about it?" he asked.

"Not necessary," said Ben, "I'm up for it."

"Me too." Teresa added.

"Okay, we just need to sort out the paperwork. I'll have to arrange some additional witnesses from the medical team as you can't use a pen at the moment Ben. But that won't take too long. By this time tomorrow…"

"… we could be up and about while the doctors get on with the repairs." Teresa grinned.

~

I thought I'd just be sleeping. Dreaming maybe. But this isn't like either. I can think but I can't see anything. Maybe this is what a coma is like? Or one of those sensory deprivation tanks? Still, I'll only be here a few days. Boring, but at least we'll have earnt enough money to cover the rest of our tuition fees. Easy money. Lend some rich guy your body while his is being repaired. Piece of cake.

I can see why the rich would rather borrow a body than wait it out in here, especially as all the courtesy bodies are guaranteed to be fit and healthy like me and Carly. Placid they called it. Tedious I'd say.

It's a shame Carly and I can't communicate, that would make the time go faster. No-one to talk to but myself. I feel like I'm going quietly mad. Or not so quietly maybe. I feel like I should shout. I'M BORED. But I know I didn't really shout out loud and no-one can hear. I'm so bored I'm talking to myself.

~

I didn't expect it to be like this. They offered us 'scenarios' like a holiday but we wouldn't have shared the experience so I thought it would be better to just sleep for a couple of weeks. Get some rest from my research. That was a mistake, I'll know for next time. I hope Carly's okay. I bet she's bored too. I wonder if she's talking to herself.

~

They should really give you some idea of time. We're only supposed to be in here for two weeks, but it already seems like forever. We must be due out soon.

I was beginning to think we'd never get called up, so it was great when that elderly couple got hurt in a car crash, needing courtesy bodies for two weeks. That came out wrong. I don't mean it was great they got hurt. I mean it was great that a couple was finally needed. I feel sorry for those two old people, waiting around for their bodies to be fixed. But I hope they look after ours. I know they've agreed not to do anything dangerous, but you never know.

~

Surely it must be time to get out of here? To be 're-united'. I can't wait to be whole again, walking around, jumping, stretching, hugging Carly. You don't realise how much you take for granted until you're deprived.

~

Something must be wrong. I'm sure we've been here more than two weeks. But there's nothing to help me gauge time. I tried counting seconds but that got really boring so I gave up after about six hundred. Everything is just as clear in my mind as it was when they put me in here, but as my memory is currently stored in a quantum computer rather than little grey brain cells they wouldn't fade anyway. I don't really remember anything that's happened while I've been here — but that would probably be because NOTHING has happened. I'm so bored.

~

How much longer can it be? This has been the longest two weeks of my life. I hope Carly's coping better than I am. I wish I had chosen one of those scenarios, it would have been so much less boring.

~

Oh! There was a funny sort of glitch just then. I think I can feel things. I must be back in my body. It's really rather a strange sensation. You wouldn't think it would seem so different after only two weeks. I can't open my eyes, there seems to be something covering them. But I can hear a noise now ... it sounds like a man's voice ...

"Good, you're both awake now. Joe, Carly, welcome back. You're both now fully re-united. My name is Benjamin Haire, I'm the Chief Executive here at Courtesy Bodies. It may take you a little while to get used to your bodies again. I'm afraid you were in there a little longer than planned, but don't worry you'll be paid the agreed daily rate for every full day you were with us. So, actually, that will make you both quite wealthy."

"Why, how long have we been here?" I could hear Carly ask.

"Ah. Well, I'm afraid that Mr and Mrs Green rather liked having the use of your bodies. You're younger than them by more than fifty years and the temporary rejuvenation went to their heads somewhat. They were enjoying themselves so much that when it came to be time to be re-united with their own bodies they decided to, shall we say, abscond. It has taken us quite a while to find them and return them to their own original bodies, but they have paid the full amount you're owed. Plus some compensation for wear and tear."

"Wear and tear? Why what did they do?" Carly sounded upset.

"You didn't answer the first question, how long have we been here?" it was my turn to ask.

"Twenty three years, seven months and four days."

Dreaming Mars

Alexander Skye

Alexander Skye has been obsessed with sci-fi since before he was born. Since those early experiments with time travel, he has read and enjoyed every branch of science fiction; from the most realistic of hard SF, through the most cynical of cyberpunk and the most Victorian of steampunk, to the most exuberant of space opera. He's enjoyed other genres besides, most especially fantasy, with which he has had a long-running affair. It began as a child, reading *The Chronicles of Narnia*, and *The Lord of the Rings*, and has never really abated. His first and greatest love, however, will always be science fiction.

Having spent so long merely reading and admiring, he decided that it was finally time to try and tell his own stories and hopefully you'll enjoy them as much as he enjoyed writing them; if not, he'll be forced to find a different job, which would be tragic since they're all so boring - after all, how many other professions let you stare wistfully at the stars on a cloudless night and call it research?

Lights blinked in the darkness. Small and in myriad colours, flickering throughout the night. Most were natural, though increasing numbers were human made – the Lagrange stations orbiting Earth and Sol, the Jupiter orbitals, the Martian relays, the scientific stations around Neptune and Pluto. All built in the last hundred years for assorted reasons, the most important being pure human curiosity and pig-headedness. If nature tells you not to live somewhere, you tell nature to fuck off and you live there anyway. The age old tale, and driving force, of the human race.

Lights blinked in the darkness. One of them was called the Pevensie, and on board the Pevensie, lights were blinking as well. The ship had recognised that it had reached Earth space, and so decided that it had been lonely long enough. It travelled alone between the assorted stations and places of the Sol system. The ship's crew spent their time between worlds sleeping in cryostasis, an artificial state of slumber keeping their youth while they spaced the years.

Lights flashed before Anna's eyes as she blinked and shivered in the stale air. Her sight took only a short moment to adjust to being awakened again after six months asleep. The cold of cryo wore off quickly, but the cold of a ship only just warming up again after months in space was far harder to shake-off. Still shivering, she half-heartedly pushed her way up and out of the cryo-cap, sending herself drifting across the room. More through luck than design, she bumped against her own locker. Grabbing at the handle to stabilise herself, she toggled the lock and made a grab for something warmer than the underwear she slept in. She couldn't pull on her jumpsuit fast enough. The metal zip was chill against her, but she pulled it up full before thrusting her hands deep into the pockets. Hugging herself close, she glanced over towards the other capsules to see who else was awake. George was still asleep, but everyone else's caps were empty and going through their cleaning routines. Anna rubbed at her eyes, trying to chase away the small yellowy sparkles which were sprinkled through her peripheral vision.

A whistling noise heralded someone's entrance into the room, and Swan's voice revealed who it was.

"I see you're all woke up now."

Anna nodded numbly as she closed her locker.

"Come on up deck, much warmer up there."

Swan smiled and rotated on the spot, reaching for handholds along the wall as she propelled herself out of sight. Anna pulled her interface glove out of the little belt pouch it lived in and strapped it around her wrist, the thin straps settling into position encircling her fingers. She touched the small screen and it activated, tiny indicators blinking as it pinged the ship's network for the time, interrogated the small chip embedded in her arm for her health, and contacted her cryo-cap to retrieve her sleeper dosage. Satisfied, Anna kicked off from the wall, sending herself pirouetting through the cold air towards the door. She caught hold of the railing that circled it with all the grace of a drunken ballet dancer, and shook her head. The drugs hadn't quite worn off yet. She steadied herself before following Swan's lead up the corridor. The metal handholds were freezing and she gasped as she grabbed the first one. On the bright side though, the chill helped her shake off the effects of the sleepers easily, and she was awake and alert by the time the handholds and the air warmed up. The bridge and engineering were always set to warm up first – sleeping quarters didn't rate as highly on the importance scale, much to the annoyance of everyone on board.

She drifted towards the bridge door as it irised open before her, and she blinked at the sudden influx of light. The sun was obviously up.

"Aha, sleeping beauty. Took your time waking up today."

"Sorry. I was just so very comfy."

Zac grinned.

"Yeah, yeah, we're gonna have to swap caps then. Mine's a piece of shit. Anyhow, as you can see, we're home…" he gestured towards the vista dominating the front of the bridge, "so it's wakey-wakey time."

Anna wasn't really listening. She was transfixed, as she always was, by the view. Earth hung there in space, aglow in the midst of a sunrise. The Pacific Ocean stretched out for as far as she could see – on the horizon she could just make out the edge of North America as clouds wound their myriad patterns across the shoreline. Much closer was Tsiolkovsky Station, the largest of man's spaceborne creations – a two-mile O'Neill tube, spinning in the Earth's shadow. As Anna watched, it edged out into the sunlight, an ocean of solar panels lighting up in a wash of dark blue.

She smiled.

"Home sweet home."

The captain glanced at her with one of his wry smiles.

"Well, if you don't mind, I'd like to park there sometime soon."

Anna made a show of a mock salute, before kicking off from the railings by the door, pushing herself through the air towards the front of the bridge. She grabbed the headrest of the pilot's seat – her seat – and pulled herself to it, before strapping down. She glanced again up at the huge viewscreen across the wall in front of her, and then back down at her console.

"Hey Pevensie, how're ya doing?" she whispered. She gently stroked the lion the captain had scratched into the metalwork for good luck, and flicked a series of switches down the left side of her station. She nodding with satisfaction at the resulting readouts.

"That's my girl," she finished with a smile.

As she did, Swan strapped herself down into her own station and began her checks. The captain pushed off towards the exit.

"I assume I can leave you girls in charge? You won't crash and kill us all?"

"Not this time Zac. Girl Scout's honour. Piss off and let us dock."

He paused.

"Do girl scouts even have an honour?"

"Out."

He grinned as he glided away down the corridor. Swan gestured obscenely in his direction as the door closed behind him.

"Right, now he's gone…" she said, turning back to her station and lifting her headset.

"Hello, Tsiolkovsky Control? ITV Pevensie to Tsiolkovsky Control?"

Anna couldn't hear if there was a reply, but since she knew Swan wasn't given to carrying on conversations with herself, she presumed there had been. The small light that came on a few moments later to indicate that the ship was receiving docking instructions vindicated her belief. She brought up the flight sticks, prepared the engines for their approach. Docking at Tsiolkovsky wasn't hard –

there was enough room inside for three military cruisers – but it never hurt to be cautious, especially in space.

The docking instructions called for her to put in at blue-9, one of the heavy cargo offload points, and indicated that it was quite close to the opening of the docking tube. This would be even easier than usual. Almost automatically, Anna lined the Pevensie up with the gaping maw of the station, gently nudging the controls until the ship assured her that they were spinning at the same rate as the station. That done, she took a quick moment to glance up at the cam feeds from the outside of the ship, watched the stars spinning lazily by.

"I love my job."

"What was that, hun?" Swan asked, yanking her headset down off her ears.

"Nothing. We good to go?"

"Yup, nice and shiny, TC says we have permission to dock."

"How very kind…"

But Anna wasn't really paying attention. Her mind was now focused entirely on the dials and numbers displayed in front of her, and the two joysticks controlling the ship's innumerable retro rockets. She nudged the left forwards, sending the ship in the same direction, the right joystick moving ever so slightly downwards. The retros on the upper hull fired accordingly. Moving at a crawl, Anna slipped the Pevensie snugly into its berth, locking the ship down onto the docking ring. She waited until she heard the safe connection alert from the unoccupied environmental station, and then felt the shudder as the large bay doors closed behind the ship. Much easier to unload cargo if there's no chance of it spiralling off into space on a whim.

Anna unbuckled herself and stood up, the gravity generated by the station's spin a welcome relief – Zero-G was fun, but nothing beat being able to stretch your legs properly. Wandering past Swan, Anna tapped her shoulder, then gestured towards the door, and, through that, to the corridor beyond leading to the engineering and cargo bays where the rest of the crew were no doubt preparing to unload the ship. Swan nodded and gave a thumbs up, and looked as though she were about to say something when she suddenly half turned and began listening intently to her headset.

Anna was making her way to the iris when Swan took her 'set off again.

"Hey, Anna! Got the usual messages from station mail, like always. There's an important message for you."

Anna turned to look at her, slightly confused.

"They said it's about your husband…"

*   *   *

"Passengers waiting to board CPV Dwarf Star leaving for Mars are reminded to have their boarding passes and luggage ready for inspection. Anyone with special requests pertaining to cryosleep is advised to speak to a member of the crew at least an hour before departure. Thank you!"

"Docking handlers required in bay green-4."

"Crewmembers of ITV Serenity are requested at…"

The computerised voice continued to speak across the boarding and customs area of Tsiolkovsky station, politely reminding civilians, and tersely ordering the staff. Anna, on the other hand, was ordering her fifth drink, and hadn't heard a single thing that the PA had said for nearly an hour. The Pevensie was due to leave in six hours, and with nowhere else to be, she had spent the last two days living on the Station, drinking heavily and staring at the cam feeds in her room.

It hadn't done any good of course. Drinking never helped anything, and staring out at the stars had lost a lot of the attraction it had held only a week ago. So different, and yet so similar. The same stars hung in the darkness, the same constellations looked down at her, but they were different. They were accusing.

She looked out at the stars she had dedicated her career to, and saw in them the time she had never spent with the husband she had dedicated her life to. Of course, she had always known, deep down, that this day would come eventually – the wife a pilot flying the JupiTerran run whilst the husband made wine in Italy? It was never going to have a – what was the old film place? Hollywood. It was never going to have a Hollywood ending. But to end like this?

Anna's head sank on to the bar.

They didn't have much family on Earth; most were back on Mars. Michael had had many friends, most of whom Anna didn't know. Being millions of miles away made it difficult to go to the Bianchi's 25th anniversary do, among hundreds of other occasions. It had also made it difficult to be there for Geoffrey's birthday parties. He hadn't minded so much when he was young. Michael simply had to point at the stars and say that mummy was up there, flying around in a spaceship; he had been quite taken with that. Then he grew up, and grew bitter. He'd been at the house three days ago when Anna had arrived in shock and despair, and he hadn't been gentle with her feelings. Completely without her noticing, her son had overtaken her in age – how had she never realised that was coming? – and he ranted at her for leaving Michael alone for so many years. Of course, as far as she was concerned, she'd only received her piloting licence two and a half years before, yet here her two-year-old son sat, thirty, crushed and infuriated about his father's death at the age of 68.

She'd never realised the gap had grown so wide, never realised Michael had outgrown her so. Modern medicine can do amazing things. But not amazing enough.

She sighed and downed the last of her synthahol whiskey, motioning at the bartender for yet another. He looked dubious, but did as she asked. Her credit was good, she hadn't caused any trouble and miserable people had been the lifeblood of bars since time immemorial. He slid the drink across to her and removed her old glass, bustling away to clean it and serve someone else.

Anna lifted the drink up and looked through the chiselled glass and the amber liquid within. She saw nothing but her own reflection in the mirrored metal behind the bar, and she barely even recognised the face she saw. She put down her glass and stared into her own eyes. There was nothing in them at all.

"Hey hun."

Anna's gaze drifted sideways along the mirror, and there she found Swan's face.

"Hey." She replied, lifting her glass once more and turning to face her friend.

"Drunk the place dry yet?" Swan ventured, pulling a hopeful smile. She made note of the fact that it wasn't returned.

"Sorry," she continued, "I just don't know what to say really. You're the first person I know in space who still has people planetside they really care about."

"Yeah, fucking stupid of me, huh?"

"What? No, I think it's amazing. I wish I'd met someone who loved me so much they didn't mind me spacing. Or someone I loved enough to not jump at the first hot dockworker on Io." Swan fell onto the stool next to Anna and rested her hand gingerly on her shoulder.

"Really. I think you're amazing. You both are. Were. Shit, I'll shut up."

Anna nodded and glanced back at her drink. She realised that she couldn't quite tell if it was looking back, and put it down.

"What're you here for Swan?"

"What else? You're the only friend I have out here you know. What family I have are on Jupiter skyhooks, and what family I have are bastards. You know that. Hell, you met my cousin that time on Jupiter One, remember?"

Anna half-smiled for what felt like the first time in a week.

"Yeah, I remember."

"Yeah, see? And he's the best of the lot."

"God only knows how you turned out so well."

"It's nice to hear someone else share the sentiment for once!" Swan returned with a beaming smile. She noticed that Anna's had faded and hers followed suit, despite doing its level best to stay in place.

"I don't really know what I can say Anna," she said, pausing to glance up at the star-field cams above the bar, "But I do know one thing. I met Michael, what, twice? And he sure's sure wouldn't want you this cut up."

"That's easy for you to say. I'm the goddamn pilot, but every time I look at the stars I see the time I should've spent with him. Didn't spend with him."

Swan winced.

"I can't imagine how that must be…but look. There's no point focusing on how things could have been. I mean, if you hadn't become a pilot, I know for a fact that me and the boys would've died last year at Big Easy. Ain't no other pilot I've known could've dodged that cargo lighter. And I've been spacing for what, seven years? I've seen a lot of pilots."

Swan leant close to Anna and her arm found its way across to the other shoulder.

"Look. Just think about what you guys *did* have. Not

what you could have had. You've told me stories about Mars when you were young. You guys had a great life together. Don't do him a disservice by drowning yourself in drink now."

She glanced at the bartender. The look he returned said everything.

"Well, don't go drowning any more at least."

Swan stood, patting Anna once more on the shoulder before turning to leave.

"I'll see you shipside in an hour, okay? You'll be there?" Swan said, holding out a small strip of sobriety tablets.

"Yeah." Anna replied half-heartedly, dropping the pills into her pocket without even looking at them.

Anna saw Swan's reflection pause and plan something to say. Then both her expression and mind changed and she made for the exit, leaving Anna alone with her thoughts, her drink and the tab.

*   *   *

Anna hung in the air before her cryo-cap, her mind a few light-years away from her body. Everyone was already asleep except for Swan and Richard who were running checks on the engines. Zac had only just clambered into his cap; he was still cooling off now. By all rights, Anna should've been asleep hours ago – after leaving berth and setting the ship on the start of its automated course to Mars, she really had very little left to do. She'd spent the better part of the last two hours sat in Zac's quarters, trying to decide what to do, and here she hung, still working it over in her mind.

On the one hand, she could take her sleepers. She'd have a nice, uneventful sleep. She'd close her eyes, feel cold, and then it would be two months later. She'd still be cold, but she'd be two months younger than the rest of

140

the universe. They'd be orbiting around Mars, and she would have to go surfaceside to see Michael's parents.

Or, she could not take the sleepers.

She wasn't entirely sure what would happen if she didn't. She knew that without them, people normally have vivid dreams, sometimes lucid. That the dreams tended to be about whatever was on a person's mind before they went in. She knew that there was a school of art devoted entirely to taking psychotropic drugs and then spending a day in cryo, just to see what kind of fucked up things might come out of it. What she didn't know was whether it might bring Michael back to her. Whether she'd spend two months living her life with him again, or just spend two months reliving the last six days. There was no way out of it once she'd gone to sleep – she wouldn't wake up until they reached Mars or everything went to hell, and she'd rather not spend that time in a personal one. Being there in reality was bad enough.

But she just might have some time with Michael again.

She decided, her fists unclenched.

Reaching out for her cap she pulled herself close to it and tapped the screen into wakefulness. It beeped readiness at her, and she touched the control for sleeper dose. It was automatically balanced, as always, in comparison to her vitals – too much had never killed anyone yet, but it woke them up with a bitch of a headache. Turning the dose down however, was unrestricted, and turning it off was easy. She slid the bar as far leftwards as it would go, and the screen flashed up a warning.

DREAMS MAY OCCUR AT THIS DOSAGE.

Good.

Anna touched the affirmative button and heard a faint whirring sound as the cap responded to her orders. She toggled the door open and clambered in. As it hissed shut she saw Swan and Richard floating in through the door. Swan flashed her a hopeful smile just before the cap closed down and the frosted plexglass blocked her from view. The world was white, then it was cold and white, then cold and black. Then just black.

*   *   *

Stars span leisurely on the cam feed across the wall.

A small transport floated past, queuing up to enter the docking tube of Tsiolkovsky station, puffs of air jetting out in myriad directions as it manoeuvred its way along the two-mile length of the station.

The lights in the room were off, the only illumination coming across uncounted light-years of space. Anna sat, wrapped up in the bed's thin blanket, staring in wonder out at the universe, wondering if it was looking back.

"I'm starting to think you love the view more than me."

Anna smiled, turning to face the door where Michael stood, wine in hand.

"Never," she ventured with a smile, collapsing forward to lie on the bed, her legs kicking into the air coquettishly behind her.

"I should hope not. You know how jealous I am," he said, mock-serious. Knocking the door-close panel with his elbow, he paused on his way to the bedside table to plant a kiss on Anna's cheek before setting down the wine.

"I managed to find real wine. None of that synthahol stuff."

"Really?" Anna rolled in order to get a better look at the bottle.

"Really. Found a little shop in the commercial zone. Wasn't much bigger than this," he said, gesturing at the room around them, "But my god that selection. This wasn't the oldest there, but I figured 'Hey, we've never had Jovian wine before'."

"*Very* true," Anna agreed, sitting up and edging along the bed whilst Michael opened the bottle.

"Jesus, an actual cork. We *are* doing well for ourselves today." He grinned.

Anna returned the smile as he poured them each a glass.

"Now," he began, climbing onto the bed beside her, "I don't know if it's true, but I've heard that if you hold a good Jovian wine up to light, it glows. Something special they do in the hydroponics labs there."

He paused for a moment, thinking.

"You know, that probably makes it really bad for you, but who gives?" he laughed, and raised his glass to Anna, who returned the salutation. As one they turned to the cam feed on the wall, and lifted the wine to it.

"Maybe it doesn't work with a vidfeed of starlight. Maybe it has to be all-natural light or…"

He trailed off as Anna shushed him, her eyes fixed on her crystal glass with an almost childlike wonder as the golden liquid worked with it to refract the stars dominating the wall of the room. He smiled and lifted his glass next to hers, turning it and admiring the way Orion's Belt bent and buckled as he did so.

They had almost given up hope that it was a 'good' Jovian when Anna gasped, holding up her other hand next to her glass. It lit up with a faint white glow, like a candle shining through frosted glass. It grew a bit brighter, and she could see it through the tips of her fingers.

"No fair! Yours is better than – oh no, there it goes."

Michael's wine began to shine dimly as well, drowning the light coming from the starfield behind.

"Well, that shows what I know. Looks like I underpaid for this after all."

Anna brought her hands down, cupping her glass gently between them. She looked up at Michael as the wine rippled, sending the muffled light dancing across his face.

"Drink that before I do."

She smiled, and lifted the glass in salute before taking a sip. It tasted somehow warm.

"It good?"

"Very. Nicest you've ever bought me I think." She replied, taking a second sip before reaching over to take Michael's glass.

"Hey, I haven't even had any yet!"

"Later." She said, turning and placing both glasses down on the table next to the bottle. She noticed with delight that the bottle was beginning to shine as well, a warm glow colouring the corner of the room.

"For now," she added, lying back on the bed, "I can think of a better way to begin our honeymoon."

She gently tugged on his shirt, pulling him down.

He broke away for a second.

"I love you, Mrs. Saint-Clare."

She smiled.

"I love you too," she replied, dragging him down into a kiss.

They tumbled down onto the bed, the thick mattress a welcome relief after a full day of walking. Light slanted in through the window, painting the far wall a glorious golden colour. It would last for a while longer before the hills in the distance swallowed up the sun and allowed the moon her chance to paint the world silver.

"I don't think I've ever walked that much in my entire life" Michael said, sighing.

"I'm pretty sure we actually walked further than the domes back home are wide. That lake alone must've been the size of our entire hab' section," Anna replied, rolling onto her side to look at her new husband. Michael looked at her with a smile.

"Beautiful, wasn't it?"

Anna nodded in agreement, before leaning close to rest her head on Michael's chest. She looked through the window, out at the vineyards that belonged to the house they were renting. The grapes were nearly in season, glowing a pale green as the sunlight made its way through their translucent flesh. The leaves were painted a far brighter shade as an evening breeze gently made its way between the branches. Despite Italy's beauty however, Anna could only think of the stars, and their evening spent in orbit.

"What was that sigh for?" Michael asked, looking down at her.

"What?"

"That sigh. If 'wistful' had a soundfile in the dictionary, that would've been it."

Anna laughed.

"What're you thinking about?" Michael pressed.

"Nothing really," Anna shrugged, "Just thinking about the other night, on the station. The stars are beautiful when there's no atmosphere to block them out."

"Very true. I always preferred this though," he said, gesturing through the window at the darkening evening, "Stars we can see back home, the dome doesn't really block them much. This much life though, you don't see it outside the 'ponics domes"

"I know, but even back home, the stars seem so far away. In orbit, it's like you can reach out and touch them. And there are so many more of them."

"Well, not to worry. We'll be back on the station for at least a day before our flight back home. In the same hotel actually, I think."

"Oh good. It'll be nice to see space again properly before we're back in the domes."

"Speaking of the domes," Michael began, trailing off as he reached over to the bedside table. Fishing a flimsy bit of paper, he tapped Anna on the head. She looked up at him as he brandished the little photograph.

"This is the family's hydroponics dome down on the flats near Pavonis Mons. Near Aldrin? It's a nice place. Great sunlight and it's near one of the terraforming stacks, so there are even clouds sometimes. Aldrin's a really nice city too actually. Pretty small compared to home, but all the more peaceful for it."

Anna playfully grabbed at the small picture, bringing it closer for a squinting look. The dome wasn't enormous, but it was clear, rather than misted like the ones they lived in.

"Looks lovely! Is it far enough outside Aldrin to get good views at night?"

"The best."

Anna snorted in mock derision.

"I suppose it'll have to do."

Michael laughed and tousled Anna's hair.

"Damn right it will!

He glanced over at his watch, and then through the window at the slowly disappearing sun.

"Time for dinner! We should eat on the balcony I think tonight, looks like it'll be a nice evening."

"They all seem to be around here" Anna called after him as he clambered off the bed and padded from the room.

"Great, isn't it? If we can make a good go of it back home, I'd love to move here properly."

"Here, you can open your eyes now!"

Anna's eyes batted open, and she blinked in the sudden

harsh light of the small vidscreen that Michael was holding up.

"It's a…screen?"

"No! You think I'd surprise you with a screen on our anniversary? Look at what's on the screen."

Anna did so, leaning back to bring it into focus.

It was a small villa, set against a hill covered in vine-wreathed frames, with more vines growing in cultured lines stretching towards where the camera had been. Then she noticed the small blinking emblem at the bottom of the image and touched it.

A small glowing box opened across the picture. It said only one word:

Purchased.

Anna gaped.

"You bought a house? On Earth!?"

"Yes! Well, no. Technically, I've put in a decent bid for it and they've accepted, pending our being able to sell the vineyard here, and you being interested in the idea. It's a bigger place than ours here, and it's lovely. It's in a small town in southern Italy – I'm told that on clear nights you can see the North African space fountain. It's a good size, and it's not really too expensive, and with the bigger vineyard, I think we could make it back in no time and-"

"Michael!" Anna interrupted, "You're babbling."

"I…I guess I am. Sorry" He put the screen down on the table, looking rather sheepish.

"I just think it could be a really good move – we both want our kids to grow up under a blue sky after all –" Anna interrupted him again, but this time with a quick kiss. Pulling away, she smiled.

"You had me at Southern Italy."

Michael grinned.

"I knew you'd like it! Just wait till you see the other pictures of it, it's a wonderful place!" He bolted to his office. "Come on Anna, I've got the rest on here. You've got to see them!"

Anna was halfway across the room when she felt faint. Her eyes were suddenly heavy, her vision blurred and as she collapsed to the floor, she felt cold. She cried out in shock and surprise, and Michael was there, kneeling over her. Before either of them could say anything, Anna knew what was happening. She could feel it. The world around her was fading out to black, yet somehow also white. She was getting colder, but warmer.

She was waking up.

"No!" she struggled to say through the strange sensation of drug induced drowsiness, "I want to stay here with you."

Michael nodded knowingly, suddenly not his energetic self now that Anna had recognised what was happening.

"Don't worry my love. I'll be here."

"You would say that. You're just my mind, telling itself what it wants to hear."

"Exactly. So, I'll always be here."

Anna started at the obvious logic. Before she could say anything, the dream of her husband leant down and kissed her forehead.

"I love you Annabelle."

The world went white.

*   *   *

Lights blinked in the darkness.

One of those lights was the Pevensie, the crew once again asleep for the long haul from Mars to Jupiter. The ship's corridors were empty, the metal cold. The captain's quarters stood unused, an antique wooden cupboard creaking in the chill. The engineering bay was empty, a single toolbelt drifting lazily about, occasionally clunking off the ceiling and floor. The cargo bay sat full of Martian crops for the Jovian colonies, ready to be replaced with He-3 and ore from the moons. The bridge's chairs were empty, Swan's headset floating gently in the cold air above her station. And on Anna's station, where the captain had scratched a lion for good luck, there was a small photograph of a man, smiling in a vineyard.

MIRROR MIRROR

ALISON BUCK

Like all of us, Alison Buck has led many lives.

One as a sensible, hard-working type, employed in financial systems, graphic design and web site development. Another as a writer, scribbling away, committing her stories to disc and eventually publishing several to reasonable acclaim. Throughout all of them, the mother of two and wife of one.

Skilled at exploring the psychology and interior lives of her characters, Alison delivers stories that range from chilling tales of horror through insightful contemporary drama to thought-provoking science fiction. Her empathy with her protagonists, her rich descriptive prose and her use of gentle humour serve to ensure that, whatever the setting, her stories are always a rewarding read.

I woke up in the dazzling glare of a laboratory. I was at least alive but, unfortunately, I now seemed to be the focus of the aliens' investigations. They had pinned me down on a narrow table in the centre of the room, my hands and legs held firmly in restraints. My head was also strapped down so I couldn't turn, but I could see all around me; there wasn't much by way of kit or equipment, just the alien scientists working quietly; all their attention focussed on me.

I'd say they were about as tall as us and of similar build, as far as I could judge, beneath their bulky suits. They were taking no chances. I don't know what diseases they were worried I'd pass on but they all wore full-cover biohazard kit at all times, long atmo-umbilicals snaking across the room behind them as they moved. Whenever they bent over me I tried to see through the dull plastic of their helmets, but I couldn't make out a thing.

At first, once I was over the shock of having been captured, I can't say I was really frightened. Their initial tests were fairly unobtrusive, avoiding contact with me as much as possible. They provided food and fluids at regular intervals and even seemed to have quiet intervals when only one or two of them would be in the room with me. They allowed me to sleep undisturbed during those periods.

However, after what I judged must have been about three days, their behaviour changed. It started when several of them appeared to be jostling each other, in obvious disagreement. At length, one of them seemed to have gained the upper hand; the other two were escorted from the room, still objecting and resisting those escorting them. From this point on, investigation became experimentation.

I was exposed first to very low temperatures and then to very high. Each time, they watched till I was almost unconscious and then returned the environment to a comfortable warmth. Next they tried to assess my intelligence or, at least, my mathematical ability. Connecting pads to my fingertips, linking me to some sort of input device, they showed me puzzles and graphical representations of numbers and mathematical problems. I played along, guiding a pointer to the correct answers. Having, I think, done very well on that test, I had rather hoped they might perhaps think me worthy of treatment as a visitor to their world, rather than an exotic creature to be studied. My hopes were not to be realised.

One of the later tests was to be the worst: my tolerance of pain. For an advanced race they have a marked propensity for barbarity. Electrodes were attached to me and the tests continued through increasing levels, again stopping only when I was about to lose consciousness. The process was prolonged and excruciating, but my screams failed to elicit any signs of pity or sympathy in my tormentors.

After that they left me for what seemed like several days. Food and fluids were provided and the catheter checked every few hours, but no more tests were attempted. I presumed they were using this time to analyse the results they'd obtained so far, so hope rose again that they might release me and try to communicate with me on equal terms. Still unable to move, I could do little more than rest and regain my strength. To pass the time I rehearsed the speech of welcome I had prepared to mark the momentous occasion of the meeting of our two worlds. So far, my starring role in this pivotal moment in world history was not going to plan. I'm not too sure if the project director and the politicians back home had specific expectations about how the First Contact would go, but I'm guessing their visions, like mine, had rather more in the way of hand shaking and the exchange of gifts and rather less in the way of invasive probing and attempted electrocution.

When they finally returned to the lab they were fewer in number and seemed somewhat agitated. There was another heated exchange, not as loud as before, which ended with one of them leaving the room. The winner of the argument, who seemed keen to project some authority over the remaining two, approached me while the others watched closely, perhaps anxiously. The onlookers apparent nervousness worried me and I wondered what this 'Boss' character was going to do. Any thoughts I might have entertained that here was the alien ambassador come to apologise, on behalf of the entire planet, for my treatment to date, were soon dashed. The Boss sidled up to the table and peered down at me. Suddenly, without notice, she jabbed something sharp into my neck and hastily stepped back. I don't know why I'm assuming it was a 'she'. I suppose, heavily disguised by those biohazard suits, it could as easily been male, but something about her build and deportment suggested that the Boss was female. She communicated some orders to the two witnesses then swept out of the lab.

Whatever it was she had injected in to me had a fairly rapid effect. Within hours I began to feel my temperature rising. I became feverish and was soon shaking uncontrollably and aching all over. My skin felt as if it were cracking and peeling away. Not in the way you might ordinarily slough off dry skin, but ripping, in large, painful strips. It was an agonising, burning sensation. My joints too were incredibly painful. Ludicrous as it sounds, I honestly believed that my shoulders and pelvis had lost any structural integrity and were breaking and reforming, over and over again. All my bones seemed to be in a torment of stretching or compressing.

Thankfully, I eventually passed out, but I do remember waking several times, always feeling terrible. My eyesight was being badly affected, with my field of vision reducing all the time. Each time I woke, I could see less and less, until I was only really able to clearly see what was directly in front of me. Around the sharp focus at the heart of this tunnel vision was a blurred area and around that, nothingness.

I was, by now, convinced that I was going to die. In my few lucid moments, I remember I felt angry that all my efforts; from my initial application to join the Space Corps, through the years of gruelling training, to the final triumph of my being selected for the First Contact programme, were now ending so pathetically. Compounding the anger was my feeling of foolishness. I, who had once been so proud to be the star of the Academy, now desperately hoped that no one back home would ever discover the truth of what had happened to me: better to be a lost hero, presumed dead in the line of duty; making a courageous step towards galactic integration, than to be an object of pity, a slightly ridiculous footnote in the half-remembered histories of generations to come.

It was during one of these brief waking moments that one of my hands became free of the restraints. I moved my arm across my body with the intention of loosening the remaining ties, but froze midway. As my free hand passed into the tunnel of my vision I had a terrible shock:

my hand was a ragged mess of green scales and livid pink! My fingers were distorted to unnatural lengths and my arm seemed wasted and deathly pale. I cannot lie: I was terrified.

I believe I must have fainted.

I have no idea how long I was unconscious. I finally awoke perhaps three hours ago and I've remained conscious since then. The pain has eased and the fire in my bones and over my skin has gone, but I don't feel that I am back to anything close to normal. My vision has still not recovered but perhaps I should just be glad I'm alive.

The scientists have been coming and going since I recovered. One by one they have been moving closer to peer at me. Whatever they've learned from this whole, dismal process, they're no more reassured that I pose them no threat; they continue to wear the full suits. One of them has just come to the table, carrying a large box. Obviously I was wrong to think the testing was over.

What now? I have to turn my head to see them opening the box and taking out something shiny: a mirror. At a guess, I'd say they're going to check if their favourite test subject is self-aware. At least this should be a relatively painless exercise.

They're fitting the mirror into a frame to the side of the table, presumably so that it can be maneuvered overhead. More scientists have come in; I can make out quite a crowd around the table now. This is very strange. Why the sudden interest? They move the mirror across and I can't but look up at my reflection.

My reflection? This can't be me. What is it?

My skin looks dreadfully pale, dull and smooth. My mouth has all but closed up and my nostrils are huge. My eyes have changed shape entirely and they're both really close together, on the front of my head.

Dear gods! What have those bloody humans done to me?
They've turned me into one of them!

The Adventures of Kit Brennan: Kidnapped!

Neil Faarid

Neil Faarid was born in the North of the UK, in a small town you've probably never heard of. He studied in Leeds but, after three years, decided he didn't like flat caps and moved away. Hoping to write a novel or two, Neil now lives in Oxford where he enjoys being unmarried and having no pets. Neil likes to write both sci-fi and fantasy, and has a few more stories he's working on, though *The Adventures of Kit Brennan* is the first to be published. He also likes to listen to music and doodle. Neil is not his real name.

Kit Brennan awoke to another noisy 'morning.'   He
groaned, turned over in his bunk, groaned again and
finally sat up and scowled at the hatchway to his room.
Any second an obnoxious robot with a faulty social-skills
chip would barge in with a hot cup of coffee; whether he
was dressed or not, whether he wanted it or not.

"Good morning, Mr. Christopher! Here's your coffee!"
The machine pushed the mug into his hands so quickly
that it spilled over and onto his sheets, staining the fabric
once again. He sighed as the robot turned and rushed out
before a word could be said.

"Good morning, Cicero," he muttered as the hatchway
slid closed.

Kit dressed quickly. He would not make planet-fall
today, just arrive at the station in orbit around Mars –
rough-casual would probably do. He donned a vest,
pulled up a grey jump-suit about his legs and tied it off at
the waist. Grabbing his well-worn mock-bomber and
throwing it over his shoulders, he turned out towards the
cockpit. He checked their progress on the Navigation
monitor, nodded his approval and headed to the back of
his ship, a Vespasian Mk. IV, to the kitchen. He sat at the
breakfast-bar, scratched the stubble on his neck and
rubbed his eyes, before bending down to tie his bootlaces
and simultaneously avoid the splash that flew overhead.
Straightening up, he stared at the plate Cicero had slid
down the counter: the scrambled egg was as sloppy as

ever, the toast managed to be both limp and badly burnt, and the bacon nearly squealed when he jabbed it with a fork.

"Thank you, Cicero. You've outdone yourself again, as usual," he muttered with a half-smile.

"'Servo ergo sum,' sir. I exist only to serve."

"Nope," Kit corrected, absentmindedly. "You *save* therefore you are. Very different meaning." Neither one spoke for a while and Kit relished the momentary peace as he ate with only the sound of Cicero washing up in the background. He stared down at his data-pad and read the news.

"The *Rotations* has really gone downhill. They're so obsessed with the Martian farming crisis there's absolutely no mention of the extension to the Patrick Moore wing at LPU," he announced half-heartedly.

"That's because no one regards Lunar Prime University as a serious centre for academia any more; not after the mammoth fiasco, anyway. The galaxy has given up caring about 'Lunies' altogether."

"Hey," Kit pointed a fork angrily at the robot. "I was a 'Luni' once! You just be careful what you say about my alma mater!" There was a brief pause as Kit chewed his bacon. Finally, Cicero chirped up again, "I suggest giving up altogether with the *Rotations*, Mr. Christoper. I recommend subscribing to the *Pent-Ident* as I do. Those fellows certainly know a gasket from a gearbox, so to speak, sir." Kit looked up, stared at the emotionless face of his mechanical companion and took a deep breath.

"Cicero, five crackpots huddled around their keyboards prattling on about how NASA lied to us all about 'Asteroid 5' hardly constitutes reliable journalism."

"But it's broadscreen at its best, sir!" the android protested.

"It is not! It is e-tabloid at its most hysterical! Now stop arguing and, here, wash this plate."

Over an hour later, he was in the cockpit and on his third cigarette. Kit heard the music player shift through his collection: the soft melodies of Beethoven's 'Sixth' jumped suddenly to the heavier riffs of 'Iron Man.' He rolled his eyes and flicked off the music unit before turning to the nav-screen. In one fluid motion, he cancelled the calm, green orbit-alert window, turned off the autopilot and reduced engine output before leisurely leaning back and taking hold of the steering handles again. Kit stubbed out the cigarette butt and kept a keen eye on the fore windscreens. Mars was now largely visible, its rust-coloured terrain stretching out before him in a wide, dark arc. He inwardly smiled as he briefly remembered his childhood of crumbly red-brown sandcastles and helping his parents on the Farm. But his reverie was interrupted by a repetitive short bleep coming from the communications unit. He span round in the chair and stretched back to reach for a handset; hesitating between the wireless headset and the removable mouthpiece, connected by a short, spiralled wire. He thumbed a button and plucked the mouthpiece from the unit, bringing it purposefully outwards and to his face.

A warbled voice crackled through the speaker, "This is a ping-call to the 'Vesp. IV' currently on entry vector, over!"

"Morning fellas, this is the Vespasian Mk. IV, ID code: Bravo, Romeo, Echo, November - 9003, over."

There was a slight pause before the operator responded, "Ah, g'morning, Kit! It's 'Coalface' Collins here, how are you? Over."

"Morning, Collins, how's the wife? Over." Kit grinned as he righted the steering handles and checked his cruising speed.

"Never you mind, slick! What're you in town for? Here

for long? Over," came the jovial reply.

"Ah, just to refuel and take on small stock. Everything clear? Over." There was an odd cacophony of sounds as Collins hummed and clicked while he looked over Kit's record.

"Nah, no problems, Kit. You're clear for Bay C-137. Listen, are you out for a drink tonight? Over."

"Maybe a quick one, where will you be? Over."

"Err, I'm usually in the Old Rust Bucket, try me there. OK, go on through, Kit! Over," there was a crackle, a short blip and the line went dead.

Kit replaced the mouthpiece and put his full attention into steering; increasing speed and guiding the ship past the gently spinning buoys, lights alternately flashing, that led to the space-station's dock midsection. The station itself was shaped like a long, thin ellipsis with a wide mid-section, a waffle-patterned equator of open docking bays and stabilisers dotted regularly around the perimeter. On either side, there were gradually raised sections of hotels and retail buildings that extended out to the communication districts on the outer arms of the station where, finally, it fanned out in two gleaming orbs of solar panels. The space-station, technically named 'Adrestia-4-001,' was affectionately called "Addy" by Martians and station-dwellers alike. Those who thought of it, knew the station as the last stop-off point for Terran settlers on their way to Mars when the major colonisation attempt had taken place in the late 21st century. In the modern age it was a mini-metropolis of mercenaries, traders and couriers that managed to turn a modest profit from passing trade between Earth and Mars. Currently it was much busier though, due to low Martian crop-yields and the resulting economic dip. *Some things never change then,* Kit had mused when he heard his parents' farm was struggling too.

He knew the station well but there was always a chance Adrestia would throw something interesting at him after the many months and sometimes years between visits. In a place where laws were fairly loose, desires went as far as they wanted, though money usually went further. For instance, as a teenager, Kit had only narrowly escaped the notorious 'Hooker-Hopper-Sachs' riots that threw the station into turmoil. Three men had been at the centre of an uproar in the red light district that sent everything into meltdown; the workers went on blackmail-strike, threats were uttered, and all the husbands on Adrestia were suddenly a little more loving of their wives.

Kit's ship landed smoothly onto the floor of bay C-137, a rushing cloud of stabiliser gas emitting as the pneumatic landing gear set down with a dull thump and a hiss. In the cockpit, Kit turned on the ship's magnetic feet and shut down the rest of the computerised systems. He called out to his solitary ship-mate as he headed for the airlock.

"Cicero! I'll go ahead and sort the shopping and admin out, then I'll head out for a drink with some Addy friends. If you can, finish up anything on the ship and meet me at the usual stop-over, I'll book a room! You're free to wander around otherwise, get your oil changed or whatever, just don't get yourself into any trouble." The android appeared in the corridor with a large wrench in hand.

"Yes, Mr. Christopher, I will see you at the Spinning Jenny later."

Kit then pulled on an oxygen mask and opened the airlock. The exterior monitor showed that the docking bay door had now closed them off from open space and bay pressurisation had stabilised; he stepped through.

After the next door, Kit was out in the cold of the spacious bay. He walked on a bit before turning to look his ship over, it still had a nice heliotrope-blue sheen to it but the go-faster stripes had almost completely faded away. Well, he had bought it over three years ago. He sighed and walked around to check the starboard side, groaned at the amount of dirt and grime that had accumulated since his last visit, and hurried over towards the station airlock. Kit waved an ID card over the reader and the small screen flashed his portrait for a moment and then a green 'Clear' box before the airlock finally opened up. He stepped through and turned to look at his ship before the doors closed again; against the bay shield-doors his ship looked tiny but not too shabby. He smiled, it may only be a rusty pile of nuts and bolts barely holding together but that did not mean he could not love it in some way. Then the airlock closed and obscured his view.

Later that evening, as the lights on Adrestia faded, synchronised with the end of the Martian day, the city gradually grew louder in preparation for a night out. Kit, finished shopping, wandered through the noisy streets and headed towards the Old Rust Bucket, manoeuvring his way through the teeming crowds and aiming for the hanging-sign bearing a faded image of a NASA space shuttle. He finally reached the door and slunk inside, jumping onto a stool as it became momentarily vacant. He gestured to the barman at the other end of the counter who nodded his acknowledgement. Within ten minutes he had a foaming pint on the bar-top and was flicking the excess from the back of his hand. He took a sip and wiped his stubble before finally looking around the bar for familiar faces. Coalface was nowhere to be seen but he suspected he might be too early – the night-shift was only just beginning and Coalface would have to make his way down from up in the communication sector. He made small-talk with the barman but, after he was called away to serve a customer, Kit did not renew the effort for more conversation. Instead he looked around the bar and took in the Old Rust Bucket again. It was busy, which he had expected, but quiet enough that he had other choices for seating. There were bigger and cleaner bars on the station but Kit preferred the quieter, familiar atmosphere of the Bucket. The regulars were good company and the drink was bad but not the worst. The décor was in the style of an old English working-men's pub and he was fairly sure the barman and at least half the clientèle were ex-Terrans. There were far, far worse people to drink away the small hours with.

As the noise level of the pub grew with the 'day-shift' influx, Kit leaned over the bar in an attempt to solidify his position, reluctant to relinquish his seat for any backwater dock-worker. Eyes trained down on the counter, the inevitable happened and he was caught unawares.

"Eh-up! Kitty Brennan! How long has it been, lad?" went the shout as Coalface Collins landed a broad hand on Kit's back, duly knocking the wind out of him. Coughing and spluttering, Kit managed a response.

"Hi-hiya, Coalface. How're you?" He stared at the Welshman whose wide grin was beaming out from his wide face. Collins was not a tall man, nor was he particularly thin, with a warm smile and a hug that could make a bear feel awkward, he was also completely irreproachable.

"Ah, all the better for the friendly faces! Stand ye a pint?"

In his mind Kit groaned, Collins only stood you the first pint for one of two reasons: either he was on the verge of another divorce (not very likely), or was not due back in work for a couple of days and it would be a long night. He made a mental note to contact Cicero so he would not waste run-time waiting up for him, and made the sign to the bartender again. Within moments the pints arrived and they moved to a recently-vacated table near enough to the bar to make buying each round easier but far away enough that they would avoid the eventual effluence of the later hours. Spilled pints, Kit hoped, would be the worst they would have to witness.

An hour or two in and the group had doubled in size. Kit had spotted another old friend from Mars in time for the second round and one of the engineers from where Coalface worked had wandered in a half-hour after that. The talk was lively and vaguely nostalgic. They each took turns with jokes and anecdotes but then the unavoidable subject came up. Kit's friend mentioned his interest in the emerging sport of Outer Space Tennis and Coalface piped up with an insinuation that only those of a certain orientation played tennis. As Kit's friend reeled from the rebuff, Coalface jumped in with the well-known Ballad of Besieged Bangor Batsmen. Kit groaned comically as Coalface uttered those five familiar syllables, "I remember when..." He ducked out of the group just as it doubled in size, those around listening keenly as Coalface regaled them with the story of how Wales revolutionised Cricket and made it the popular sport it is today.

"Well the Cardiff lot had never seen anything like it!" he heard as he reached the bar and leaned over to shout for another drink from the obliging tender. Happy for the custom Coalface usually brought, the man beamed as he slid the pint down the counter.

Kit scanned the pub as he took a sip and found that most of it was now clustered around Coalface. A few groups had preferred to keep to their own guffaw-inducing tales while some solitary drinkers remained at the bar, apparently worried that it would fall down. It was then that one of these gloomy figures caught his eye, as he heard her sigh loud enough to be ignored by all. When she found no one responding, she sighed again, even louder. By this point Coalface had reached the point in his story with the speciality cheeses and Kit knew from experience that that bit was best avoided if possible. He glided smoothly over to the woman and sat on the vacant stool next to her.

"Go on then," he conceded. "Tell us all about it – there's a drink in it, if you want." She seemed startled for a moment and piped up with a claim that she desired to just be alone. Kit rolled his eyes and went to leave but she caught his arm suddenly and pleaded with him to stay. He looked at her tired, watery eyes and shot her a 'Well?' expression. She turned to the barman and urgently ordered a tall gin as if the world were about to end. Kit looked over to Coalface for a moment and caught his eye. The Welshman, noticing the slender figure beside him, winked and grinned before turning to the rest of the group to begin what Kit fondly referred to as the 'dolphin denouement' of the story. He rolled his eyes again and paid the bartender at the arrival of the woman's drink. She reached for it with an odd, hungry expression and turned to him with a smile.

She spoke with a clear English accent, bearing a slight home-counties twang, "It all began last June..."

Kit awoke to the horror he had expected. It was late in the morning: he could guess that from all the noise rattling in his ears. He turned over slowly, taking care lest his head explode completely. Moving even slower again, he raised himself up into a sitting position and held his skull. He made the habitual groan and whispered the mantra of the hungover, the beginning of the healing process: "Oh, never again..."

Then some of the roaring in his ears stopped. Puzzled, he looked about himself. Cicero had not been making the noise, he was probably still in the charge unit outside; (their arrangement being that if Kit was staying in a hotel, Cicero was allowed a long charge and extended down-time for his circuits). No, something else was moving in the hotel room. His eyes wandered and vague, distorted images of reaching the hotel room came back to him. They seemed somehow incomplete, some vital component missing, like a combustion engine without oil. He gently rubbed his face and held his hands over his eyes, letting his mind warm up. There was the hushed sound of a door opening and, startled, he froze. He dared not look as he heard the padding of approaching feet on the carpet. A cold sweat seemed to cut through the hangover and a tingle of anxiety shot down his neck as he heard a feminine voice speak.

"Good morning. You don't have to hide your eyes, you know, I *am* wearing a towel."

Kit gulped drily and said a mental prayer as he opened his eyes and moved his hands away. There before him was a slender woman in her mid-twenties wrapped in the usual way in a white towel, smiling at him. She had olive-green eyes and long, straight, jet-black hair which she was now towelling off. With a mental bump, his mind sharply remembered where he had seen her before – the woman from the Old Rust Bucket, the one with the sob-story he could not quite recall. *Oh, what have I done?* He thought to himself in a panic. *Oh hell, oh f-*!

"Did you sleep well?" she unknowingly interrupted with a coy smile. "You were certainly knocking them back last night. Didn't stop you being a gentleman though." His eyes went wide, as she smiled sweetly at him for a moment, taking a break from drying her hair.

"Listen, err, last night," he stammered. "I don't-"

"Remember? Well, I'm not surprised, really. Well, I told you everything that had happened to me over the last couple of months and you took me out for a couple of drinks to cheer me up. Some of your friends came with us but something happened with the Welsh man, I think, and most of them went home."

"Oh, no. Collins, what have you done now? I'd better call him! I hope he's not gotten himself into trouble like last time!" With that he moved to get out of bed.

With another flash of anxiety, Kit quickly checked himself and looked down before rising; a pair of shorts, happily, maintained his dignity. He looked at her for a moment, and fought for a name. She sat on the opposite side of the bed, away from him, humming as she continued drying.

"Erm, look, Miss Kent-"

"Sussex," she corrected.

"Yes, sorry, Sussex. What exactly happened after all that?" His hangover was threatening to return as he tentatively tried to walk over to the suitcase Cicero had left for him. "I mean did we, well, actually sleep together last night?" He was sure it was the hangover but he felt himself blush. Kit hated having to ask, hated the *way* he was asking. A brief silence held between them. Sussex turned to look at him with a quizzical expression.

"Of course we did," she said calmly.

"Oh, right, well, I want you to know I don't exactly make a habit of doing this kind of thing. I mean I don't just sleep around or have tons of girlfriends or anything like that." She stared at him, his head was not clear enough to make decent excuses.

"Alright," she said slowly. "It's OK, you know. You don't have anything to be embarrassed about."

She turned away again and that seeming an end to the conversation, Kit moved towards the suitcase, stooping to pick out a faded pair of jeans and trying to ignore the rush of blood to his face. As he stood to slip them on he heard the soft fall of a wet towel, some rustling of fabric and a zip being done up. He half turned to look at her and she walked over to him, fastening her belt and adjusting her bra as she did so.

"Do you have a shirt I can borrow?" she inquired, staring down at the suitcase. "Some arse got beer all over me last night."

Kit felt his heart beat faster in his chest and thud in his ears. *That's not fair*, he thought. *She's got her wiles and the whole damsel in need thing while I'm embarrassed, hungover and not even dressed over here!* Sussex looked back to him, smiling sweetly, innocently again. He could feel heat radiating from her body, she was presumably still warm from the shower. He was suddenly struck by the inviting scent of soap on her skin, caught himself gazing at the graceful curve of her neck as she bent to look at the neatly-folded clothes. His heart was still playing the drum solo from 'Free Bird' when he decided that, whatever exciting moment of proximal intimacy he was supposed to be enjoying, he was putting an end to it.

"Yeah, sure, just pick one out," he blurted before quickly about-facing and doing up his fly. When she had selected a shirt, he reached down for a grey t-shirt and they simultaneously pulled shirts over their heads.

Finally dressed, Kit muttered an excuse and stumbled out of the hotel room, into the corridor. From there he found the small closet-sized room next to his own. He opened the door and tapped the android on its head unit.

"Wakey-wakey!"

The lights in the robot's eyes blinked on and a second later its voice module shakily activated.

"Good morning, sir!"

"Not so loud!" he hissed, "Now, come on. I've got a terrible hangover and I need to go out and get in touch with Coalface about last night. And erm," he hesitated,

"I need you to take care of someone for a while."

The robot assented and stepped out of the unit with slow, deliberate steps. Then he followed Kit into his room and greeted Sussex ambiguously. Kit was not known for keeping much female company and certainly none that was particularly intimate. Cicero instantly evaluated the situation and assumed the woman currently wearing his owner's shirt was a friend of the new, clothes-borrowing type. He adopted a polite, formal tone.

"Sussex, this is Cicero my helper; Cicero, Sussex is a, erm, friend. Sussex, I'm very sorry but I really should go check on Coalface about last night. Would you mind waiting for me with Cicero? Unless you've got things you need to do..." He held his head and waited a beat; Sussex simply smiled.

"Right, then. I'll go check on Collins."

With that he smiled weakly, grabbed his jacket from the back of a chair and darted out of the room before woman or robot could protest.

As Kit headed out of the hotel, he winced at the noise of midday traffic. The station was busier than an anthill in picnic season and his head was still pounding. He headed for a coffee bar before wandering back and rummaging for his mobile communicator in his pocket. With some mental difficulty he retuned the device and called Coalface. A dial-tone sounded in his ear.

"Hello?" Kit winced: it was Pandora, Coalface's current wife and she did not sound pleased.

"Hiya, Panny, it's Brennan. Is he up yet?"

"Don't you 'Panny' me, Christopher Brennan! He was out all night with you lot before *stumbling* into my bed at bloody *six* o'clock this morning?!"

Kit groaned audibly but it did nothing to appease her.

"Look, Panny, I didn't mean for him to come back like

that! He took it on himself to go out drinking last night, we all just got caught up with it – you know what he's like!"

"Well that's as maybe but would you mind explaining who this other girl, this '*Kitty*' is? Hmm?" He looked about helplessly and decided to buy himself time with a sip of scalding coffee. He hissed and tried to answer with a burnt tongue, "I, err, I don't know. He's not the type to juggle two girls at once, you know," he proffered.

"Isn't he? That's how he met me!"

Kit winced again.

"Oh right, erm, well I don't think he is cheating on y- Wait! Did you say 'Kitty'?"

"Yes. He's got himself a new tattoo and it says 'Kitty'!" He laughed to himself.

"It's me, Pandora! The daft bugger's got me on his arm!" He heard only silence for a moment.

"What?! But Chris, why?! And it's not on his arm – Oh, hang on, here he comes! Don't be long, Chris, I still want to chew him over about last night!" She called incredulously.

Kit grinned as the phone went quiet, there was some mumbling and he was passed over to the groaning Welshman.

"Hullo?" Coalface said in a husky, strained voice.

"Morning, Collins, how are you feeling?"

"Like I got hit round the head by Swansea's entire batsman reserve team! What can I do for you?" Kit was momentarily distracted by a muted boom in the distance, a far away crash and vague sounds of shouting. There was a slight tremor beneath his feet but he was called back to the conversation with Collins, though he continued to look about himself. He was now at the hotel again, standing outside the doors, about to light a cigarette. Those around him were all starting to head into the hotel in a rush and others across the street seemed to be

174

running in every direction. He was distracted by Coalface calling to him.

"Lad?! Oi, Kit!"

"Yeah, sorry! Listen, Collins, how are you after last night? You haven't got into any trouble, have you?"

"Erm, no, I don't think so, no," his voice sounded confused.

"Well, what do you remember about last night then?" Kit heard him swear.

"Hell, Brennan! I've *just* sodding woken up, you know!" There was an aggrieved sigh and he went on, the mental strain evident in his voice. "Well I remember getting the first round in and you chatting up that lass. We all went for a curry and ended up in Akbar's for a bit. You disappeared somewhere along the way. Listen, Kit, I'm not being funny lad, but can this wait? I've got it pretty bad here and a horrible stinging pain in my-"

Kit did not hear the next word under the sound of approaching gunfire; he watched as a crowd surged towards him. He was jostled and nearly knocked over by people sprinting past him. He was just about to dive out of the way, into the hotel, when he was knocked down by a huge mass of a man. He looked up to find a bulky goliath standing over him with a wild look in his eyes and an annoyed expression on his face; he wore a t-shirt that looked three sizes too small for him, army fatigues and hard-looking, rubber-heeled boots. He towered over Kit, staring down at him before then looking satisfied, as if he had made a decision. The giant plucked him hastily from the ground. Kit called out, kicking and waving his arms but the man threw him over his shoulder without a word. His thick arms squeezed a gasp from Kit's lungs and he ran on. Kit tried to yell with what remained of his breath but, in the midst of all that chaos, no one could possibly have heard him. In a mad rush the giant carried him down street after street. The motion swung Kit about violently, making his attempts to break free utterly futile. Nevertheless, he continued to strain against the iron grip and beat his hands against the man's thick skull. The giant seemed not to notice.

He ran quickly down the street, losing no speed as he turned corners and dived down alleyways; before long, Kit realised they were headed for Adrestia's warehouse district. The sounds of calamity seemed far away, Kit heard only a low rumble of running feet and the fading roar of terrified screams. He tried to look around him in case he needed details later but the shaking motion of the giant's running and the panic in his own head meant his eyes could not make sense of what street they were in or any numbers on warehouse doors. He tried to look over his shoulder and found they were in front of a large iron and concrete warehouse, its retractable metal shutters slowly descending over the doorway. It looked too low for the giant to get under with Kit on his shoulders. He yelled out but the giant had no time to listen as he threw Kit through the opening, sliding through himself afterwards. Kit rolled, groaned and began to pick himself up off the floor. The giant was quicker though, gripped him hard by the back of his collar and dragged him further into the warehouse. Kit took in his surroundings with little hope. The warehouse was dim but he could see it was completely empty except for a small striped tent in the centre, the sort road-workers might use. He heard the sound of running feet echoing and he turned to see another man, more his own size, following them. He was decked in the drab, dark grey uniform of a civic maintenance worker. Kit had a feeling that, whatever was going on, the third man was probably not going to be any help to him. The evil grin on his face as he noticed Kit confirmed it. The giant pushed him towards the tent harshly and, finding it covered a manhole, Kit followed the uniformed man down the maintenance ladder. At the bottom he found himself in the access tunnels that ran in between levels on Adrestia, the air was suddenly thick and clammy as Kit realised he was surrounded by power conduits and heating pipes. The giant landed next to Kit and looked past him to the other man who was checking a data-pad and nodding. The giant grunted and Kit turned around just in time to see him swing a large, meaty fist at him. Kit slumped against the tunnel wall and the darkness enveloped him.

A hard slap across the face brought Kit back to consciousness. He looked about and found he had been handcuffed and strapped to a chair, he was also facing a video-camera. A bright light was shining in his eyes so he saw nothing beyond it but he could feel the presence of other people in the room with him. He also felt a chill and guessed he was probably in a ship out in space somewhere. An angry male voice, accompanying a handgun muzzle pressed hard against his temple, corrected him.

"Open the Docking Bay doors or handsome here loses his head!" It had been said towards the camera but Kit did not doubt he was the intended victim. Heart racing, Kit looked on towards the camera, and tried to look up to the man holding the gun. He breathed frantically and strained to break free, craning his neck away from the weapon. He tried to yell out but realised there was strong industrial tape clamped over his mouth. Before long, the gun was removed as a shout sounded from somewhere far off in the ship. Fear gripped his heart as unseen hands dismantled the camera equipment and he heard bodies moving behind him. The bright lamp was switched off and Kit blinked the light-spots out of his eyes before he tried to look around again. He felt the bonds around his ankles loosen and he was pulled up into a standing position. He checked his situation and found he was surrounded by a handful of men busily moving large, full holdalls about.

"A good 25 million? Oh, this is the sweetest haul ever!" he heard one of them say. Kit calculated and realised the situation. *Kidnapped to help thieves escape?! Oh, wonderful!* He thought. *Mum'll be so pleased to hear what I've been up to this Summer!*

"Alright Twinkle! Move it!" Before he could mumble or do anything though, he was roughly manhandled out of the room. He heard the powerful roar of the engines and laughter from the men as he was led down a dimly-lit ship's corridor. Then he was hauled into a small canteen chamber, his handcuffs and the tape were removed unkindly before he was pulled over to a wall, a door slid open and he was tossed through it.

"Keep quiet! If we need you again, we'll come and get you! Until then, sit quiet and say your prayers 'cause as soon as we get back, you'll be taking a stroll out the airlock!"

He found himself in a stock cupboard, barely wide enough to contain him though quite empty, save for an old crate. He held his head with one hand while bracing himself against the wall with the other. Resting his arms on a shelf for a minute, Kit tried to bring his thoughts to order. The panic set in as he realised he had been dragged onto a ship full of homicidal maniacs. His heart began to pound in his ears. *They're going to kill me! I need a way out! I need an escape pod or a signal for help or something to get me away from these lunatics!* As the pounding grew louder he realised there was a terrible, mechanical screech coming from all about him. He heard it worsen and go up in pitch before finally there was a loud thud and Kit heard the screech become a whine and eventually whimper away. The pounding also began to subside but not the cold sweat that had set in. Kit's eyes darted around the gloomy cupboard, searching every corner for an opening or some sign of corroded weakness. The door bore no handle and though it had small cracks allowing thin shafts of light through, there was decidedly no way to open it from the inside. The only hole in the ceiling was a small fan unit that was definitely too small for him to fit through. He sighed and slumped against the wall, sliding down to a sitting position. *There's no way out* he screamed internally. *There's no way back to my ship, to Cicero, to Mars! There's no way to-!* He stopped as he realised he was doing himself no favours. He had to take a minute and breathe. *OK Kit, calm down. Take a deep breath. Try to think calmly*, he told himself. *There's always a way.*

Kit checked the crate of dusty packets and found nothing useful. Only long-outdated dried food samples, no good. Then he checked himself over. He found his heart was beating a much calmer rhythm now, his jaw was sore from the punch but overall he was unharmed. He could think clearly enough and his limbs all stretched and flexed with their usual dexterity. He rubbed the goosebumps on his arms to try and block out the cold of unheated atmosphere before, absentmindedly, going for a cigarette in his pocket and finding a squashed packet there. Next to that was his mobile communicator. *The fools haven't searched me!* He grinned. Kit was about to pull it out when he heard heavy footsteps approaching the cupboard. Quickly dropping the communicator inside the old crate, he stood up just in time to see the door open with a small whoosh.

"Come!" It was the giant again. Kit found him different though. Instead of a feeling of subdued rage,

Kit could feel a repressed vibe coming from him. Like a child after being scolded. He stepped out of the cupboard cautiously, eyeing the giant carefully, and turned out into the small canteen. He felt a large finger prod his back in the direction of a wide corridor. He could hear distant shouting now from somewhere in the ship and hoped it was nothing to do with him. The giant overtook him, muscling him out of the way, and he followed after him silently. *If I'm going to survive, I have to either be important or useful.* He took a quick look over his t-shirt and worn jeans. *Useful then?* he hoped. The giant led him into a wide antechamber filled with bulging holdalls; this stretched out to the cockpit where he could see the five men of varying sizes and ages arguing over the engines.

"I'm telling you, she won't take it!"

"Bull! Push her into it and she'll get us there! I didn't waste thirty grand on a piece of crap, Skinner! *You* must have buggered her up!"

"Chief, he can't have! You don't bugger up a ship this size, it just gets old and rusts!"

As he entered, the giant merely grunted at the man who had been addressed as 'Chief,' and sat in one of the pilot-seats taking no part in the argument. Kit could see that they were now out in open space. Something in him sank a little, the rest stayed on edge as he felt more of an intruder than a hostage. He watched as they continued to argue over the state of the ship, trying to take in as many details as possible. As far as he could tell there was six of them in total. The man called Skinner was stringy, wearing dark coveralls as Kit often did, and covered in what looked like grease; he identified him as an Australian from his accent. The Chief was much older but stood much straighter and wore an eye-patch on a scarred face that Kit guessed had seen plenty of combat but not enough sun. He was dressed in a rough, cheap suit with an open-collared shirt.

Ex-military, he considered. *Probably a UCAF soldier, old enough to have seen the second Space Race, and then some.* The third man was dressed in a like suit of lighter hue. He looked slippery to Kit, confident with a gun in his hand but he doubted his bravado without one; he guessed it had been his gun pressed to his head before. The fourth man looked much the same but was noticeably taller, slimmer, wore a sharper suit, and had not said a word since Kit arrived. Kit recognised the fifth man as the fake maintenance worker the giant had met. The giant made it six. Kit considered the group again and came to one conclusion. *Thieves, more specifically, bank-robbers.*

"Well maybe it's the extra weight we're hauling!" Kit took a step back as the slippery thief advanced on him, an accusing finger jabbing sharply at his chest. The giant turned in his seat to look at the Chief but all eyes eventually settled harshly on Kit. His hands went up in protest but before anything could be said, the Chief spoke in a stern, defensive tone.

"Kong brought him on my orders, to use as a hostage to get out. No one has a problem with that." It was no question: there was an almost tangible battle of wills going unsaid. As if the atmosphere weren't heavy enough, the giant, Kong, then rose slowly from his seat. A moment of silence passed before Skinner made an attempt to break it.

"That's fine, Chief. But why is he still here?"

"We're holding him until we get back. We might need him," he said slowly, staring icily at Kit. "Especially if the engines are buggered."

There was another extended silence as no one would comfortably admit they were on the run and not doing it well.

"For the moment we're on repairs until we can get going again. Skinner, you're on that! It doesn't have to be perfect, just working. Finn, keep an eye out for STARS.

Kong, he's your responsibility for now." Gesturing at Kit, the Chief had the final word. He finished his sentence and pushed his way out of the room. The oily thief, Finn, sighed, bumped past Kit and moved to slump in the chair Kong had vacated. Skinner turned to Kit for a moment and looked him over.

"So what good are you?" he asked with an evaluating look.

"His ID says his name's Brennan. He's a greaser," Finn said over his shoulder. Kit's hand immediately went to the back pocket of his jeans with a jump. Finn held up a small square of rough leather, Kit's wallet. Instinctively he dived for it, Finn did not resist and a small chuckle went through the group. Checking it over, he found everything there but for a small amount of cash. It was not much so Kit let it slide and replaced the wallet in a front pocket.

"I used to be a mechanic. A few years ago," he muttered. Skinner looked to Kong who had been examining his fingernails. The giant shrugged and Skinner nodded to himself.

"Alright. What would you do if you've got a leak in your lubricant feed-line?" Skinner threw the question sideways at Kit. He considered it a moment, figuring this was how he would make himself useful.

"What pump model are you using, African or European?"

Skinner grinned.

"You any good with antiques?"

"My parents have a farm in the Dust Bowl. There's nothing *but* antiques down there!" Kit offered. Skinner nodded again and turned out of the cockpit, gesturing for him to follow. No one else objected so he matched pace with Skinner. They walked down a curved corridor and found the engine room.

Skinner led him into a double-door sealed room and Kit

marvelled at the enormous engine that filled it. It was a very early nuclear engine with a tiny amount of radioactive material powering two huge thrusters. Both machinery and design were old but Kit guessed the high-output thrusters, as well as the well-armoured design of the ship, were what had caught the Chief's eye when he had bought it. They offered him good acceleration and long-lasting fuel. Kit guessed he was not much of an engineer though, this engine needed a complete overhaul and a lot of replacements before it would be serviceable for any great length of time. Hundreds of pipes and cable conduits were hanging from the ceiling and large housing panels had been left gaping open. Kit whistled through his teeth and Skinner grinned at him as he plucked a tool kit from off the floor.

"Luckily, the containment unit's fine. It's the focus converters that were making all that noise." Skinner paused as he checked a gauge. "Coolant and ventilators could do with a check-up too," he said, suddenly, despondent. The Australian sighed, released the latch on a maintenance hatch and slid the heavy door back along its track.

The thief set Kit to work on the failing port-side modulator while he worked to repair a feed-line next to it. Kit never shook off the feeling that Skinner was keeping a cold watch on him all the time. They worked for what seemed like hours, mostly in absolute silence, before Skinner ordered a break and a grateful Kit slumped down against the side of the coolant unit.

"Nearly there, I reckon," he muttered.

Skinner grunted an acknowledgement while standing over the open panel Kit had worked at. He surveyed the work quickly and made a point of absentmindedly poking a thumb through his belt and letting his hand fall over the gun-holster he had there. He nodded his approval.

"Listen, I'm not being funny but why exactly have you got me here working on this piece of junk?"

Skinner looked at him and mulled it over for a second.

"I'd say mainly 'cause the Chief doesn't like admitting to a mistake. Besides, if you're useful, he might keep you alive!"

"And is that likely?"

Skinner grinned and Kit felt a shiver run down his spine.

"Was it worth it? The job you pulled?"

Skinner, who had been checking a readout, suddenly turned his head to glare at him. There was silence for a long moment.

"Yeah. Well bloody worth it! Now come on, you're no use if you're slacking. And if you're no use, you're dead." They went back to work, but not before Kit subtly pocketed a small screwdriver from off the floor.

They went on and on for another few hours and Kit reckoned that they were finished on the port-side focusing unit when Skinner called it a day, giving up and sending Kit back to his cupboard. Kong was there in the canteen and was happy enough to seal him in. He also threw a dust-sheet in with him and ordered him to sleep. Kit sighed with great relief when the door finally closed. He listened out for Kong's fingers at the keypad but heard nothing beyond the basic locking mechanism. *Great, if I can get into the panel I could probably get the door open.* He paused for a moment. *If.*

Kit chose the cleaner side of the dust-sheet to wrap closest around him before fishing his communicator out of the old crate. Using the screwdriver, he prised the casing off and looked hopefully at the gold lines flowing up and down over the green plastic. He had to work quickly, had to get off the ship before they got too far away from Adrestia. Kit located the signal-output circuitry and tried to work out the right parts to fiddle with. Removing one or two components that limited the range of signal, Kit worked hard and fast for an hour before he felt fatigue make his hands unsteady and his sight unreliable. He finished quickly and reassembled the device. Lying back and staring at the ceiling, he tried to think about the next step. Even if he did manage to get the signal to work as he wanted, it did not necessarily mean his guaranteed escape. He would have to survive long enough to be rescued and, if the thieves picked up his signal as he suspected they would, Kit would have to avoid them until help came. At last he gave up and let the final wave of fatigue wash over him.

A few hours later, Kit awoke to the sounds of the thieves congregated in the canteen outside. They were muttering and chatting lightly and Kit's brief shock of panic was short-lived. They seemed happy enough to be eating breakfast out there so he sat up, stretched the kinks of his back and rubbed his face. He then went back to the communicator and switched it on. The screen blinked into life and Kit quickly pushed it through the loading screen to get to the settings menu. He recalibrated it and began to type an SOS to his own ship's ID code but doubted it would get straight there so set the wave wide in the hope of it being picked up by others. Kit just had time to save the settings and turn the device off, pocketing it, before Kong's footsteps could be heard again at the door. He led Kit past Finn and the other unnamed thieves, who were smoking and playing poker over milky bowls and greasy dishes. They eyed Kit coldly, as they had before. Kit may have been repairing their ship but if he could not be trusted, that was that. Kong led him back to the engine room and he rejoined Skinner's efforts on the engines. They worked for about four hours without interruption before an opportunity arose. The Chief called Skinner out of the room suddenly to go fix the radar and, glancing back at Kit, he left, sealing the double doors to the engine room behind him.

Kit moved quickly. He shut the maintenance hatch and jammed a wrench in the runner to clasp it in place. Looking around, Kit found what he was looking for and slammed his boot against the flimsy vent cover that led to a conduit access-shaft barely wide enough to crawl through. He dived in without hesitation and struggled past fittings until he found he could shuffle about with some efficiency. He was just about to turn a corner when he heard the shouting begin. He turned on the communicator and sent the message he had prepared before, sending out a short prayer with it. Skinner was now banging heavily on the maintenance hatch and Kit pushed on until the access shaft opened out enough for him to crawl quicker and quicker. Suddenly another shout went up. Kit dropped his belly to the floor. He guessed it was the scanners picking up his message. Moving on slowly, he strained his ears to listen for what was being said or done to thwart his escape. But he shuffled louder than he meant. There was a loud click, the shaft-ceiling above flew open, a thick arm plucked him from the shaft and set him shakily on his feet. It was the Chief. Kit swore under his breath and turned to run but the Chief was faster.

"Get back here!" he roared. The older man threw him to the floor and placed a hefty boot on his chest. "You've got some answering to do, Brennan!" Spitting the words like acid, the Chief once again picked him up and held him by his collar. He was ready to swing a fist when Kit ducked out of the way and threw his weight to the side to unbalance the Chief. Kit's collar ripped and he was again flown outwards, down what he realised was the corridor to the cockpit. There was only the loud muttering of curses coming from there but Kit knew he was outnumbered if he backed in.

With a growl, the Chief raced after him in a bull-charge but Kit found he was faster. He dodged, the Chief skidded, Finn emerged to see what was going on. Before he could evade him, Kit was charged again by the Chief, only to be knocked over by Finn. He rolled and was up again in a flash, but Finn was still on him. Fists flew at his head, one dodge only lining him up for another strike. He ducked and weaved as only Addy street-fighters knew how before gripping Finn by the arm, holding his shoulder straight and wheeling him around to fall into the watching Chief. Finn rebounded and twisted backwards but a ready fist connected with the thief's jaw and he went down in a slump. The Chief advanced on Kit with a terrifying grin.

"You know, I could've used someone like you as backup, but now you've just pissed me off!" The Chief threw another fist at Kit, all his weight rolling with it. Kit tried evading but was caught in the gut. Winded, he staggered back into the cockpit, the hard metal of the control panel jutting out at him. The Chief was on him in a second, strong fingers grasped tight around his throat. Gasping for air, Kit's arms flailed about. He kicked at the Chief's legs, arms knocking a joystick out of place, fists flying off the Chief's arms to smash buttons on the dashboard. He heard a shout from Skinner as the ignition sequence started up and the engines began to hum at the back of the ship. The other thieves had begun to cluster around too to see what the noise was about. Skinner raced in, barging past Kong on the way to try and disable the unready engines. But it was too late. An explosion rocked the ship. Meanwhile, Kit's vision began to blur and he felt the last gasps of air waste away inside his desperate lungs.

Another explosion rocked the ship. This time the force was enough to knock everyone off their feet. Kit's sharp gasp of air was louder than the thieves' angry mutterings and as his lungs tried to catch pace he rolled onto the floor and gripped the pilot seat to steady himself. There was a third explosion and the ship shook hard before a hailing bleep sounded on the dashboard communicator. A stern, authoritative voice came through the speaker. Kit sighed with relief as the matter-of-fact tone of the "STARS" officer officiously called for engines to be deactivated and weapons to be stood down. The Chief wheeled, yelling at the unnamed thieves to man the guns but they were too late. The cavalry had arrived. Kit saw his own ship fly in a sharp arc over them and round to face their windscreen. He saw his small EMP cannon spark up on the hull and waited for the disabling wave to rush through the ship's systems. Screens sparked and blinked before fading, the lights dimmed, the engines finally shut down and suddenly they were completely alone in silent space. In the darkness, Kit heard curses, then the Interstellar Police clamp fit itself over the airlock and begin to force the opening. Within moments, the STARS were inside the ship, tasering the giant Kong and knocking Finn back down to the ground again. Breathing a sigh of relief, Kit went on panting on the ground.

Much later, Kit had escaped both the confines of the thieves' ship and the bureaucracy of Interstellar Police witness-statement protocol. He walked with the lightness of a man released from prison back to his ship, where he found Cicero and Sussex Coleridge waiting for him. The woman beamed, flew over to squeeze him tightly and plant a happy kiss on his cheek. Cicero shook Kit's hand mechanically and said he was very pleased to have him back. Kit slumped into his pilot-seat and looked at them both; Sussex grinning widely, Cicero standing with a somewhat triumphant stance.

"I'm glad you turned up when you did, Cicero! Thank you, old boy! How did you manage it?" he asked, the fatigue heavy in his voice.

"Not at all, Mr. Christopher. I was helped a great deal by Miss Sussex here. She saw your picture on the news and we realised that the hostage on a ship forcing Station Control to open their bay-doors was actually you," the robot intoned.

"Wow, well, thank you Sussex! It seems I owe you a drink, next time I'm in town." He smiled, waiting for her to accept it. She only looked at him quizzically. Awkwardly, he looked to her, then to Cicero, then back again.

"That reminds me, Mr. Christopher. As we're leaving straight away, which room should I bunk Miss Sussex in?" Cicero asked.

He knew it was impossible but Kit suspected somewhere deep inside his CPU, Cicero loved pushing him into awkward situations like this. He stammered for a moment.

"You do still want a mechanic, don't you?" Sussex asked, the first sign of worry appearing in her features. Like a car-crash, the memories flooded back to Kit. The night they had been drinking, her need for a place to live, his passing statement about pilots always needing dedicated mechanics, her misreading of the situation... He remembered it all up to stumbling back to his room at the hotel. They had kissed, if rather drunkenly, but after that he remembered nothing until the morning after. She watched him colour and half turn away in his chair. He stammered again.

"Cicero, would you mind making up a pot of coffee, please?"

The robot complied and left the cockpit. Kit stood and stepped nearer to Sussex, she looked up slightly into his eyes. He had not really noticed how similar in height they were before, now he saw she could only be an inch or two shorter than his six feet.

"Sussex, I... When I said- Well I can't pay you, and there's not really all that much to fix up," he began. She moved closer to him. "And about before, I mean I wasn't really looking to start a relationship, you see. That night in the hotel room, it didn't necessarily mean-"

She looked at him quizzically.

"What-? Do you think that we-?" then she grinned as if realising something. "Oh, Kit, you thought we'd had one mistaken night of drunken passion and I was going to take that as a declaration of love?"

He felt the blood rush to his cheeks again. She stepped back, smiled and shook her head playfully; then turned on her heel and sauntered off in the direction of the bunk-rooms.

"Hey, wait!"

"Cicero, would you be a dear and bring me a cup when it's done brewing, please? I've got to unpack my things," she called out for both of them to hear.

"Hey! Sussex! Are you saying we didn't then?!" Kit shouted frantically, rushing to the corridor opening.

"With two sugars please, Cissy!"

"Sussex!" Kit threw his arms up in exasperation and finally gave up, flinging himself back into his pilot-seat. He flicked the engines on and prepared the ship for leaving the station. *Then again, another person around wouldn't be so terrible. And a mechanic could be quite useful...*

"Oh, the hell with it!" He shouted to no one in particular. "Fine, Miss Mechanic! Welcome aboard!"

BlueWinter

Alexander Skye

Alexander Skye has been obsessed with sci-fi since before he was born. Since those early experiments with time travel, he has read and enjoyed every branch of science fiction; from the most realistic of hard SF, through the most cynical of cyberpunk and the most Victorian of steampunk, to the most exuberant of space opera. He's enjoyed other genres besides, most especially fantasy, with which he has had a long-running affair. It began as a child, reading *The Chronicles of Narnia*, and *The Lord of the Rings*, and has never really abated. His first and greatest love, however, will always be science fiction.

Having spent so long merely reading and admiring, he decided that it was finally time to try and tell his own stories and hopefully you'll enjoy them as much as he enjoyed writing them; if not, he'll be forced to find a different job, which would be tragic since they're all so boring - after all, how many other professions let you stare wistfully at the stars on a cloudless night and call it research?

A small blue light flicked on in the corner of the screen, blinking slowly. In fact, it was more like breathing; gradually pulsing, like a heart slowing down for cryo, so faint and unobtrusive that Alice didn't notice it.

It was time for her half-hour lunch break before she did realise it was there. She blinked in surprise – Gray wasn't meant to be in touch for at least another three days. That must mean… it's important! She half-stood in her seat and looked about the room – most of her workmates had already disappeared down to the cafeteria. Perfect timing. Alice bent down to the bottom drawer of her desk and withdrew her VRD 'set.

She flicked it aside, and unwound the headset's thick cables. Carefully untangling the blue vis-feed from the green and pink sound I/O wires, she placed the 'set gingerly on her head, and flipped open the socket covers on her computer tower. Flicking the adjacent switch from VIDEO ONLY to FULL VRD, she plugged in the assorted cables. A faint pulse went through the headset to inform her that it was active, and Alice brought down the small eyepiece – power was fine, vid was working properly, sound and input were working properly, VRD wasn't yet active. She hadn't encountered a problem with it, almost brand new as it was, but it couldn't hurt to check.

With the 'set in place and ready to go, she pressed the small breathing light that signalled Gray's message. The computer screen flickered for a moment as it detected the VRD 'set, and up popped a small message window:

VRD Equipment detected. Would you like to use full virtualisation dreaming for this session?

Alice tapped the 'Yes' button, and settled back into her seat. The computer's screen went dark for a moment, and then flickered to life in miniature on the headset's eyepiece.

It counted down from 3. She absentmindedly brushed something unidentifiable off the coiled cabling – no matter how vigorously she cleaned that damn drawer, some bit of fluff always found its way in. There was a faint tingling sensation at her temples and the world went away.

When the world came back and Alice opened her eyes again, the office was gone. In fact, so was Alice. Here she was BlueWinter, a highly styled version of herself. Her avatar would usually be decked out for a night in the Spider's Web club down on the 12th floor, outlined in various kinds of blue. On this server however, the admin forced a dress code. He was something of an Ancient Rome fetishist and so everyone wore togas. Whether they liked it or not.

And in fact, whether they clipped through their avatar models or not.

Either way, it made for an interesting site. The forum was designed much like the Roman equivalent, with marble columns and pillars lining the sides, small subfora curtained off with great swathes of red cloth and a ceiling opened up to the finest skybox artwork the Admin could find. In fact, but for a few small details, it was a picture perfect replica of a Roman forum. The main issue was the medieval kite shields over the 'entrance'. She'd never worked out how someone so interested in the Romans could make such an obvious mistake – maybe they were the only decent resolution model he could afford. Regardless, they rather killed the Roman immersion. The fact that half the people in the forum had hair in every single shade other than natural, a fair number had wings and a couple were cel-shaded didn't help to keep up the illusion. Nevertheless, it was a fun place to meet, and one where it was hard to seem out of place – perfect for what Alice needed.

She moved forwards through the 'building', pausing to wave briefly at a couple of the regulars, and checked the two subfora nearest the rear wall. No sign of Gray. While peeking into one of the smaller side rooms, she spotted Redshift at the back, plugging away at a keyboard only he could see. She brought up her 'board and tapped out a quick message; he was in one of the smaller rooms, he was busy with something. Probably a client. Either way, it wouldn't do to just go blustering up to him.

Message written, she gestured minutely at him and then, once he was limned with a pale blue, she hit send and waited. She saw him notice her message immediately; he glanced up at the curtain and smiled. He nearly went to wave, but then remembered what he was doing. He held up a single finger, and went back to typing.

A moment later, a response pinged up in her peripheral vision.

Sorry Blue, gimme a min, workin on a quick job for this ugly fuck.

She glanced back at where Red was sitting. The 'client', an avatar doing his level best to look as though he wasn't watching Red like a hawk, was definitely no model. BlueWinter stifled a chuckle.

I did get the info you wanted though. Ill get it to you in a bit.

Gray wanted to see you btw.

She nodded, and wrote back.

Thanks Red. Ill catch you later then – gonna look for Gray.

She sent it off, watching only long enough to see Redshift glance leftwards in his HUD, then she slipped back out of the subfora and looked about the server again. No sign anywhere. Where on earth was Gray?

Even as she thought it, a flickering white coalesced at the 'entrance', and there stood Grayscale. For a moment his avatar displayed its normal outfit – a surprisingly sharp suit, lined and highlighted in white strips; he looked like something one of the old school electronic bands might've whipped up. Then the server's custom rules took over and his clothes popped out of existence, revealing a toga. Blue noticed that he now had purple lining to it – he'd donated some money to the admin for running costs. She'd been meaning to do the same – it only seemed polite, considering the way she used and abused his forum.

She quickly shrugged off that train of thought and waved at Gray, pinging him with a quick preset 'Hello' message. She needn't have bothered, since he saw her wave and batted away the message ping as he made his way across the forum to her.

"Hey Blue, long time no see!"

She smiled and quickly threw him a hug.

"Too long, Gray. How have you been?"

"Not bad, not bad. I'm sorry Blue, but we'll have to be quick here – I've only got a bit of time to spare. Would've been longer if you hadn't ignored me for an hour."

"Oh fuck off, you knew I was at work!"

Gray smiled.

"Yeah, any excuse. Come on, let's find somewhere to sit."

They wended their way to the nearest of the subfora, and slipped in past the hanging red drapes. There was a free bench up against the rear wall, so they both collapsed onto it and settled down to chat.

"Same as usual I take it, Gray?"

"Of course," he nodded, summoning his 'board so they could share a private conversation. BlueWinter brought hers up as well, manipulating the language presets toggle to set the keyboard to an abnormal layout, just in case anyone decided to try and watch what she was typing. Probably a pointless precaution, since she and Gray always used Esperanto anyway.

« I got that stuff you were asking for, about the big clampdown in the Michaelson arco. Some pretty nasty stuff here. »

« I don't doubt it. I suppose you'll be after your usual fee? »

« But of course! » Gray furnished himself a grin, but quickly sobered.

« I do wish you'd leave SK alone Blue. They're not particularly nice people. »

« I know that Gray. Why else would I be after this stuff? Someone has to get it out there, and if anyone can, it's me. »

« Yeah yeah. I'm just worried about you girl. »

« I'm touched » Blue tapped out, putting on a faux-pout.

« No, seriously. Sigma-Kross have done some seriously bad shit to people before. Hell, I'm a bit scared just passing this stuff on. »

« Look, it'll be fine. They only get away with that stuff when it's in the background, in countries no one gives a damn about. We're fine here. We have to be, that's the whole bloody point of the free world isn't it? »

Grayscale sagged in his seat, though what that expressed, Blue couldn't tell.

« I just hope you're right, girl. I really do worry you know. Especially after reading some of the shit they did in Michaelson. I didn't read the whole thing, but it's pretty clear that the explosion was no accident. »

« *Jesus. Speaking of, might I have a copy?* »

Grayscale nodded. His hand swirled in midair while he summoned the file, and then with a non-existent pop, it was in his hand – a sheaf of papyrus, with indecipherable script across them, another of the server's whimsies. BlueWinter watched as he glanced over what she guessed was a file listing hovering alongside. Satisfied, he held out the documents, and BlueWinter reached for them in return. They even felt like papyrus as she bundled them up and folded them away into her toga. They vanished as soon as they went out of sight, disappearing directly into the passworded documents folder stored on her VRD 'set.

« *Thanks again Gray. You're a darling.* »

« *God don't, it makes me sound like some 1950s toy boy.* »

Blue laughed aloud at this, the sudden noise sounding strange after time spent silently typing.

« *Either way, this should hopefully be more than enough for me to finish up the piece and report. Then, in less than a month, it goes to the front page of every damn thing I can get it on.* »

« *You really think it'll do any good? I mean, I know you're an idealist Blue, but still. Stuff about how shitty SK are has been on the 'net since they started up. Why should this one be any different?* »

« *Because the average public read the papers, they don't trawl hacksites and conspiracy forums. And the average public vote. If I can get people pissed off enough at SK, parliament will have no choice but to do something about it.* »

« *Jesus, you really are optimistic. Good luck with that I guess.* »

« *Filling me with confidence here, Gray.* »

« *If I thought anyone could do it it'd be you, girl. But I AM serious. Play it safe. SK are proper bastards.* »

Blue nodded and blinked away her 'board.

"Thanks again Gray, much appreciated."

"Anytime girlie. You know how to contact me if you

need anything. And I'll ping you if anything good shows up around the place."

"You're the best." Blue paused a moment while she glanced up at the time. "I'd better be off, lunch is nearly up and I was pretty hungry before I slept."

Gray nodded, and stood, batting away his keyboard interface while he did so.

"Good to see you again Blue. Stay safe."

"I will, I promise," she replied, before blinking out of existence.

Gray sighed to no one in particular as he logged off as well.

Alice blinked herself to wakefulness. She looked about in surprise and hurriedly glanced at her watch – almost the end of lunch! Of all the times to catch a nap!

She stood quickly, her VRD 'set yanking on her head as she played out the full length of the cables. She started in surprise – when had she put that on? Then it came back – Gray sent a message, she sat down to answer it, and…and then she had woken up.

Oops.

Gray would be angry. Hopefully he'd be around this evening when she could dive again from home. For now though, Alice had less than ten minutes to grab some food, so she bundled the VRD 'set back into its drawer, and made a beeline for the stairs down to the cafeteria. She was in such a hurry that she almost bowled over the security guard who was coming through the doors. He just managed to keep a grip on his sandwich, as well as the banister, while Alice fell backwards.

"God, so sorry miss!" he said as he bent to help her up.

"My fault, it's fine," she said as he pulled her to her feet, "Are you okay?"

"I'm just fine," he smiled, hefting his intact lunch, "How about yourself?"

"I'm alright. They haven't stopped serving food have they?"

"Sorry, wouldn't know, the wife made me this one. You doze off or something?"

"Yeah. I hoped it wasn't that obvious," Alice laughed.

"You'll be fine miss, just look a little sleepy is all. Besides, I didn't see a thing."

He winked.

"Thanks," Alice smiled.

"Not to worry. Now get downstairs and get some lunch before it goes cold. God knows it's bad enough warm," he smiled again and moved aside, gesturing down the stairs.

Alice nodded her thanks and sped past him.

He waited until he heard the door at the bottom fly open and slowly swing shut, his smile gradually fading. Then he tapped twice on his lapel and, turning his head to speak into it, reported in.

***

Gray sat back in his chair and removed his VRD 'set with a heavy sigh. It got harder and harder to lie to the poor girl as time went on. But this would be the last time, he thought as he tapped out his report on the meeting.

Met again with Winters, Alice. Passed on doctored reports on Michaelson Arcology incident, included standard program to inhibit VRD memory recall and delete the reports. Subject claimed that she would be going to the presses with the story within a short time frame. Further observation recommended.

He paused and rubbed his eyes, swearing softly under his

breath. He knew exactly what the response would be, and knew exactly what it would mean. Nonetheless, he tapped 'file report', and watched Alice's fate disappear for review. The speaker next to him crackled to life, and he jumped, momentarily forgetting standard operating procedure.

A security guard's voice echoed through the small device.

"She seems to have had a nap. Showed no sign of nervousness talking to me, didn't seem worried about anything other than missing lunch. I'd say, no memory."

Gray nodded to no one in particular.

"Thank you, might as well head back to your patrol now."

"Yes, sir."

The small red light on the speaker died, and Gray sagged in his seat, reflexively rubbing his eyes once more. This wasn't going to be good. He had barely a moment for rumination before his report received the response he had known it would.

Something more permanent must be done about Ms Winters.
See to it.

Gray closed the message and sat in the red glow of his monitor for a moment before bringing up the programs and requisitions he needed. No point disobeying this order – someone else would just do it in his place. He sent orders and personnel requests out across the whole city, calling in sections of the company that weren't supposed to exist. As they all winged their way across the company 'net, Gray muttered to himself.

"I warned you about SK, girl…"

***

Alice yawned as she stepped into her apartment, pausing only to close the door and throw her coat across the sofa before collapsing bodily beside it. It had been a long day, even with the short nap at lunch.

She groaned; Gray would be put out, at best, at having to wait this long. 'No point delaying any further', she decided as she dragged herself to her feet and made her way over to her computer desk. She hit the power toggle and busied herself with digging her personal VRD 'set out while the computer booted up. It was newer and fancier than the business model she used during the day, with better built-in security. She usually preferred to talk to Gray from home because of it, but sometimes he had to pass things on quickly. Impatient man.

The computer beeped its readiness at her as she unwound the cables and jacked them into the small I/O panel on the front. Alice settled the headset in place and brought up her 'net browser, answering the affirmative when it asked about VRD. She had an uncomfortable sense of déjà vu as the set counted down from 3 on its HUD visor, but then there was a tingle and she was in a toga, standing in a Roman forum.

She glanced around quickly, just in case Gray was standing about the main room. When he wasn't, BlueWinter moved to check the subfora, working her way around the forum nodding and waving at the regulars. She was just peeking into one room when there was a hand on her shoulder.

"Heya Blue! Sorry we couldn't talk much earlier, guy's a real slavedriver. Didja find Gray in the end?"

She turned round and smiled at Redshift, moving almost automatically to give him a quick hug before she paused.

"…Earlier? I've not been on in nearly a week."

Red frowned.

"Sure you have. I was in the back room there?" he pointed to one of the fora she hadn't yet checked, "I was working for the fuck ugly guy? Told you Gray had been asking for you?"

He paused for a moment, taking in the confused look on Blue's face.

"Seriously, it was like six hours ago. I'll ping you the chatlog."

His eyes flickered to one side and he manipulated some invisible controls. A moment later, there was an incoming file blinking in Blue's peripheral vision, and she accepted it. A small log popped out of the file and displayed itself to her.

BlueWinter:
Afternoon, Captain Scarlet.
Redshift:
Sorry Blue, gimme a min, workin on a quick job for this ugly fuck.
I did get the info you wanted though. Ill get it to you in a bit. Gray wanted to see you btw.
BlueWinter:
Thanks Red. Ill catch you later then – gonna look for Gray.

She checked the time stamp in the corner. Eleven minutes after lunch started. About three after she reckoned she had fallen asleep. She frowned, reading the log again, and then twice more. Every time she read it, it seemed more and more like she could recognise it, that she had indeed written it. But she had absolutely no memory of writing it. Of being online at all to have written it.

"What the fuck is going on here."

Red started in surprise.

"You okay? Tired or something?"

"I…I don't know. Look, Red, did we talk about anything else earlier?"

"No. Though I did see Gray a bit after we spoke. Don't know if you spoke to him though. He looked…angry. Or sad maybe."

Blue mulled it over for a moment, but then there was an ethereal beeping noise.

Scrolling green text appeared in the edge of her vision:

Loud noise detected in vicinity; disengage VRD?

It had happened a few times before. The last time, it had been the girl who lived in the apartment next-door exploring new and interesting ways to have sex with her boyfriend. But now Alice had a sick feeling in her stomach.

"Red, I've gotta go. I'll try to get back in contact, yeah?"

He began to ask what was wrong, but Blue didn't hear him – she was already busy waking up from VRD to hear a loud banging on her front door.

She slipped off her 'set and stood, all the tiredness from the day forgotten as she moved, as quickly and quietly as she could, towards the door. She paused for a moment, shaking, as she tried to steel herself to see who was outside. Alice breathed deeply and closed her eyes, reaching out to touch the small panel by the door as she opened them again. The small screen whirred gently as it came to life, the dark grey being replaced by a flat image of the corridor outside her apartment. She blinked – there was a lone man outside. She took a closer look at the screen, and then jerked back as the man looked up at the camera. He froze for a second, then held a hand up, reaching into his pocket with the other. He withdrew a persopad and she watched as he hit the sleep key, tapping his foot as he waited for it to awaken. As soon as it did, he began stabbing away at the keys with a furious speed. A moment later, he held it up to the camera.

blue its me gray. you have to let me in shit is going down.

Alice froze, eyes locked on the screen and the man who shouldn't be there. She remained perfectly still as countless warring thoughts flew around in her head – how the hell could Gray be here, what was going down, should she open the door? She squeezed her eyes shut and moved her finger over the 'open' key. It hovered there for a moment, the indecision wracking her head.

"Fuck!"

Her finger stabbed down on the door release.

The door hissed open and Gray bundled himself through, closing it quickly behind him, before running over to the windows and carefully sneaking a glance down at the street outside. Satisfied, he pulled all the curtains closed, and was halfway to the light switch when Alice stepped in his way.

"What the hell are you doing here. And how the fuck do you know where I live!?"

Gray was taken aback for a second, as if he was surprised that she had asked. Then he blinked and held his hands up.

"I'll get into the how later, but right now, I'm here to save your life."

Alice didn't respond. Her shock must have been evident however.

"Look, SK know about the files I gave you earlier. They also know that you shouldn't remember that I gave you files, and they rely on that to buy them time to get things into position. I'm here to make sure that you aren't by the time they arrive."

With that he continued to the light switch, and the room went dark.

"No…wait…I," Alice paused a moment to try and collect her thoughts.

"I don't remember anything from earlier. I know I was online but…I can't remember anything."

"I know," Gray replied, "But don't worry, it should come back to you. For the moment, we have to get out of here, and we have to take the files I gave you with us."

"What files! I have no idea what the hell's going on, and I have no idea about any fucking files!"

"Alice! Stop freaking out, we can't afford the time!" he practically shouted as he moved back to the window to peek out into the road.

"What do you expect me to do, goddamnit? You just showed up at my apartment telling me that Sigma-Kross are coming to kill me. How the fuck do you even know where I live?" She collapsed into a chair, with her head in her hands. Then she realised what Gray had just said.

"How do you know my name, Gray." Her voice was completely flat.

Gray froze for a second, then she saw him sigh. He turned from the glass and looked at her.

"Because I know you. You're Alice Winters, you work at Picard & Samuels, an SK subsidiary, in HR. I know that you're never late to work, that you get on well with everyone in your office, and I know that this is just who you are during the day. The rest of the time you're a 'net reporter called BlueWinter, known for punishing exposés on big corps."

Alice just watched as Gray spilled out the details of her two lives. One he knew, one he couldn't have known.

"And I know this," he paused, closing his eyes briefly before staring directly at her, "Because I've read the file

SK keep on you. Because I wrote most of it."

"You what?"

"I work in Sigma-Kross security. Division for 'net-based subversion and counter-espionage."

"You fucking what!?" Alice screamed, leaping up from her seat and backing across the room.

"I work at SK. Or I do, until they find out what I've done. Look, Alice, I – "

"No, I don't want to hear it! Get the fuck out!"

"Alice, if I leave now, the SK team will arrive in fifteen minutes and there will be an inexplicable fire in this building. There will be no casualties other than the woman who lives on the third floor in room 6. There will be absolutely nothing left of her, or her computer, and the media will assume she was one of those Third Front crazies who managed to blow her own apartment up. And that will be it. They've done it before, Alice, and they'll do it again. I know, who do you think cleans up the 'net backlash?"

"Then what the fuck are you doing here? Why are you helping me!"

"Because I'm goddamn sick of it. I want out, and I want SK to go down, and those files I gave you earlier about Michaelson were the real deal. I was supposed to give you duds, and they were supposed to delete themselves the minute you left VRD, but I gave you the real files."

Alice was about to respond when Gray swore and turned to the window. A large van was pulling up outside, and a small car behind it. The car emptied first, two men in sharp suits stepping out on the pavement, followed swiftly by another seven men climbing from the van.

"Shit, they're here. Look, Alice, I'm here to help. I'm here to get you out, and then we can take the files from your VRD and blow SK out of the fucking sky."

"My VRD? My VRD's at work, the one here's my personal one. It doesn't have anything on it!"

"Fuck! Goddamnit! Shit!" his hands clenched a moment and he breathed.

"We'll have to worry about that later. Right now we have maybe a minute before they're up here."

"How can I trust you?"

"If I wanted you dead, I'd have just left you to them."

Alice blinked, the bile in her chest that had been building for the last few minutes threatening to escape her throat as tears began to well from her eyes.

"What do we do, Gray?" she asked, her voice breaking as she tried to subdue the terror she was beginning to feel.

"Follow me," he said, reaching into his jacket and removing a small pistol; she didn't know what kind. Gray tapped the door release, and edged outside, his grip on the gun tightening. Alice could hear noises from the corridor beyond, people coming up the staircase, slowly by the sound of it. Gray reached into his jacket again and seemed to be fiddling with something. He grunted, and then smiled as a humming noise emanated from his left breast pocket. Alice watched as his face seemed to blur and censor itself. She tried to blink the sensation away, but to no avail.

"Right…" Gray muttered, his voice distorted, "The stairs are out."

He glanced the other way down the corridor.

"There, the window! When I say go, run for it and jump out."

"We're on the third floor!"

"Yeah, and that restaurant out there has those awnings up all night. So long as we miss the support poles, we'll be fine."

Alice gaped.

"Won't they have people outside in case we try that?"

"They don't know it's we, girlie. As far as they know, you're about to go to bed. They should all be coming up the stairs, going nice and slow so no one wonders what's up."

At that moment, the first of the SK enforcers appeared around the top of the staircase. He instantly ducked back and swore as Gray fired down the corridor at him, the bullets kicking huge clumps of plaster from the wall as they just missed the man's head. Gray fired two more shots to keep them back, then spun and fired three more through the window at the end of the corridor.

"GO, GIRL!" he roared to Alice as he stepped out of the doorway, firing again at the stairs. Alice didn't need to be told twice.

She ran out of the apartment, stumbling as she caught her shoulder on the doorframe, and dashed down the corridor towards the window. The next door along opened as her neighbour came to see what was going on, then slammed shut with a scream as further gunfire echoed along the hall.

Bullets whirred their way past Alice and thudded into the wall beside the window. She glanced back and saw Gray running after her, firing over his shoulder as the SK enforcers piled out of the stairway.

"Oh god…"

The shattered window loomed in front of her, and she leapt out into the night.

INTERVENTION

ALISON BUCK

Like all of us, Alison Buck has led many lives.

One as a sensible, hard-working type, employed in financial systems, graphic design and web site development. Another as a writer, scribbling away, committing her stories to disc and eventually publishing several to reasonable acclaim. Throughout all of them, the mother of two and wife of one.

Skilled at exploring the psychology and interior lives of her characters, Alison delivers stories that range from chilling tales of horror through insightful contemporary drama to thought-provoking science fiction. Her empathy with her protagonists, her rich descriptive prose and her use of gentle humour serve to ensure that, whatever the setting, her stories are always a rewarding read.

My heart was thumping, my chest heaving. Icy air was tearing at my throat.

I looked at Gibbs. The kid was gulping air just like me, his face slick with sweat. He wiped each palm in turn and renewed his grip on the gun, looking left and right, his eyes wide with fear.

"What the hell happened?" he gasped.

"Someone sold us out," I told him, "That was an ambush!"

"A trap?"

I nodded: didn't seem much point wasting breath to talk. We'd been set up, no question.

"Who?" he snatched the word between gulps of air, "Who knew we were here?"

"Who d'ya think?"

He frowned. He didn't know.

"Hatcher."

"Who?"

"Shh!"

I raised my gun to signal silence. Gibbs' mouth snapped shut. Biting his lip, he was struggling to control his breathing. He was trying not to make a noise now because we could both hear them: two, three, maybe more, moving slowly, cautiously, sliding over and around the tangle of pipes, concrete and twisted metal of the barricade. They couldn't know where we were, but they were definitely moving in our direction.

Gibbs' eyes were panicked now. I made the slightest shake of the head to reassure him while I tried to scope an escape route. We were hidden, for the moment, by a liquid oxygen storage vessel. As tall as a man, it was coated in thick hoarfrost. The low temperature would fox the scanners until the Stalkers were almost on top of us, but I reckoned we had only a few minutes before the lead Stalker's scanner was that close. We had to move.

A narrow corridor extended away to our left, featureless. There was no cover but, right at the end, was the door to the loading bay and, even from that distance, I could see that it was ajar; a shaft of weak sunlight drawing a thin bright line across the floor. The Stalkers wouldn't risk following us in daylight: if we made it out of the door, we'd be safe.

I turned my head. There were several doors across the open area to our right, but I had no idea where they led or whether they were locked. Making a run for any of them, we'd have to break cover. Exposed, we'd be easy targets for the Stalkers' guns. Unless we made it through the first door, we'd both be dead before we even got to try the handle of the second.

There was no choice: the corridor was our only hope. Gibbs was grimacing as the pain in his shattered leg cut through the morphine. I nodded towards the corridor and his eyes followed mine. He swore, soundlessly and began to shake his head, but I was in no mood to argue: I wasn't about to leave him here. He winced as I put my arm around him and hoisted his weight against me. He made a weak attempt to shrug me off, but we both knew that, without my help, he was dead; he couldn't make that run alone.

I took a deep breath and hurled myself forward, dragging Gibbs along beside me.

Like some grimly desperate three-legged race we

staggered in a stumbling dash along the corridor. Alerted by our sudden movement, a terrible chorus of alien shrieks and screams went up behind us as the Stalkers gave chase. In seconds they would reach the end of the corridor and have a clear shot at us; we had to get to the door. Beside me, Gibbs was in agony. His eyes were almost closed and his cheeks ran with tears, but he never made a sound.

We were only maybe three feet from the door when a blast slammed into the wall ahead of us. The shock knocked me back a stride but I threw myself forward and bundled the kid through the gaping door. My back exploded in pain as a second, better-aimed, blast hit me, propelling me forwards and out, into the daylight.

We were free!

Ignoring the burning in my back, I quickly forced myself to get to my feet; we had to move away from the door. Gibbs was lying on the ground and he wasn't moving. I grabbed his arm and dragged him to the lee of a burned-out car. Clapping my hand over his unconscious mouth, I ducked my own head down behind the battered and rusted wheel arch just in time. The door crashed open.

Thankfully, we were hidden from the Stalkers; our location effectively masked by the overload of data swamping their sensors from every angle. I could hear their grunts and the electronic whining of their scanners, overwhelmed by the light and heat flooding this man-made environment beyond the confines of their carefully modulated hive. The sound woke Gibbs with a start. Holding him tightly, I slowly turned his head so he could see my face. The panic in his eyes seemed to ease. Our faces only inches apart, I raised a finger to my lips and assured myself that he had both seen and understood before I took my hand from his mouth.

We stayed there for several more minutes until I was sure that the Stalkers had retreated back into the corridor. Only then did I let myself focus on the pain in my back.

"You're hurt," Gibbs whispered.

"No shit!"

"Mac, you're bleeding."

"You're not doing so great yourself, kid." I managed a grim smile, "I'll give you another Morphine shot, but I need you to stay with me. We've got to get some distance between us and this place. Once it's dark the whole swarm will be out hunting for us and we don't have anywhere to hide."

"I don't understand. Can't we just go back to the House?"

"No, kid; someone there set you up to be Stalker-fodder today."

I hated to have to tell him, but he had to understand the danger he was in. The poor kid was in shock.

"Gibbs, someone you know arranged all this. They arranged to have you killed, or maybe captured to coerce your father. There's no way you can go back to the House. Not now, maybe not ever."

Gibbs was pale.

"But you said you knew who did this," he said, trying to make sense of it all, "You said it was someone called Hatcher."

"As far as I know, Hatcher's the only other person who knew we'd be here, but I don't know that for a fact. I do know that I promised your father I'd keep you safe and I aim to keep that promise."

"Safe? Mac, I've been shot in the leg!"

"OK, not 'safe'. 'Breathing'? How does 'breathing' sound?"

"I guess that sounds OK," Gibbs forced an anxious smile.

"Sure it does," I said, breaking open the Morph shot and giving it to him to drink, "And it sure as hell beats the alternative!"

Buoyed up by my own slug of morphine, keeping low and out of sight, I managed to half-carry, half-drag Gibbs a mile or more out of the city before nightfall. After clambering up the steep, dry walls of the cliff overlooking the road, we finally rested on a rocky outcrop from where I could keep a watch on any traffic below.

"I could take first watch," Gibbs offered.

"You're a good kid, but no; I'll take first watch. You get some rest."

"It's no trouble, Mac, I'd like to take the first watch. I feel OK. And, Mac, you're still bleeding."

For a moment I was sorely tempted. Even with the morphine, I was in a lot of pain and I was bone-weary with all but carrying Gibbs up to the top of that rockface. But I'd made a promise and I knew my duty.

"Thanks kid, but no."

"Mac, please let me help you."

"Look, kid, this isn't some game. This is life and death. They'll keep looking for us and if they find us... Well, like I said, it's life and death."

"I could use your gun."

"You've got your own gun."

"What? This?" he held up his gun, "This isn't a gun. Your gun's a proper gun."

I lashed out, pushing the barrel of his gun to one side.

"Soldier, look where you're pointing that! That's a loaded gun! Shit like that tells me you've got a long way to go and a hell of a lot to learn before you'd be safe using a weapon like this."

"But Mac -"

"Gibbs, I said no! Now let it go."

Gibbs looked hurt. The kid had guts and I admired that, but he had to learn that, no matter how important and vital his father might be to the Resistance, out here I was in charge.

Far below us, in the city, I could see lights moving back and forth as the Stalkers searched for us. Eventually the activity eased off; they'd called off the search. All was quiet for several hours.

Then, just before dawn, I noticed something on the road below. No sound, no warning, just a twitch of movement, a minute shift in the darkness, out of the corner of my eye. I nearly missed it. The Stalkers were coming. Those bastards never gave up.

I grabbed the kid, my hand over his mouth. He was awake now, and terrified.

"It's OK Gibbs, I won't let them take you. If it comes to it, I've got enough ammo in this for both of us. If there's no way out, I promise, I'll do what needs doing."

His eyes opened even wider. He was in blind panic; began struggling and making angry, muffled noises. I held him more tightly, pressing his arms to his sides and closing my hand even harder over his mouth. I really didn't have time for this; Stalkers were closing on our position. I could hear them scrambling over the scree at the base of the cliff. I needed to reassure the kid. I needed him to calm the fuck down.

"I'm only saying, if it's necessary, kid. A bullet is quick. You wouldn't even feel it and, believe me, you do not want these monsters to capture you alive boy."

His struggling was manic now. I had to shut him up. I couldn't defend myself, and him, if he carried on struggling like that.

"Sorry kid."

I hit him over the head with the butt of my gun. His body went limp and I lowered him to the ground. I felt for the pulse at his neck. He was OK. He'd have a headache when he woke up, but he was OK and I could get on with saving our lives. I readied my gun and began to straighten up, raising my head slowly to peer down the slope, into the darkness.

In that instant I heard a sound behind me. I span round. A Stalker towered over me, the moonlight bright on the scales of its skin and on the evil-looking gun in its claw. I knew I had no chance but I raised my own gun. There was a terrific noise. I'd been hit.

I fell back, muscles pulsing with pain.

I could feel myself slipping into darkness.

I should have been dead.

But I was alive. I woke up on a pallet, my arms, legs and chest pinned down; in restraints. I was still alive. How could I still be alive?

All I could see was white and light; a ceiling above me. I twisted my head to left and right. As far as I could tell, I was in a small, featureless room. A cell?

I thought I was alone, until a familiar voice suddenly came from behind my head.

"Hello again Mr Macintosh."

"Hatcher!"

"How are you feeling?"

I struggled with all my strength to get free, to get at the bastard who had betrayed me.

"Where's the kid?" I spat the words, "Hatcher, so help me, when I get free, I'll kill you with my bare hands. Where's Gibbs? Where's the kid? If you let the Stalkers have him, so help me!"

"Stalkers?"

"You bastard! Tell me where he is!"

"Calm yourself, Macintosh. Gibbs? If you mean Gibor Mendes; he's back with his family. And safe, no thanks to you."

"What! What the fuck? What are you talking about?" I was now struggling so violently that the whole pallet shook, "Let me out of these, Hatcher, you son of a bitch!"

"Gibor Mendes, the boy you kidnapped, is back with his family and you, Macintosh, are incredibly lucky to be alive; the police were armed and had instructions to shoot you if necessary to save the boy."

"Police? What the hell are you talking about?"

Hatcher ignored me.

"When Gibor went missing, his father called in every favour and pulled every string to get him back alive and, let me tell you, Anton Mendes has some very rich and powerful friends. No one would have looked too hard or asked any awkward questions if you'd been shot dead resisting arrest. You're lucky they couldn't risk hurting the boy; they only fired warning shots."

"I was shot."

"No, Macintosh, you were not."

"Stalkers shot me in the back."

"No, Macintosh, you ripped open your own shoulder on a broken metal hinge as you forced yourself through a vent in the wall of a storage facility. I'm told the opening was barely wide enough for the boy, never mind a grown man."

"What the hell are you talking about, Hatcher? What's going on?"

"You really don't remember? Anton Mendes. Do you remember talking to Anton Mendes?"

"Gibb's father?" a memory of our conversation came

into my mind, "Yes, I remember Mendes: leader of the Resistance.   I promised him I'd look after his son," another memory flashed back, "And you betrayed us to the Stalkers, you bastard!"

By now my wrists were torn and bleeding, but the restraints held.

"Mendes senior," Hatcher continued, sounding almost bored, "Is a businessman. He is, or was, a patron of this institution, a very generous patron.   Before you absconded, we have you on CCTV, breaking into my office and stealing some files. I'm guessing you took Mendes' file and used it to find him, snatch his son and make the calls to the family home threatening to kill the boy."

"Me? Kill the kid? What the hell? That's bullshit and you know it!"

"Macintosh, you did threaten to kill their son. The boy confirmed it. He said you threatened to kill him and commit suicide yourself, just before you were caught."

"No. No, that was only if Stalkers over-ran our position and were about to capture us."

"Then perhaps we should all be grateful it didn't come to that."

"Is Gibbs OK?"

"Well, I daresay the trauma of all this will last several years and make some lucky analyst very wealthy, but his doctors say his leg will heal completely, given time and rest."

"His leg! They shot him in the leg."

"Ballistics say the boy was probably shot accidentally when you wrestled his bodyguard for the gun."

"Bodyguard? No, it was the Stalkers."

"Ah yes, the Stalkers. Lucky for you the 'Stalker' who 'over-ran your position' chose to use his Taser or, right now, I'd be short one patient."

Everything was beginning to unravel. I didn't understand. None of this made any sense to me. I remembered the Stalkers. They were real, very damn real, so why was Hatcher trying to deny it?

My head was spinning. Feeling weak and nauseous, I banged my head on the pallet, desperate to clear my brain.

I trusted my memory, I'd been through too much to doubt it, but it made no sense that Hatcher would make all this up. The Stalkers could be forcing him. But why? If they wanted to keep their existence secret, why hadn't they just killed me?

I needed to look into Hatcher's eyes. I needed to know if he was lying to me.

"Hatcher?"

He corrected me, but without any hint of irritation in his voice.

"Doctor Hatcher."

I didn't know what game he was playing, but I went along with it.

"I'm sorry. Doctor Hatcher?"

"What is it Macintosh?"

"Doctor, could you come round to the side, where I can see you? It's really weird talking to a disembodied voice."

"Very well."

I heard him get up from his chair. A few paces brought him into sight. He stopped a few feet away from the pallet, lowered his glasses and smiled.

"Is that better, Macintosh? Do you remember me now?"

"I do. I do, sir, and I'm sorry."

"It's alright, Macintosh," he sighed, "In a way, you know, I blame myself. Clearly supervision was lacking in the administration of your medication. In short, Macintosh, I believe you were not always taking your pills."

"I'm sorry, Doctor. I will take them from now on."

"Good man, good man. That's the attitude. We might perhaps look at upping the doses for you; help you keep things straight."

"I'm so grateful, Doctor."

"No need, no need. Let's just get you well."

He took a step forward.

"We'll make a start on that, first thing tomorrow, eh, Macintosh?"

He smiled and took another step. I could feel my hand slowly beginning to slide under the restraint, lubricated by the warm blood coating my wrist,

Hatcher hadn't noticed.

"For now," he said, "I just want you to try to get some rest."

In a final, foolish, inattentive lapse, Hatcher moved to give my hand a reassuring pat. In the instant that he felt the wet blood on my skin and before he was even fully aware of the movement of my hand, I had already grabbed his glasses, smashed them on the pallet and driven the twisted metal frame into his eyes. As he screamed, I clamped my hand across his mouth and began to scrape some of the skin from his face.

I knew now. I'd seen it in his eyes. They weren't human eyes. Hatcher wasn't just working for them; he was one of them. He was a Stalker. Somehow he'd adopted human form, but I knew I'd find his lizard skin underneath. Once I had the proof, I'd get out of here and rescue the kid.

I'd promised his father. And I always keep my promises.

On the Game

PR Pope

After a typical and uneventful childhood PR Pope entered the world of scientific discovery through a science degree and subsequent research. Content to remain behind the scenes and avoid the limelight he has been quietly involved in many of the greatest advances made in recent years. Discreetly amassing a fortune he was defrauded out of most of it when responding to an urgent email requesting aid for an ill member of the royal family of a third world nation. In despair he retired to a semi-autonomous geo-stationery satellite positioned above Lake Victoria where he currently lives by synthesising protein from particles in the solar wind using a process he himself developed to exploit cosmic rays.

Tim opened his eyes to an unfamiliar ceiling, viewed from an unfamiliar bed. The room had the unmistakeable aura shared by hotel rooms the world over, sanitised, air-conditioned, comfortable yet not comforting. The curtains were obviously not completely closed, as enough pre-dawn light was trickling in to illuminate the room. He could see an anonymous painting of a ship, hanging above the head of the bed. Even upside down the 'man of war', for that is what it was, seemed both out of place for a bedroom and yet typical for a hotel chain. He turned his head and gazed at the fine brunette hair, long lashes and still glossy lips of the beautiful woman asleep on the pillow next to him. A narrow band of yellow light, that heralded the sunrise triumphantly breaking through the crack in the curtains, fell across her neck like a wound running from down-turned chin to earlobe. Her small diamond stud earring glinted and sparkled in its spotlight. He marvelled at the perfect smoothness of her skin and the lack of wrinkles on her neck as he watched her breathing gently, oblivious to the attentions of both the sun and Tim. The rumpled sheets did a poor job of covering her modesty. Tim's attention shifted to the pert pale breast and cherry red nipple that was exposed.

He would have to get used to this sort of situation now he had chosen to play this dangerous game. The rôle of gigolo brought with it not only the frisson of sexual excitement that he felt looking at this delicious woman, but also a tinge of the fear of discovery. He knew that, as he moved through this new world, a world he had not even realised existed until a mere five days ago, he would have adventures – the wild sexual adventures that had attracted him to the rôle in the first place, but also more perilous adventures in this precarious existence. While he was with a client she would be engrossed in him and by him. He was a plaything, but well rewarded. However, he knew that some, if not most, of his clients would be using him in private while still maintaining their marriage or other relationship in public beyond the door of the hotel room. The room was a different, secret, place within the alternative world he had decided to enter. Outside, many of his clients' partners would be oblivious, others would be suspicious, some would be jealous. Those who didn't take kindly to being usurped as sexual gratifier, may even try and take revenge. He had been prepared for the consequences of playing this game. He had chosen to join this world with his eyes open.

He continued to gaze at the serene beauty lying beside him. Frankly he was amazed that anyone this gorgeous should need the services of a gigolo. Surely she could have her pick of men. Men who would be prepared to spend a fortune to impress her, please her, seduce her and pleasure her. Why did she feel the need to pay? He was intrigued, but knew he would never ask. Could never ask. The rules of the game were perfectly clear to everyone. No questions asked. A good time is what she wants, a good time is what he delivers. Her requirements are satisfied and his credit goes up. He had expected to be spending at least some of the time with women who would have trouble finding anyone to make them happy. Older, plainer (he had been tutored to say plain, not ugly), or with unusual (he meant repellent) habits or features. However, so far, it appeared the new world he now inhabited was populated by rich, beautiful and lusty women who found him attractive. The contrast with his normal (should he say normal, past, previous or other?) existence was quite breathtaking. What had surprised him was that they wanted to wine, dine and talk to him. They knew nothing about him and yet they wanted to talk. He had never mastered small-talk, yet in these scenarios he had suddenly found his tongue. He had invented a persona that would be infinitely more interesting than the small-town pharmacist living in a bare, featureless apartment in a bare featureless street. His character was larger than life. More than three dimensional. Did anyone believe a word he said? He had no idea. Did it matter? Not really. They wanted excitement, or attention, or affection. Most of all they seemed to crave sincerity and he had already learnt how to fake that. That surprised him too. If you were paying for someone to satisfy you, why would you ever think they might be sincere. Surely that was what real relationships provided? He didn't have real relationships here, in this secret place, in this alternative world. It was all just a game. None of this was genuine. They would leave to go back to their husbands, partners, friends as if nothing had happened. He would leave and go back to his apartment. It seemed at once clinical, impersonal, unreal yet also sensual, erotic, even loving.

He shifted position slightly under the sheets. He was supposed to be awake when his client awoke. Yet he mustn't wake her up. When she was ready to get up, they would get up. When she was ready to leave, they would leave. He was hoping to have time for a shower, but it all depended on what she wanted, and when. He was still gazing at her breast gently rising and falling with her breathing. He realised he was getting aroused. It would need to be a cold shower then! It wasn't the done thing to walk around like that in his small town. People would talk. He would get noticed. There would be trouble. Still, he continued to watch the rise and fall, rise and fall. He could hear the gentle sound of her breathing. He wished that he could smell her perfume, taste the light sprinkling of sweat still glistening on her body as he watched so avidly, breathe in the musky smell of satisfied beauty. But he knew he couldn't. He desperately wanted to reach out and touch her. Trace his finger around the beautiful curve of her throat. He would love to be able to gently caress that alluring breast, run his fingertips around the areola, stroke her nipple with his tongue, tease it and gently suck. But he couldn't. She must wake up in her own time. He had no choice but to lie here quietly and wait. He could at least watch her, desire her. He wished that he could wake up to someone like this in his other life (he'd decided to settle on other – 'past' and 'previous' weren't accurate as he still inhabited that life when he wasn't here, 'normal' seemed to suggest that this was somehow abnormal; all in all 'other' seemed to be the best choice). When he awoke in his own bed, his featureless bed, in his own, featureless, room, there was no one else there to look at. But he would be able to shut his eyes and remember this image, this scene.

She stirred a little. He held his breath, watching her eyes to see if she would open them. They flickered briefly behind the eyelids, but remained closed. She moved her arm and in the process dislodged more of the sheet. Now he could see both of her breasts rising and falling with her still gentle breathing, as well as her stomach. The soft downy hairs on her abdomen shone golden in the sunlight that was increasingly filtering in between the curtains. The curve of her stomach, the dimple of her navel, all reflected the perfection of form that characterised this enticing woman. He let himself breath again and found that he was straining to see what else he could make out under the edge of the sheet. Like an adolescent schoolboy he was staring hard to decide whether he could see the beginnings of her pubic hair, the mound of Venus they always called it in those awful books he'd read as a teenager, or merely shadows. He couldn't decide. Perhaps she would move again. He suddenly felt pathetic. He was supposed to be a gigolo. A professional. Yet he was thinking like a spotty youth furtively flicking through porn pictures in the park. He shut his eyes and took a deep breath.

Just then there was a gentle tap at the door. A disembodied voice, muffled through the door and the short hallway past the bathroom, told him that breakfast had arrived. There was a click as the door was unlocked, followed by a slight creak from the hinges. Footsteps, soft on the plush carpet, but still audible, preceded the appearance of the waitress carrying a large tray. He watched as she put it down on the table in the corner of the room. A slight blonde girl, probably not yet even twenty, she looked at the woman in the bed as she turned to leave and struggled not to raise her eyebrows. He was surprised that she had so studiously avoided making eye contact with him. Was she embarrassed, or just more attracted to the beautiful creature laying at his side. Maybe she knew who he was, or at least what he was and why he was here in bed with this woman. He watched her walk back towards the door, appreciating the tightness of her uniform and the tautness of her slender young body inside it. As she disappeared from view he waited for the sound of the door closing. But it never came. Instead, he heard heavier footsteps approaching. Surprised, confused, he stared at the end of the hallway waiting to see who was coming in now. Suddenly a man in his mid thirties was standing there. He was obviously not hotel staff as he had no liveried uniform, just a loose jacket over an unkempt shirt and a pair of matching trousers. Tim couldn't see his feet, but from the look of him and the sound of his footsteps he guessed he was wearing brogues. As Tim watched, unsure what was happening or what he should do, the man gazed at the supine woman in what looked like a mixture of disbelief and shock. His mouth had opened involuntarily and was now gaping. Tim could still not decide whether his best option was to remain in the bed, keeping his dignity under cover, or whether he should try and leave now. The credit transactions would be settled separately so he had no need to stay if this scene was likely to get unpleasant. By now he was sure that the man must be the husband or lover of his client; she was still serenely sleeping through the, albeit quiet, drama that was unfolding around her. It had to happen at some point, he just hadn't expected it to be this early on. He had very little experience yet, compared to the others he had met who were doing the same as him. They talked in terms of levels, classifying themselves, as most societies do, to determine a hierarchy. He was the lowest level. A newcomer who had only just joined the game. Others had much more experience. But they had all been happy to give him advice in advance. At the moment, though, he could remember none of it. Fear was now kicking in, fear of the unpredictability of a jealous lover. He knew that French law had a specific name for it, *crime passionnel*. He wasn't in France. He'd never even been to France, although his newly adopted persona had many tales to tell of days spent in Montmartre and nights in Pigalle. But both crime and passion knew no borders. He decided that he should not stay any longer than necessary, but at the moment the man was blocking the only exit from the room. He assumed that, as the room had air-conditioning, the windows would not open wide enough to make an escape that way – what's more he had no idea how high up they were, he couldn't even remember the room number let alone the floor. Watching the man carefully, Tim formulated his plan. As soon as this interloper moved away from the hallway towards the woman, who was on the side of the bed nearest to him, as he inevitably must, Tim would slide from the bed and run away as fast as possible. Was he still wearing any underwear? He didn't know, he'd soon find out. Maybe the waitress would still be outside and she could help him to hide somewhere. Otherwise he would need to head for the stairs and find a store cupboard on another floor where he could get a uniform or at least a towel.

While Tim was planning his escape, the man had closed his mouth. He hadn't completely regained his composure as there were tears in his eyes and he was shaking, although he was trying hard to control himself. In a quiet voice he was saying "Katherine, Katherine." He reached down and grabbed her left foot through the sheet, shaking it to wake her up. Tim could see a thin wedding band on his third finger. She slept on and he became louder, calling her name over and over like a mantra or a prayer. When she still didn't awaken he dropped to his knees and crawled along beside the bed until his tear stained face was next to hers. He leant forward and kissed her on the cheek. She responded by absent-mindedly batting at her cheek with her hand, as if to wipe away an irritating insect. He caught her hand and, through his tears, called her name again, louder still, his voice choking. Meanwhile, Tim had seen his chance. He knew he would only have one opportunity to get out. As he was aiming himself across and out of the room, he suddenly realised that there may be other people in the way. Would Katherine's husband have brought someone with him to help deal with the situation, or would he not have wanted any witnesses to his shame and despair. Hoping for the latter, Tim looked towards the door as the hallway came into view. As he sped past the end of the bed, he could see the man look up abruptly at him. He could feel the hatred in those eyes even in that split second. He kept going. He must get out of the room. The hairs on the back of his neck prickled, as if those hate-filled eyes were already burning into him like laser beams. Once through the door he looked along the corridor and saw a sign pointing to a staircase to his left. He knew he had to run as fast as he could and as he made it to the stairs he looked back to see his nemesis stumble out of the room into the hallway. Tim dashed through the doorway, and, glancing both up and down, decided that down would offer more options. As he started towards the first step down he thought he heard a sharp crack behind him. He raced down the stairs, images of steps, banisters and walls flashing in front of him. After eight flights, which he guessed must be two storeys, he stopped and opened the door to a corridor. Stepping out gingerly he noticed a door with no number, right next to the stairs. It opened for him and inside were supplies of toiletries, tissue and towels. Immediately behind the door was a mop in a bucket, a dustpan and brush and a broom. On the wall next to the broom handle were half a dozen towelling dressing gowns hanging on hooks. Just what he needed.

Some thirty seconds later he was out of the store cupboard and racing to the lift wearing one of the dressing gowns. If he could get downstairs to the lobby and outside he was sure to be able to find a taxi to get away from here. He watched the lights above the lift doors slowly count down, then heard the double note chime as the lift stopped at this floor. The doors opened, he walked in, turned around and breathed a huge sigh of relief. Feeling the tension subside, he was sure that his escape was now inevitable. But the lift doors didn't seem to be in any hurry to close. Starting to worry again he looked at the floor indicators to see what was happening. As he turned his attention back to the corridor stretching away from him, though, he saw the stairway door fly open and the man who he was now assuming to be Katherine's husband run through. Desperately hoping the doors would soon shut he was appalled when he realised that the man was now carrying what looked like a gun. He'd never actually seen a gun in real life, so he had no idea what sort of gun it was or what its range or accuracy might be. He stepped backwards, as if that might make any difference, watching in impotent horror as the man raised his weapon, aimed it straight at Tim and fired. What happened next seemed to Tim to be in slow motion. He could almost see the bullet heading for him but couldn't move fast enough to get out of the way. Finally the doors of the lift slowly started to shut, but he knew the bullet would get to the opening before they could close it. He held his breath one last time and, in dumbfounded anticipation, waited for the inevitable. He felt nothing but knew the bullet had hit him. As the doors slid shut he heard the canned music fading along with his vision until all he could see were two words glowing. "GAME OVER".

Exploring the Heavens

Alexander Skye

Alexander Skye has been obsessed with sci-fi since before he was born. Since those early experiments with time travel, he has read and enjoyed every branch of science fiction; from the most realistic of hard SF, through the most cynical of cyberpunk and the most Victorian of steampunk, to the most exuberant of space opera. He's enjoyed other genres besides, most especially fantasy, with which he has had a long-running affair. It began as a child, reading *The Chronicles of Narnia*, and *The Lord of the Rings*, and has never really abated. His first and greatest love, however, will always be science fiction.

Having spent so long merely reading and admiring, he decided that it was finally time to try and tell his own stories and hopefully you'll enjoy them as much as he enjoyed writing them; if not, he'll be forced to find a different job, which would be tragic since they're all so boring - after all, how many other professions let you stare wistfully at the stars on a cloudless night and call it research?

It was thirty-eight years after our initial extra-terrestrial contact that we met our first humanoid aliens. By that time we had treaties and trade agreements with aliens of every colour and form – the Shethi, a race who look for all the world like billowing sails attached to some limbs; the Bradan, a race descended from the avian predators of their world, more like sentient dinosaurs than anything else; the Kor'van, a psychic race who appear as humans to us, as Bradan to Bradan, as Shethi to Shethi and so on – a very useful natural defence which also means that, to this day, no one knows what the Kor'van actually look like.

However, one fateful day in July of 2473, by Earth calendars, we met the Aardosh. They are a race rather more similar to us than any we had met before, and also rather familiar. Our first contact had some interesting and important repercussions.

The exploration vessel that originally met the Aardosh was the UES Sparrow, a small scouting ship designed specifically for frontier exploration. The Sparrow was one of many ships which the United Earth Coalition's scouting division employed along the many borders of human-explored space, but one of a select few that actually contacted alien races.

All such ships had a small diplomatic group on board, just in case, and all were trained in 'First Contact Protocol', a set of rules, regulations and customs honed from nearly four decades of alien interaction and negotiation.

Being on the rim of the galaxy as we are, we had links to only a few alien races. Nearer to the centre of the galaxy where there are far more stars, there are, accordingly, more populated planets, most of whom know each other well. However, out in the galactic sticks, as it were, the interstellar alliances are less a huge block of races, and more a daisy chain of inhabited systems who reached out to one another. Eventually the chain reached the centre, and from there, our arm of the galaxy was linked to galactic society.

Thus, there were standard diplomatic practices which we had been taught by other races; many were just phrases in a standard language originating from the centre. Some had told us it was the language of the first race to enter the stars, but by this point, it didn't matter. It was, effectively, the language of interstellar diplomacy, and all our diplomats had been taught to speak it with at least partial fluency.

However, another important facet of interstellar doctrine was that no race should be artificially advanced beyond its own means. Thus, the myriad races of the galaxy were at quite different levels of technology. Scout ships might encounter a race who had vessels the size of a continent which could accelerate to interstellar travel in less than twenty seconds, while on the other hand, they had met races whose only method of interstellar travel was slow enough to require cryo-sleep.

Every race traded in music, literature, art, manpower and materials, but never in technology. Of course, this meant that closer to the rim there was a booming black market in smuggled tech; the human race has taken advantage of it on many occasions, always being careful to keep it as secret as possible.

The other main thing that races would not share was contacts. Part of the same doctrine of 'if a race can't do it themselves, don't tell them how' kept diplomatic ties between races effectively secret. A race could give you the whereabouts of other species they knew, but they wouldn't put you in contact.

Our first contact outside the Sol System, the Hagane, were more than happy to tell us that the Shethi were in 'that general direction', but were not willing to tell us exactly where, nor to put us in touch via their own diplomats.

Really, it's a good system; a game of galactic survival of the fittest. Each time a race meets another, their contact is based entirely on that meeting – no preformed opinions based on other races' information, no technology beyond their own ken. This made it easier for each race to decide whether the other was a reasonable alliance prospect.

All of this was why the UES Sparrow was exploring a small star system in the 'general direction' of the Aardosh.

The small ship, more framework and solar panels than anything else, was actually pausing to recharge its solar batteries and refine some fuel from the large gas giant in the system. It was during this refuel that another ship appeared in orbit of the same planet.

The command crew only took a few seconds to react, activating the ship's blue alert – red is of course, danger, and blue is encounter. Sadly, blue is used far less often.

Either way, the crew of the Sparrow presumably flew into action.

The actual meeting between the Sparrow's diplomatic team and the team from the Aardosh vessel was not of real interest; just short discussions in galactic politalk deciding when and where the full diplomatic teams would meet and discuss the terms of any possible treaties between the UEC and the Aardosh Council.

However, the important thing was the informal report

written by one of the diplomatic aides. He was a practising Hindu and so, when he wrote a letter home to his mother about the last few months and mentioned that the Aardosh diplomat looked like an angry god, she understood his meaning. However, once the contents of his letter got out, due to some illegal hacking on the part of a sensationalist newscast service, some very vocal minorities across the Sol system grabbed the wrong end of the stick and went wild.

The bible belt of the old United States went on marches across the country. Some protested that no aliens could be Gods, since theirs was the one and only. Others were demanding that any and all contact with these aliens happen on American soil, since these aliens were evidently the Biblical God and his angels and that America was holy land for reasons they left unexplained. Sects of multiple religions protested, in multiple countries, demanding that there be no contact with this race at all for fear it would insult their own gods. Nothing that had been written in the original letter ever mentioned the Aardosh as literal gods, but such is the way with the lower orders of news reporting. However, the media frenzy caused something else; it was as if people had suddenly awoken to the possibilities of deep space again. Recruitment for the Coalition's diplomatic and scouting divisions soared to new heights, even while the few remaining zealots protested across the Sol system.

And so, when the Aardosh finally arrived on Earth, it was to considerably more pomp and ceremony than had been seen in years. The whole system tuned in to watch, simply to see what all the fuss had been about. Practitioners of every religion held their breath, some more bated than others, some secretly hoping that the tabloids had been right all along. Most of the human race was just interested in finally seeing this alien race who had turned around an entire culture by their merest existence.

However, a great many of the insanely zealous of almost every religion waited to see their own god step forth from the Aardosh transport, each equally sure that it would be his God, her prophet, their angels.

So, when a chest-high humanoid with smooth blue skin and four arms stepped out, most of them felt incredibly sheepish.

The Dragon and the Rose

GINGERLILY

So you want to know something about me? You nosy lot! Well what can I tell you… Age? – Old enough to know better by now (or so my Mum says). In fact old enough to be a grandmother if I had got around to having children at any stage. Work? – well I do some, but it's so boring you would fall asleep if I told you, so make something up yourself, it'll be much more fun. In fact – write and tell me about it to alleviate the boredom of my job! Interests? - reading, photography, reading, playing guitar, reading, Formula 1, Dragon taming, Underwater knitting… Are you still reading? Last life lesson learned – There is no such thing as a quick game of Angry Birds before I catch my bus. I will miss the bus. And probably the next one as well. And I can get by on 4 hours sleep.

Once upon a time there was a moderately beautiful princess called Rose. She lived in the middle of a dark forest. Sounds like a pretty unlikely place for a princess to live, doesn't it, but hey, this is a fairy tale and doesn't actually have to make sense.

There was one major problem with this location - at least she blamed the location for this problem. There really wasn't a good enough supply of tall dark handsome princes for her to marry. She insisted on having a tall dark handsome prince, as she thought she was really a lot prettier than she actually was. There was no shortage of princes, which again seems strange for the middle of a dark forest, but there you go! The problem was that none of them really came up to her exacting standards, in fact most of them didn't even get anywhere near. The average prince that happened along was of medium build, probably an inch or two shorter than her, with sort of brownish hair and a vacant look.

The real reason for this was Rose herself. She was moderately beautiful in looks, but let's say she was a little spoiled. OK, let's be honest and say she was a total brat and no-one could stand her! Her reputation had spread far and wide and any half-decent prince wanted nothing to do with her. She, of course, wouldn't have believed this even if anyone had dared to tell her, as she was as vain and self-deceiving as she was bad-tempered. Had she any redeeming qualities, I hear you ask? Of course she had, she was very fond of her second cousin, Lily. This might, though, have been because she only saw her once a year, for a couple of hours at a time. Apart from that, she was very good at writing dirty limericks, which she really didn't like to talk about too much in case she gave the wrong impression.

When she was about 22, and she still hadn't managed to find herself a handsome enough prince, she decided it was about time to try something new. She was also completely fed up with living in the middle of a forest, and wanted a change of scenery. As the King had banished her to the forest at the age of 16 (Ah, that's why she was there - I did wonder!) and told her not to come back until she had copped onto herself, she couldn't just head on back to the castle. She sat and thought about this for a while. By the time she had reached 24 (she wasn't too intelligent either) she had managed to work out a cunning plan. She would go somewhere else!

She rummaged around in the cupboard under the stairs for a while and managed to find a dirty old backpack, with a tattered map in it. She looked at the map in puzzlement for a while, before she realised that it was a map of the palace, which wasn't much good to her. Then it occurred to her to ask the kitchen-maid for directions. Even though she did live in the middle of the forest, it was in a biggish and fairly comfortable house, with at least a few servants to bully and order around. The maid, when asked, told her that she had heard of an enchanted city somewhere in the wood, but of course she couldn't say where it was or how to get there. Rose decided that this was a much more sensible idea than following a map, which would only get her to some other boring place with no decent princes.

She made some careful preparations. These mostly consisted of sending the maid out to buy her some new and extra dazzling clothes, and getting a completely new hair-do. She found a book on market gardening, which she decided she might need when her food ran out. She tried to think of what else she might need, and eventually added in her MP3 player, in case she got bored on the journey.

The next day she intended to get up at first light to set off on her journey, but she slept in until second light. It was actually about 3 in the afternoon by the time she started off, because she kept on thinking of more stuff she wanted to bring, and she had to go back for it. In the end, she had about four servants carrying all her luggage. Of course she couldn't carry anything herself - she was a princess after all, and a very spoiled and bratty one at that. She wanted to ride off on a magnificent white horse, but as she had never learned to ride, she had to make do with a bicycle instead.

She decided which way to go by closing her eyes, spinning round and pointing. This nearly led to immediate disaster, because she was on the bicycle at the time. When she had picked herself and the bike up, she tried again, and ended up pointing straight at the biggest tree she had ever seen. The third time was a bit better, as there was actually a path going in that direction, so off they went.

She very soon got tired of the whole thing, as she had not realised just how difficult it was going to be. She wasn't exactly dressed suitably for this kind of activity, her silk dress kept on getting caught in the bicycle chain, and her high heeled sandals didn't really give much protection to her dainty feet. After about an hour of this she was bruised, hot, tired and very hungry. She decided she needed to stop and go home to see if she could borrow a car, preferably a chauffeur-driven Merc.

She turned round to tell her entourage to stop and go back, and got a very nasty surprise. They weren't there. Not one of them. No luggage either. No clothes, no food, and more worrying, no path. She looked in total confusion at the bramble hedge in front of her eyes. A very big bramble hedge. With lots of very sharp-looking thorns. And no gaps whatsoever. She decided to turn round again, then look back a second time. As soon as she looked forwards again she got a second very nasty surprise. Right in front of her, about 3 yards away, was a dragon. Actually it was a DRAGON. I say that because it seemed to fill the whole forest, and there was absolutely no chance of not noticing it.

At this stage she started to realise that something slightly odd was going on. She was still trying to make sense of it, when something else strange happened. The dragon spoke to her. It said,

"Is this the best this tatty old forest could come up with?"

Rose said, "?????"

The dragon said, "What was that? Speak up girl, I'm a little deaf after flying through that thundercloud this morning."

Rose said, "!!!!!!!"

Then she said, "Heeeeeeeeelllllllllllllllllllpppppppppppppppp somebody!!! Get me out of here!!!!!"

The dragon winced and said, "No need to shout, I'm not that deaf. Anyway, there's no-one else around here any more. I've eaten them all."

Rose said nothing - she was, for once in her life, struck speechless. The dragon looked her over carefully, the more he saw the less impressed he was. He finally gave a big sigh, reached down and ate her in two quick bites.

"Hey - you can't do that, she's not allowed to die yet!"

"Who says! It's my story, and I can do whatever I like in it. I was getting totally fed up with her, so I decided to kill her off. Why shouldn't I - and anyway, just who are you????"

"I'm the spirit of narrative, and I watch over all stories being written to ensure that none of the rules of narrative are broken. You've been just about getting away with it so far, but that is way too much of a broken rule to let off this time."

"Yeah, and just exactly what do you intend to do about it?"

"I have great and arcane powers, in this case the power to inflict a major case of writers' block on anyone who won't go by the rules."

"Uh-oh, I'm in trouble. OK, you win, she doesn't die yet. Rats. Looks like I'm stuck with her now."

There was a massive flash of light, a loud bang, and a very nasty smell. Rose appeared on the ground in front of the dragon, in one piece, but totally disoriented. The dragon looked pretty unhappy too. He tried eating her again, rather slower this time, and exactly the same thing happened. He looked at her very confusedly, which was nothing to how confused she was.

Then there was another loud bang, and a cloud of green and purple smoke appeared from nowhere. It slowly cleared to show a man, rather short and fat, with long white hair and smoking a very fat cigar. He was dressed in a check suit which was louder than any of the bangs had been, in a virulent green and a sort of salmon pink. He had a pair of extremely shiny black patent leather shoes, with about 4 inches of snowy white sock showing. His shirt was shiny and purple, and he was wearing a wide tie with some unpleasantly bright fractal patterns on it. He had more rings than the average rapper, and his tiepin was a positive masterpiece of bad taste.

He smiled widely and bowed to Rose and the dragon.

"Meldephus X. Carthington at your service," he

proclaimed, "But you can call me Mel C."

Rose instantly regained her voice.

"Certainly not, you don't look a bit like her, and I'm sure you can't sing or dance either."

He looked very pained.

"I most certainly can sing, and dance too! I do, however, see that this could cause some confusion. Maybe you could just call me Doc. C. Or maybe not that either. Ah! How about Doctor Mel."

He beamed happily at his two companions.

Rose said doubtfully, "Well alright, but just who are you anyway, and where do you come from? And did you have anything to do with the dragon not being able to eat me?"

Doctor Mel smiled again and seemed to expand.

"I did indeed my dear. That was just a little sample of a vast range of wonderful magic spells I have for your delectation! That was but one of the marvels in store for you if you would just put yourself in my hands and let yourself be taken on a tour of my marvellous wonderland of mystery and magic!!"

Rose groaned.

"Oh no, I don't believe it - a salesman! I should have known. Well not today thank you. Goodbye and close the door behind you when you leave."

Doctor Mel put on his best shocked and horrified look (number 6 in the training manual), put his hand on his heart and murmured brokenly, "I am shocked and hurt that you should insult me so. How could you mistake me for such a cheap and common person. I am much more than a mere salesman. You wound me deeply."

He wiped a tear from his eye with a large bright yellow silk handkerchief.

Rose looked at him in deep disgust, and turned to the dragon, who had been very quiet up till now.

"Can you eat him?" she said hopefully, "I think he

would make you a better meal than I would, and I would really like to get rid of him sooner rather than later."

The dragon eyed him up and down rather doubtfully, then snapped him up and gulped. He swallowed, and then a very peculiar expression came over his face. Steam came out of his ears and he sneezed violently several times. The now familiar loud bang came and a very cross-looking Doctor Mel landed on the ground in front of him. Rose began to feel a little bit sorry for the dragon - he was having major problems with his food.

Doctor Mel stood up and gave Rose a very dirty look.

"Hmmph, I can see that I am not welcome here. You are obviously not the kind of person that I am accustomed to dealing with. I shall remove myself from the vicinity and seek out the company of those who value me as they ought. You will regret this I'm sure, you have no idea what I could have done for you. It's too late now though."

With this there was another cloud of smoke, this time in pink and yellow, and he disappeared. Rose tossed her hair and sneered, "Good riddance! We don't want any slimy salesmen around here. Nothing but a bunch of lying scum they are."

The dragon turned his head towards her and rumbled.

"I wouldn't have been so quick to get rid of him, you do realise that there's nothing to stop me eating you now, don't you?"

Rose looked at him thoughtfully.

"How do you know that?" she said, "The charm might still be working. Anyway, do you really want to take a chance on it?"

The dragon pondered this for a while.

"To tell you the truth, no I don't. It might be a good idea to hold off on eating you for a while, at least until I get desperate."

Rose heaved a sigh of relief. Then she started thinking. It had just occurred to her that even without the dragon eating her, she was still not in a good position. She was lost in the middle of the forest, without her luggage or her servants, and most importantly without any food. She was starting to feel a few hunger pangs herself, with no prospect of a meal anytime soon. She looked about for ideas, but all she could see was a lot of trees and brambles, and a very large and disgruntled dragon.

This was actually the first time in Rose's life that she was really and truly in trouble, and she was not at all enjoying the experience. Her brain was working as hard as it was able, and she was beginning to panic. Suddenly a genuine inspiration hit her - why not ask the dragon for help! She could vaguely see a couple of potential problems with this, but she dismissed them impatiently.

"Dragon" she shouted in excitement, "take me to somewhere I can get some food."

The dragon looked at her in astonishment and anger.

"What! You have a nerve you scruffy little thing! You've already messed up my day with all those bangs and stuff, and now you have the colossal cheek to demand that I do something for you. You don't seem to realise just who you are talking to!" He subsided into menacing mutters and pointedly looked away from her.

Rose realised that she might have made a bit of a false move in her enthusiasm. She scraped up her courage and walked around to where the dragon's head was pointing.

"Dragon, I'm sorry about what I just said, I was very rude. Please forgive me."

This must be put on record as the first time in her whole 24 years that Rose had ever apologised for anything. It's amazing what the presence of a large dragon can do for your acting ability!

The dragon looked moodily at her and sighed.

"I suppose you think it's all alright now do you? That I'll do whatever you want and be at your beck and call? Don't count on it kiddo!"

Rose swallowed and tried again.

"Dragon, will you please help me. I'm stuck here in the forest with no food and I don't know what to do."

"Well what do you expect me to do for you? I don't carry a pack of sandwiches round with me in case I should meet a hungry girl. If I do meet one I usually tend to eat her rather than treat her to a picnic lunch."

Rose considered this in silence for a few minutes. Then she remembered what she had started out to do.

"Dragon, do you know about the enchanted city that's supposed to be hidden in the forest somewhere?"

"Yes, I've heard of it, what about it? You do know that no-one has ever found it - if it really exists at all."

"Well how about we go and look for it together? We could end up becoming rich and famous."

The dragon suddenly got a very thoughtful look on his face. Famous he could do without, but rich was very much a word that caught his attention. Dragons and riches go together like fish and chips, and he could always do with another ton or so of treasure for his hoard. He suddenly started to look a bit more cheerful. Rose breathed a sigh of relief - she was good at seeing the signs of another sucker who had just been caught. She started to develop the theme a bit more.

"We could charge a lot of money bringing people on sight-seeing tours to the city - tourism is always a big money-spinner! This could be the new Dizzyland, and you know how much money that makes!"

The dragon was by now well and truly hooked, so they settled down to make plans. Fortunately, the dragon was rather better at planning than Rose, being a bit more experienced in adventures and travelling. In spite of all his grumbling, he was quite looking forward to this.

"Ahem, I'd like a word with you."

"Oh no. Not you again. What do you want this time?"

"It's a little matter of character development, Rose's to be exact."

"Her character is developing quite well thank you. What's your problem?"

"A little too well I'm afraid. She started off totally thick and obnoxious. I will grant that the presence of a dragon will probably deal with the obnoxious side fairly fast, but how on earth did she suddenly become a lot smarter? You can't start off by saying that she took 3 years to think up a plan, and then have her thinking on her feet and outwitting the dragon, it just won't wash. You'll have to change things round a bit, won't you."

"Not at all - it makes perfect sense to me. The spell that was cast by Doctor Mel didn't just make her dragon-proof physically, it also enhanced her intelligence as well. Good thing too, she'll need everything I can give her if she's going to come out of this alive, and you DO want her alive, don't you."

"Alright, alright, I suppose you get away with this one, but be warned, I have my eye on you."

Rose and the dragon talked late into the night, after he was persuaded to go and catch a rabbit for her. He even roasted it as well. She swallowed her pride and ate it with her fingers, getting rather burnt and messy in the process. She was hungry enough not to care too much about that, and she hadn't exactly been in a state of pristine perfection to start with. Then the dragon lit a fire and they sat round it, well he sat most of the way round it and left a space for her. They introduced themselves, as she felt it would encourage friendly relations if she wasn't calling him 'dragon' all the time.

"My name is Princess Rose," she said, "What's yours?"

The dragon looked a bit sheepish (now that would be worth seeing!) and muttered something about dragon names being too terrible for human ears.

"You can call me Al," he said eventually, as he couldn't think of anything more imposing.

"Hello Al, pleased to meet you," she said. She didn't think much of it as a name, but she wasn't going to start making nasty comments. It was becoming more obvious to her that she was totally dependant on Al to have any chance of getting anywhere alive, let alone finding her prince.

The next morning Rose woke up horribly early, feeling cold, stiff and uncomfortable. This was the first time she had ever slept in anything other than a cosy feather bed, and she had not enjoyed a good night's sleep on a pile of grass and leaves. She had eventually managed to get to sleep, but only because she was exhausted after the eventful day. She staggered to a stream that was a little way away, and splashed her face with cold water. This at least woke her up fully, but she still felt very sorry for herself. There was nothing for breakfast either, which depressed her even further. Al was eager to get going, and she was eager to get closer to anywhere where they might find a half-decent hotel with a Jacuzzi and a French chef.

Soon she was on his back and they were in the air, and Rose had changed her mind. She was finding it hard to hold on, she slithered around on Al's scaly skin, and on top of that she was feeling severely airsick. She shouted at Al to stop, but he couldn't hear her with the wind in his ears. He flew higher, and to add to her misfortunes she was getting cold and wet flying through some big grey clouds. She hammered frantically on his impervious back, but he didn't even notice it. She tried kicking, no response there either. Just as she thought it couldn't get any worse, he dropped sharply and swung to the left, throwing her violently against his wing. She lost her grip and slid across his back, falling through the clouds. She screamed in terror as she plummeted towards the trees.

Just as she reached the top of a tall pine tree, Al swooped under her and she landed neatly on his back. This didn't last long, she started sliding again, and was falling off just as they touched down. She fell headfirst into a large bush and ended up with her nose about six inches above the ground. After a few minutes of catching her breath, and trying to figure out which way up she was, she pulled herself out of the bush and sat down. Al looked on in concern, she did not look at all well and there was a large jagged scratch across her face.

"Are you all right Rose?" he asked worriedly, "That was a nasty fall you had there."

"No I am not all right, I am frozen, bruised, totally miserable, and I think I'm going to throw up!" she replied, all thoughts of being friendly and co-operative having vanished in mid-air.

"Oh dear. I am sorry, I had no idea it was going to be that difficult," said Al.

"What on earth are we going to do now?"

At that moment there was a loud bang and a cloud of familiar looking smoke. The florid figure of Doctor Mel emerged from the cloud with a beaming smile on his face.

"Hello my dear friends," he said jovially, "And how are we getting on today?"

Rose and Al turned slowly to look at him, then at each other. The same thought had crossed both of their minds at the same time - how had he known exactly the right moment to appear? And why had his attitude changed so much since they had seen him last?

"Oh dear, you do look like you are having one or two little problems?" said Doctor Mel in a voice that oozed synthetic sincerity and sympathy. "How lucky that I chose this moment to drop by and see how things were."

Rose's toe itched to plant a nice juicy kick on his ample behind, but she stifled the impulse, for the moment anyway. They were in quite a jam, and it was just possible that the intrusive salesman might actually be able to help them.

She smiled sweetly at him and put on her best little-girl voice.

"Oh how nice of you to come and see us, we are always pleased to have a helpful friend drop in."

He showed no sign that he had noticed any change in her manner, but he was well aware of it, and that it was just as false as his own. He had been closely watching the pair, and had chosen his moment quite carefully. He bowed in his best and most elaborate style, and played up to her magnificently.

"My dear, I am delighted to get such a warm welcome from such a charming young princess. I am always eager to help beauty in distress, and on this occasion it is an unparalleled pleasure. Now, what can I have the honour of doing for you?"

Rose weighed up her options, and decided a little consultation was in order. She turned to Al, to discover him frantically trying to speak to her. He seemed to be unable to open his mouth. She turned indignantly to Doctor Mel and asked him what was going on. He looked rather embarrassed.

"Yes, well, it seems to be an effect I have on dragons I'm afraid. I've done everything I can to find out what causes it, but it's a total mystery. It seems to be impossible for a dragon to speak in my presence! But there, what can you do about it?"

Rose was highly suspicious of this, but she really couldn't think of anything she could say without offending the Doctor, and she still had hopes of his producing a solution to their problems. She let it go, and launched into a tangled explanation of their dilemma.

"But nothing could be easier, my dear," he exclaimed, "I can send you to the enchanted city in less time that it takes to say the words!"

She was highly relieved to hear this, although a remnant of caution held her back.

"What is this going to cost me?" she asked. "I don't actually have any money with me you know."

"No problem, no problem at all, my accounts department will be in touch with you in due course. You'll have plenty of money to pay me by the time that happens."

Rose wasn't totally happy with this, but she didn't see any other choice.

"Thank you very much, I'll take you up on the offer," she said.

"A good choice, my dear, I'm sure you'll be very happy with the results. A pleasure doing business with you."

With that there was yet another loud bang, a cloud of green smoke surrounded Rose and Al, and they disappeared from sight.

The smoke slowly cleared, to show them an amazing sight spread out in front of them. It was indisputably a city, but it was like no city either of them had seen before. It shone, it glittered, it sparkled and even coruscated! It seemed to be made entirely of mirrors and very large brightly coloured stones. It was extremely tacky. Rose fell instantly in love with it. This was her kind of city. Al wasn't quite so impressed, in fact he was totally disgusted with it, it hurt both his eyes and his artistic sensibilities. He looked at Rose and saw the look of total rapture in her eyes, and groaned.

He then thought back to the conversation he had tried so hard to take part in and groaned again, rather louder. He had a very bad feeling about the whole arrangement, and he also had a strong feeling that he had seen the Doctor somewhere else. He was not at all happy about the situation, and he really couldn't do anything about it. He looked back at the city, wincing as the sun came out from behind a cloud and the resulting dazzle brought tears to his eyes. This was the absolute pinnacle of bad taste - no, make that execrable taste. He looked at Rose in disgust as she gazed spellbound at the city.

"Shouldn't we be making a move here?" he said, as she showed no signs of emerging from her trance. She looked round at him with a dazed expression.

"Oh, yes, I suppose so. Actually, now that you mention it, I am kind of hungry, and tired too. Let's go and see who lives here."

Rose started thinking of all the wonderful things she expected to find in the city, like comfortable beds, hot meals and bubble-baths. From this you can see that her priorities had changed slightly in the last day or so. She hadn't quite lost sight of the prince she had set out to find, but for once in her life she was willing to put off the search for a day or two in favour of other more important things.

They started down the road towards the city gates, which were directly ahead of them. These were in keeping with the rest of the city - totally tacky and overdone. It was a little surprising to Rose and Al that there was no sign of any guards or gate-keepers, or anyone else entering or leaving the city. It was also very quiet, and they began to have an uneasy feeling that something was not right here. They eventually reached the gates, and stood waiting for something to happen. After a few minutes nothing had happened, so they tentatively walked through the gates. Still nothing happened. There was an eerie silence and stillness hanging over the city. As the minutes passed, they slowly worked their way through the glittering streets towards a large castle. Still nothing happened, but this did not reassure them, in fact they got more and more jumpy the further they got.

They had almost reached the gates of the castle, when they both had a feeling that something was watching them. Rose froze in terror, but Al, who was rather too big and fierce to admit to being scared, looked around to see what was happening. At first he could see nothing unusual, but after a while he noticed a large black cat sitting smugly on one of the castle gateposts. Al tapped Rose on the shoulder and pointed to the cat. They both felt unwilling to break the silence that was so total it seemed to weigh them down.

Rose saw the cat and immediately felt there was something very strange about it. It looked perfectly normal, but there was a very un-catlike feeling about it. She couldn't describe what it was that gave her this feeling, but she was sure that this cat was not at all what it seemed. She walked towards the cat, without really being aware of what she was doing, until she was about 3 feet away from it. The cat's glowing green eyes seemed to see right through her, and shivers ran down her back. The cat abruptly jumped down from the gatepost and walked through the gate. Rose followed as if mesmerised, and Al couldn't see anything to do except to follow her in his turn.

The procession passed through several huge rooms with enormously high ceilings, and ended up in a rather smaller room. This was about 50 feet square and at least as high, built entirely of bare dark stone and with no furniture apart from a plain wooden, throne-like chair. The cat stopped here, and sat in the middle of the floor with its back to them. Rose stopped and stood behind the cat, and Al behind her. They waited for what seemed like a very long time for something to happen.

After an unknown amount of time had passed, a white shimmering light started to glow around the wooden throne. This slowly spread to the rest of the room, until nothing could be seen except what looked like a pearly fog, with flickering lights moving around in it. This abruptly cleared to show what appeared to be a completely different room. It was the same size, but it was now richly decorated - by someone with the same taste as whoever had designed the city. Sitting on the throne was a tall thin woman dressed entirely in white, but with a lot of unnecessary decoration - lace, frills, pearls and some over-large diamonds. She also held a long ivory rod with a silver bow on the end. Rose stared at the woman in amazement for a few moments, and then cried out in delight.

"Lily, I don't believe it! How on earth did you get here?"

It was her second cousin, whom she only saw once a year. She had never wondered why this was, but she now began to get an idea.

"Are you actually the Queen of the Enchanted City?" she asked excitedly.

Lily sighed.

"Yes Rose, I am actually, and you wouldn't believe how boring it is here. There is no-one else in the whole place except the cat, and he isn't really much company. You have no idea how pleased I am to see you and your friend. Won't you introduce him to me?"

Rose remembered her manners and introduced Al. She gave Lily a quick summary of all that had happened in the last day - although it felt more like a week to her.

Lily was fascinated by the story, but she almost seemed

more interested in Al. She was most friendly to him, to the point that Rose started to feel excluded. This would have led to trouble if Rose hadn't been still rather under the spell of the cat. She kept staring at him and once or twice almost lost the thread of the story. There was something almost hypnotic about the steady stare from those unblinking green eyes.

When the story was finished. Lily asked for more details about Doctor Mel, she was most interested in the description of him.

"I'm sure I have heard of him somewhere, and I have a feeling it wasn't very good either. Rose, are you sure you haven't got into trouble here?"

"I knew it!" shouted Al.

"There is something wrong with him - I had a very bad feeling about him from the beginning. Rose, I think we could be in big trouble."

Rose looked doubtful, but she was outnumbered. Even the cat gave a loud miaow and waved his tail at the sound of the Doctor's name.

At this moment there was a loud bang, and the man they were talking about appeared in person. This time the smoke was multicoloured, and he looked rather more imposing than he had done on the previous two occasions.

"Well Ladies and Gentlemen, I am pleased to see you all getting on so well!"

He rubbed his hands together and gave a sort of sneering laugh. He continued.

"It makes it so much easier for me to get you all under my control."

He gave a maniacal cackle, and with a flash and a bang he re-appeared, looking rather different. He was taller and considerably thinner, dressed in a long blue robe with silver symbols all over it. In fact, he looked like a Hollywood producer's idea of an evil magician. To complete the picture, he had a beard as worn, more successfully, by Ming the Merciless.

The entire company had been struck speechless, apart from the cat, who already was speechless. They looked at this new Doctor Mel in horror, especially Rose, who suddenly had a feeling she was in BIG trouble. She was quite right.

"Rose, my dear, could I trouble you for immediate settlement of a certain trifling debt?" he asked with a knowing smirk.

She found her voice with an effort.

"Er... how much exactly would you be looking for?"

"Oh nothing too much, only £100,000, in Sterling or US Dollars, used notes only please."

She stared at him in horror, this time with much more justification.

"What??? How on earth could I owe you that much for one travel spell?? I can't possibly pay you that - it's outrageous!"

He smirked even more horribly and rubbed his hands.

"You most certainly do owe me that, and if you don't pay, well I'll just have to invoke the penalty clause, won't I."

"P-p-p-p-penalty clause...."

"Yes my dear, I get to keep you as my slave for the rest of your life. And believe me, you won't enjoy it."

He was most certainly enjoying it, as he contemplated the shocked and horrified princess in front of him. He rubbed his hands a bit more and looked her up and down. She turned imploringly to Lily.

"Can't you do something about this - please stop him."

Lily slowly and regretfully shook her head.

"Rose, I'm terrible sorry, but he is legally entitled to do

this. You really should have checked the conditions a bit more carefully before you agreed to his terms. I'd lend you the money gladly, but I haven't got even a tenth of that amount."

Al, as usual in the presence of the Doctor, couldn't speak. He wasn't going to let this stop him from doing something though, so he took in a large breath and prepared to incinerate the Doctor. As he was about to breathe out, the Doctor negligently waved a hand at Al, and he flew through the air and hit a distant wall with a loud thump. A large ball of flame gushed from his mouth, and a gaudy, gold-embroidered tapestry caught fire and fell on top of him. A smell of lightly-toasted dragon drifted around the room. At this Lily lost her temper in a big way.

"Right, that does it!" she shouted in a royal fury.

"Nobody throws Al around and gets away with it. I'm going to stop all this nonsense right now!"

She raised her ivory wand and pointed it at the doctor.

"LET ALL SPELLS CEASE," she shouted in a voice that thundered and echoed round the room.

Oh dear, she really shouldn't have said that. Really, really shouldn't....

The Doctor stared at her in horror.

"The Great Unravelling," he whispered in a shaking voice, "We're all doomed now."

Lily looked at him and swallowed.

"I've really done it now, haven't I?"

He looked at her in disbelief, and turned away.

There were a series of loud pops, and clouds of smoke began to appear, as spells abruptly undid themselves. The first results of this took some people very much by surprise. Rose was shocked to discover that she had just grown a few inches taller, and a look in a mirror told her that she had also become even more beautiful than she thought she was. Her intelligence suddenly seemed to expand too, which enabled her to deduce that someone had put a spell on her when she was a child.

She was distracted from this discovery by the even more amazing changes that were happening to the cat. It appeared that he actually wasn't a cat at all, in fact he turned out to be the most incredibly sexy man that she had ever seen. He was tall, with shoulder-length wavy black hair. His eyes were the same mesmerising green, and his face still had a cat-like shape to it. His shoulders were wide, and he had a slim build with more than a suggestion of strength. Dressed from head to toe in black leather and silk, he had an air of animal magnetism about him, and Rose found herself drawn helplessly towards him.

"Hah - I've really got you this time!"

"Oh no, what is it now? Look I'm nearly at the end of this, and I haven't got time for these stupid interruptions."

"This is serious. Does the word plagiarism mean anything to you?"

"WHAT! Where on earth did you get that one from? Who am I supposed to be plagiarising?"

"You ever heard of Perry Tratchett?"

"Of course I have, I have all his books - he's one of my favourite authors. What of it?"

"Does the description of the cat turned man in your last paragraph sound a little familiar by any chance?"

"Oh. I see. You're talking about Nanny Gogg's cat Greedo being turned into a man."

"That's right. I don't think Perry would be too happy about the major similarities here, do you?"

"I don't see why, after all he was talking about a real cat that was temporarily turned into a man, I'm talking about a man temporarily turned into a cat! Not the same thing at all."

"It's more the description I was thinking of."

"Well all I was doing was describing the sexiest man I could possibly think of. I can't help it if my taste in men is the same as Perry Tratchett's, can I."

"Now you're really going to be in trouble, making comments about his sexuality!"

"Well you just go and check it out with his agent, while I carry on with my story. You have to get your facts right before you start saying things like that you know."

While all this was going on the dragon had changed a little as well. He was now a tall, well-built, blond handsome hunk with a small crown on his head. He still looked rather dazed though, and his clothes had a few scorch marks on them. He got unsteadily to his feet and looked in Lily's direction. She had not altered very much, apart from her tacky white outfit. This had changed into a shabby white nightgown, with a few sad-looking ribbons dangling limply from the neck and sleeves. She ran over to Al and flung her arms round him.

"Are you all right, my handsome prince?" she cried.

He looked even more dazed, but managed to pull himself together enough to give her a passionate kiss. She returned it with interest, and they promptly forgot about what was happening around them.

This was well worth paying some attention to. The Doctor who had turned wizard was now turning into something rather less dangerous - a pile of bones. He definitely had met his doom, as the life-spell he had put on himself several hundred years ago abruptly ran down. The castle itself, with its surrounding city, was quietly fading away to a run-down stone fort and a cluster of shabby mud huts. As the circle of cancelled spells widened, a lot of very strange forest creatures were either disappearing totally or changing into rather more ordinary forms. The effects of Lily's words were going to have a very far-reaching effect, probably changing the whole country permanently. She didn't really care much about that right now though, as the ex-dragon prince was at that moment proposing to her, and she was delightedly accepting.

Rose was not really paying attention either. She had not noticed the dragon turning into a prince, and she wouldn't had been that interested anyway. She was far too caught up in admiring the sexy ex-cat, he was far more to her taste than any wimpy prince. He seemed to be very taken with her too, in her new and very beautiful body. They slipped out and went in search of a spare bedroom.

****
*
****
*

WARNING! WARNING! GRATUITOUS SEX SCENE

****
*
****
*

Oh just use your imagination. I can't be bothered with this stuff.

****

*

****

*

END OF GRATUITOUS SEX SCENE

****

*

****

*

And did they all live happily ever after?

Well you'll just have to read the sequel to find out, won't you. It will chart the long and eventful journey taken by Lily and her Prince to find his home in a world without magic. I could do another one, about Rose and her cat-man. Or maybe I would have to get someone else to write that one, as it would be verging on pornography.

Hey - I could do a prequel as well, or several. There is the story of Doctor Mel and his evil deeds to be told. The dragon and the cat should also have their stories told; how they came to be enchanted in the first place.

Then there's the movie rights and all that. Could be a lot of money in this...

Elsewhen Press

Look out for the first volume in PR Pope's thrilling new trilogy:

QUEENS OF ANTARES:
BLOODLINE

PR POPE

A new fantasy trilogy for readers of all ages from 8 to 80. Already compared to CS Lewis and CJ Cherryh, PR Pope weaves an enchanting tale around three young people who are accidentally transported from their mundane lives to a new world, where they must find the strength to lead a revolution in order to make their way home. On the way they discover who they really are, where they belong and the enduring power of a bloodline.

Volume I **Bloodline Returned**
coming soon
For more information visit www.queensofantares.co.uk

Visit the Elsewhen Press website www.elsewhen.press
for the latest information on our titles, authors and events,
to read the blog, or to place a order